The Party

Curtis Adler, originally from Wisconsin, USA, now lives in Dublin. He is married with two young children.

The Party

Curtis Adler

**POCKET
BOOKS**

LONDON • SYDNEY • NEW YORK • TORONTO

First published in Great Britain by Pocket Books, 2004
An imprint of Simon & Schuster UK Ltd,
and in Ireland by TownHouse Ltd, Dublin

Simon & Schuster is a Viacom Company

1 3 5 7 9 10 8 6 4 2

Simon & Schuster UK Ltd
Africa House
64–78 Kingsway
London WC2B 6AH

ISBN 0 7434 9219 6

www.simonsays.co.uk

Simon & Schuster Australia
Sydney

A CIP catalogue record for this book is available from
the British Library

TownHouse Ltd, Trinity House, Charleston Road
Ranelagh, Dublin 6, Ireland

ISBN 1 903650 32 1
www.townhouse.ie

Typeset by SX Composing DTP, Rayleigh, Essex
Printed and bound in Great Britain by
Cox & Wyman, Reading, Berkshire

ACKNOWLEDGEMENTS

First the science: To get the basics of this story right I consulted a number of guidebooks on schizophrenia, but the source I relied on the most was the excellent website maintained by the British Columbia Schizophrenia Society. I mined *The Complete Guide to Psychiatric Drugs* by Ron Lacey for medications, and I acknowledge Dr Tony Bates for confirming that my prescription, if a bit passé, was not entirely unfeasible.

Then the art: I acknowledge Tim and Anne Thurston who, despite suffering through an early draft of this book, still remain close friends – both with the author and with one another. I am deeply indebted to Treasa Coady for her patience and perseverance; to Siobhan Parkinson for her clear understanding of what was wrong and clear guidance in setting it right; to Hugh and Ella for their good-humoured support (over and over again); and most especially to Gráinne for so generously believing in this thing.

Finally, to those friends and relatives who so consistently enquired after the health of this uncooperative patient, my belated but heartfelt thanks.

ACKNOWLEDGMENTS

To my mother, Helen

PART I:

THE WEEK BEFORE

CHAPTER 1

Julia flicked off the television. She wished Denis was home.

She felt like she used to feel back in college after a good concert, Bruce Springsteen or The Police, when her ears still rang and her eyes still burned from the blinding stage lights. She felt again that emptiness that came afterwards – after the show, after the good-byes, after the drive home – back in the apartment, drained but wide awake, too alert to go to bed. That's how she felt now, stretched out on the sofa in the large sitting room, gazing up at the high ceiling. Restless and deflated, irritated by the silence.

Evening hung in the sky over Kenilworth Square and the setting sun glowed through the tall bay window. Her dressing gown was too heavy for the unusually warm weather.

She glanced at her watch. She got up and left the sitting room, climbing the stairs to the ochre-tiled bathroom. Reaching into the mirrored cabinet, she found a bottle of scarlet nail polish. Nothing like painting your toenails on a Saturday night, she thought. For the sheer excitement of it.

She wished she could tell Denis about her presentation that day. The cosmopolitan, high-powered atmosphere of the con-ference – 'Making Immigration Work: Europe's New Labour Force'. She wanted to tell Denis how she had enjoyed presenting in that large, comfortable room in that expensive hotel, behind a proper oak lectern and before an expanse of silver screen, speaking to two hundred well-groomed Europeans, almost all men, who watched her, taking notes from their padded seats. So different from her usual routine, so far removed from her talks to po-faced teachers on plastic chairs in dirty school halls.

She'd been asked to make the presentation by John Quilty, a business associate of Denis's whom she had met once at a reception. He had phoned her one night out of the blue, all charm, asking her about her work. Probing whether any lessons she had learned from her experience advising teachers might apply to the workforce at large. He said he was organising a conference. He had a budget for speakers.

Julia was flattered. She accepted straightaway.

She'd prepared hard for the day, over-prepared in fact, as she always did. She doctored up her tired old slides. She put in a colourful graphic about 'Spheres of Influence' and a quote from a professor at Harvard Business School. She rehearsed, several times, in front of the mirror, with a stopwatch in her hand. She soul-searched about her appearance. She knew she would be representing the department but she wanted to avoid the frumpish stereotype. She decided to wear heels, show some leg. She spent most of her honorarium on her outfit. In the end, she didn't have time to get her hair done but she knew it would do. Loose, but not out of control.

But as John introduced her and she crossed the stage, she wondered if perhaps she had overdone it. Two hundred men with their antennae raised, gaping with that blonde-on-stage stare. She inhaled deeply as she faced them, feeling, for an instant, like an expensive whore. But then she cleared her throat, thanked John for inviting her, and launched into her presentation.

After the first few slides she felt right at home. She paused at her three points of irony and they laughed like trained monkeys. She spoke directly to the audience, gauged their reactions, set her pace to ensure they came with her. These guys were the lucky ones, she thought. The ones with the BMWs and the Jaguars, the ones who didn't get wet in the rain. She knew they cared about profit, not about immigrant workers. She knew they would remember what she looked like, not what she said about EU policy, or cultural awareness, or group integration techniques.

She wondered, as she spoke, if Denis was like these men. She wondered if he laughed like they laughed, with that deep, posturing, my-laugh-is-louder-than-your-laugh voice. She wondered if he would have stared that way when she crossed the stage to indicate a particular point on a particular graph? Would his questions, at the end of her presentation, have been so simple, so inane, so narrow-minded?

No, she thought, as she smiled across the applauding room. Denis wasn't like that. He was a gentleman. An independent type. Never had that herd mentality.

Maybe Denis did look at women, though, she thought, as the presentation ended and she put her gift pen in her bag and walked out of the foyer and towards her car. In some ways, she hoped he did still notice women. She wanted him to stay alive, to stay hungry, even now as they were entering their forties. She didn't want him to slow down or lose the edge he had when they were first married. But she knew that if Denis were to look at another woman, it wouldn't be to ogle her. He would do it for a purpose.

To communicate. To lock her in with his blue eyes and get into her soul. The way he used to look at Julia, peering into her mind. He could still do it. But it had been too long, she thought. Far too long.

She was sorry Denis hadn't seen her today, looking pretty damn good for her age. Not quite the youthful bride he'd married, but not too bad all the same. She wished he had seen her walking out the door to her conference, looking like, well, like someone to be admired. Or perhaps too much time had passed. Perhaps he was beyond admiring her any more. Perhaps that was the problem.

A car drove by outside the open window and then the house was silent again. She leaned forward and rested her feet on the coffee table, painting her toes one by one. Bright red. If it was nice again tomorrow she'd wear her white sandals when they went into town.

She paused for a moment to listen for the boys upstairs. Jimmy was probably asleep. He'd been at a friend's house all day, playing hard. All that energy packed into an eight-year-old body. Such good humour he had, such a little charmer. When he'd come home she was still wearing her outfit and he greeted her with bright enthusiasm: 'Wow, Mum! You look like a model!'

Good old Jimmy, she thought. Always gets it right.

Barry was probably still awake, probably studying in bed. A few more exams to go before the summer holidays. Then one more year at school, and then, my God, university. Almost grown up. Still so dreamy, though, still spending Saturday nights at home. It had been a difficult transition for him, coming back to Dublin two, almost three years ago. The move from the States had sent him into himself. He still hadn't emerged from the protective cocoon he had woven about himself when they first came back.

Julia worried about Barry. She wished things would work out for him. She wanted him to fit in and to find his own course through life and make more friends. To be happy.

She had seen Barry earlier, as she drove home from the conference. She knew his routine on Saturdays, knew he would study until late in the afternoon and then cycle to Bushy Park to do some training. She decided to pull over and see if she could spot him exercising on the football pitches. She parked the car and walked beneath the tall beech trees through relaxed groups of parents and children and elderly women. Everything was green and the mid-summer sun shone brightly beyond the shadows of the trees. For a few minutes she walked slowly, scanning the fields until she saw him back towards the beech grove on an empty football pitch. She watched him in the sunshine in his running gear, carrying out his routine: sprinting the length of the pitch, fast and hard, holding his head and body erect until he passed beneath the crossbars, then slowing, and turning, and jogging slowly back the length of the pitch until he caught his breath. And then, when he reached the starting point, turning and sprinting again up the field, running hard, like an animal on a race track chasing some sort of prize. Up and back. Over and over.

She wished Denis was home so they could talk about Barry. She wanted to tell Denis about how strong Barry was, and how athletic he looked today with his blond hair and tanned skin as he ran like a champion up the field. She wanted to tell Denis how proud she felt then but how worried too, because she felt that Barry used his running to cope, to burn off his frustrations with this life of theirs, a life into which he simply hadn't settled. She wanted to talk to Denis about it, to discuss what they should do to help Barry, to give him more confidence, to help him to socialise better and perhaps to protect him from himself.

She sighed now in the silent house, leaning back on the sofa, letting her toenails dry in the warm evening air. She wished Denis would come home. He was out at some launch, some new campaign that was kicking off for the summer season. Julia hated when he had to go to these things without her, especially on weekends. She imagined what it would be like if he came home now, as she sat on the sofa letting her toes dry, and he sat across from her in his dress suit with his bow tie undone. He would be tired. He would tell her some funny story about someone making some faux pas during a speech, or share some juicy bit of gossip about someone in the business world. And then she would tell him about her day, teasing him about all those men staring at her on stage, and she would see him trying not to be jealous, trying hard to be the wise, caring, counselling husband, even though he would hate to imagine her in front of all those men. And he would listen like he used to do, back when they were in Massachusetts, and she would look into his face and hear his soft, Donegal accent as they talked. And then their voices would get lower as he noticed her there on the sofa, in her red silk dressing gown, with her legs stretched out before her, her red toenails shining, drying in the still, heavy air.

'Oh well,' she sighed to herself. 'Perhaps some other time.'

She stood then and crossed the room to go into the kitchen. The light was fading now, the back garden falling into shadows. She switched on the light. Jimmy's shoes were on the floor and his

T-shirt was draped across the back of a chair. The table was covered with playing cards, Jimmy's creations: little two-card tepees and square huts made from cards leaning against one another. There were piles where cards had fallen over, remnants of Jimmy's attempts to go higher, to put the cards together into something stable and strong, which had then fallen, and scattered, leaving behind a fragment, a sad ruin.

Julia began to gather the mess together. Tidying, she smiled sadly. No matter how you spent your day, you could be the president, the president of the world, and yet you end up gathering clothes into piles, tidying away toys. Keeping the house in order.

She glanced at the luminous clock on the door of the silver oven: 9:47. Saturday night. The excitement of it all.

She was just about to head upstairs to bed when the phone rang.

CHAPTER 2

On Sunday morning Denis glanced at the clock on his bedside locker. God, he groaned. There's half the day gone.

He leaned forward in bed. The bright sunshine flooding the bedroom hurt his eyes. He rubbed his face slowly, trying to rouse his skin from sleep. He had dreamed of frantic activity and now his thoughts flitted uncomfortably through the events of the launch last night. The models, the photographers, the jokes about Donegal men. The endless greetings, the empty conversations. Feeling tired, wanting to leave the party, getting stuck beside Jack O'Shea who was quite drunk, blathering on about the government and the EU and the corruption of it all. Finally piling Jack into a taxi and paying the driver, looking at him there in the back seat half asleep, hoping he'd get home safely to his lovely wife, whom he didn't deserve. Pain in the arse, Jack O'Shea.

Denis got out of bed carefully. His mouth was dry. He took his dressing gown from the hook on the door and shuffled downstairs. He paused before the French doors into the kitchen. Barry sat at the table with his feet up on a chair, his attention focused on the school textbook in his lap. He pulled at a strand of his hair with his fingers, rolling it slowly, over and over. The sun shone from the skylight across his long legs.

He's like a lion, Denis thought. Lying in the African sun.

He stepped quietly into the kitchen. 'Study going okay?' he whispered.

'Yeah,' Barry mumbled without looking up.

'Where's Mum?'

'She's out. She's getting the paper.'

'Right. Can I get you anything?'

'What? No, thanks. When's lunch?'

'I don't know, I'm just up.'

'Oh,' Barry grunted as he returned to his book.

Denis crossed the kitchen and flicked on the kettle. He pulled a mug from the cherry-wood press. Barry hasn't lost his accent, Denis thought. Almost three years back in Ireland and he still talks like a Yank.

Denis spooned coffee into the cafetière and then filled it with boiling water. He quietly left the kitchen, carrying the coffee and his mug out into the sunny garden. He sat on an iron garden chair, setting the coffee on a low iron table beside him. The big chestnut tree cast a shadow across the grass, but the chair was positioned directly in the sunshine. He squinted as he sipped his coffee. He began to perspire. He sat quietly watching as a blackbird landed on a nearby bush, picking blue berries off one by one.

A minute later, he heard the door open behind him and Julia stepped into the garden.

'So, you're awake,' she said.

He looked up at her as she handed him the newspaper. She had showered, her hair was gleaming, she looked wide awake. He couldn't remember the last time he had seen her in loose summer clothes. But she didn't smile as she met his gaze.

'Is that coffee fresh?' she asked.

'Yes, I just made it.'

'Good, don't move, I'll get a cup. And I need something to wipe off this chair.'

He opened the newspaper and scanned the business section, looking for stories of his clients. He came to the 'People' page. His eyes were drawn to a colour photo in the upper corner.

'My God,' he said softly. 'There I am.'

The photograph had been taken early in the evening. He stood in his dress suit with his eyebrows raised in a wry smile. Before him were three tall, thin women in designer lingerie. They smiled broadly, leaning forward, their mouths hanging open with laughter, their long hair brushing their bare shoulders. The caption mentioned the launch of the new ad campaign.

Nu U Lingerie. For today. For tonight.

Denis shook his head in disbelief. Just what I need, he thought. How did they get that in so quickly?

He leaned back in his chair and squinted towards the house. He tried to see Julia through the windows but the bright sunshine hid her behind the glare. He looked at the photograph again and then folded the newspaper beside him.

A moment later Julia returned. He could sense her distant mood, she seemed to be working out a puzzle in her mind. She sat down stiffly on the edge of the chair.

'So, when did you get in?' she said coldly.

'It was late.'

'It certainly was.'

'It was our launch,' he said. 'I couldn't leave until it was wrapping up.'

'Did you enjoy yourself?'

'Not especially. You know how these things are.'

Julia nodded unsympathetically. They gazed across the garden in silence for a moment.

'Julia, are you okay?'

'Michael phoned last night.'

'Oh. Is everything all right?'

'Yes,' she said. 'Yes, I think it's okay. But I'm not sure. He said there's going to be a party. Up in Ballyfinn. But he couldn't be right. He kept talking about Stephen Deane.'

'Yes?'

'Stephen Deane. The actor.'

'I know,' Denis said flatly. 'His people are from Meenbane. Just outside Ballyfinn.'

'Does Michael know him?'

'Yes, he was in the house with us. At college.'

'You actually lived with him?'

'Yes.'

'You never told me that before.'

'We weren't very close.'

'But you lived with him – before he went to Hollywood?'

'Yes, that's what I said. Michael and I both lived with Stephen Deane. For three years. Before he went to Hollywood.'

'You should have told me,' Julia said. 'I thought Michael was, well, imagining things. I didn't believe him. I must have sounded like some kind of . . .'

'Why did Michael phone?'

'I told you, there's going to be a party, on Saturday night. He said Stephen Deane is in Donegal this week. He's buying a house or something. Apparently your gang from college will be there. And all the big knobs from Ballyfinn. And we're invited. Michael wants us all to come up.'

'Saturday?' Denis asked. 'This Saturday?'

'That's what he said. He said we could drive up on Friday. We can spend Saturday together. Barry is invited to the party too, and Michael says we can get a sitter for Jimmy.'

'Typical Michael,' Denis said with annoyance in his voice. 'How can he expect us to drop everything and . . .'

'Your brother didn't arrange the party,' Julia cautioned. 'Stephen Deane did. It's not Michael's fault.'

'Oh. Still. He could have given us a bit of notice.'

Julia thought for a moment. 'But Denis, if Stephen's throwing the party, why didn't he invite you himself?'

'I don't know. He probably didn't have my number.'

'But we're in the phone book.'

'I don't know,' Denis repeated.

'Anyway, if it's true, it's kind of exciting. It might be fun. We'll have to go.'

'We don't have to do anything,' Denis said testily.

'Michael really wants us to come up. You could show the boys your old haunts. And besides, how many times do we get invited to a party with a movie star?'

Denis folded his arms and studied the ground. 'How did Michael sound?' he asked.

'He sounded okay. A little nervous. But okay.'

'Jesus,' Denis said. 'You know Michael. He might have the dates wrong.'

'He sounded okay,' she repeated.

'And what about Anne? You haven't seen her since that school thing . . .'

'I know,' Julia sighed. 'It's going to be uncomfortable. At least at first.'

She paused for a moment then, looking down into her coffee. 'Denis,' she said softly. 'We should try to go. We've nothing else on. Maybe it's an opportunity.'

'For what?'

'You know. To get together. With Anne and Michael. It's been two years now.'

He looked across the garden. 'Friday,' he sighed. 'I'll have to check my diary. Are you sure you want to do this? My old gang from college. You'll be bored.'

'Oh God, how can you say that? It's not just the party. It's an opportunity. To fix things up.'

Denis stared across the garden. 'I'll check my diary,' he said again.

'Denis?'

'Yes?'

'We have to go,' she said.

'Right,' he exhaled. 'I'll check my diary.'

That afternoon they walked together down Grafton Street: Denis and Julia, and Barry and Jimmy. The day was mired in hazy sunshine and the shop windows glared with heat. Slow-moving shoppers, overdressed for the warm weather, shared a sense of irritable discomfort.

Sweat glistened on Jimmy's forehead. He carried a strawberry ice cream cone and it was dripping down his hand onto the hot pavement.

'Why don't we split up?' Julia said. 'I'll go with Barry. You take Jimmy. We'll finish quicker.'

'Mum!' Jimmy called out.

'Just a minute,' she said impatiently. 'Now, when should we meet?'

'Mum! Do you see that sign?'

'Jimmy, please, just a minute. Let's meet back here at three. Is that okay?'

'But Mum, look how they spelled it!'

Jimmy pointed to a sign above a boutique. Pynk. As he swung his arm around his ice cream brushed against Julia's white trousers. A circle of strawberry glowed from her inner thigh.

'Jimmy!'

'Ah, Jimmy!' Denis snapped. 'You have to be careful!'

Julia inhaled sharply. She dug into her handbag for something to wipe off the mess. And then, with her head still down, she heard a woman's smoky voice: 'Well, if it isn't Denis O'Donnell!'

Julia looked up to see a woman extending her hand towards Denis. She was shorter than Julia and had thick, dark, smartly styled hair. She wore a man's-style shirt that strained at each button and had large eyes and wore no wedding ring.

'Ah, no,' Denis said. 'It couldn't be! Catherine Sweeney! How are you?'

'Sure I'm only the best!' Catherine exclaimed. 'And what about you?'

Denis took her hand and then kissed her cheek. Julia felt ice cream dripping down her leg.

'Sure you seem to be everywhere,' Catherine said. 'I saw you in the paper this morning, with that gaggle of half-dressed hussies.'

'In the paper?' Julia interrupted.

'Now, Denis,' Catherine scolded. 'Where are your manners?'

'Sorry, what am I thinking? This is my wife, Julia.'

'How nice to meet you,' Julia smiled stiffly.

'You're American then?' Catherine said brightly.

'Yes.'

'But you haven't a strong accent.'

'No, I suppose after a few years . . .'

'Sure my accent is everywhere,' Catherine said to Denis. 'Donegal and Dublin and London, the lot! Sometimes I don't know where I am. But what about these fine fellows – they couldn't be yours?'

'They are indeed,' Denis said. 'This is Barry and this is Jimmy.'

'My God,' Catherine intoned, fixing her eyes on Barry. 'Two fine boys. Sure you didn't waste any time, did you, Denis?'

'Are you living in Dublin now?' Denis asked.

'No, just passing through. I've been in London, it must be twelve years now.'

'That's a long time,' Denis said.

'The money's good, of course,' Catherine continued, 'but they make you work for it. You've no life at all. So I'm testing the waters in the auld sod. Checking out my options. But listen, what about the big reunion? Surely you've heard?'

'We only got the news yesterday,' Denis said.

'I can't wait,' Catherine said. 'Imagine our Stephen Deane,

hitting the big time! Who'd have thought? And you'll all be there?'

'Oh yes,' Denis said. 'We're all looking forward to it.'

'Well, well,' Catherine flashed a practised smile at Julia. 'I'm delighted to meet the woman who could tame this wild Donegal man. Lovely to meet you all. And sure we'll see you on Saturday night?'

'We'll be there,' Denis said.

'Lovely. Ta-ta, chaps!'

They watched as Catherine walked away, waving with her fingers, a gold watch glinting on her wrist.

'Right,' Denis smiled nervously. 'That was Catherine.'

'Yes,' Julia replied. 'I'm so pleased I met her. Especially with ice cream all over my pants.'

'Dad,' Jimmy piped up. 'Is your picture in the paper?'

'Yes, Jimmy.'

'Wow! Can I see it when we go home?'

'Why didn't you tell us?' Julia said.

'It must have slipped my mind.'

'That's great,' Julia said. 'She must think I'm the world's greatest idiot. Now I really am looking forward to this party.'

'No one's forcing you to come.'

Julia glowered at him, then looked down and rubbed furiously at the stain on her leg.

'Are we going to Donegal?' Barry asked.

'Yes, I guess we are,' Julia replied.

They stood in the centre of a young man's clothing store. Full-sized images of slim, aggressive-looking men stared at them from the surrounding walls. Julia wished Barry would buy his own clothes. He was nearly seventeen but he still seemed incapable of deciding what to wear. It didn't matter what he got, everything looked good on him. She riffled through a rack of shirts.

'So when are we going?' he asked.

'Probably Friday.'

'This Friday? Why didn't you tell me?'

'Uncle Michael only called last night. Dad said he didn't want to go. But something seems to have changed his mind.'

'Oh,' Barry said, a look of confusion crossing his face.

'Is that okay? Do you have something else on?'

'No, I do want to go. Why? Don't you?'

'I'm not sure.' Julia picked a shirt from a rail and held it up to his chest. 'How about something like this?'

'No.'

'Okay, well . . .'

'What about these?' he pointed to a display. 'It's what the guys at school are wearing.'

'Okay . . .'

'This one,' Barry said. 'And maybe this one too.'

'I've never seen you pick out your own shirts before,' she said. He looked at her as if he'd been reproached.

'But it's okay,' she said. 'They're very nice.'

'Well, can we get them?'

'Both?'

'Yeah. This one for Friday night, and this one for Saturday night.'

'Okay,' she said, examining the price tags. 'I hope you have a chance to wear them.'

'Me too.'

She looked at him blankly as he studied the shirts, sensing something in his thoughts that he wasn't willing to share.

Jimmy and Denis walked beneath the high glass ceilings of the Stephen's Green shopping centre. The air inside was hot and stagnant. Jimmy talked continuously as they threaded their way between the crowds.

'When are we going, Daddy?'

'Probably Friday,' Denis replied distractedly.

'Are we staying with Uncle Michael and Auntie Anne?'

'Yes.'

'Will I have the same room as last time?'

'I don't know. Probably.'

'And can I go to the party?'

'We'll see.'

'Who's going to be there?'

'People I used to know. Stephen Deane will be there.'

'Who's he?'

'The actor. You know, the one in the film about the nuns. With the waterfall.'

'Really?' Jimmy said, wide-eyed. 'Wow!'

'I'll introduce you.'

'That's cool.'

Jimmy paused for a moment as if imagining the meeting. They passed through the entrance of a large department store.

'Didn't Nanna Jennie used to live there?' Jimmy asked.

'Sorry?'

'In the house. With Auntie Anne and Uncle Michael.'

'Oh, yes,' Denis said. 'Uncle Michael and I grew up there. With Nanna Jennie.'

Jimmy thought for a moment. 'But now it belongs to Uncle Michael and Auntie Anne,' he said.

'That's right.'

'All by themselves.'

'Yes. Why?'

'Oh, nothing. Why don't they have kids?'

'Lots of couples don't have children,' Denis explained. 'Some couples have children and some don't. It depends on what they want.'

'Oh,' Jimmy said thoughtfully. But then he brightened. 'Well, it's a lovely big house anyway. I love the back garden. It's massive.'

'Yes, it is. I'm surprised you remember it so well.'

'I remember everything,' Jimmy said earnestly.

'I see.'

'Do you?' Jimmy asked.

'Sorry?'

'Do you remember everything?'

Denis looked down at him. His eyes were focused into a serious expression, waiting for an answer to this important question.

'Yes, I do remember,' Denis said. 'I remember most things.'

'That's good,' Jimmy said. 'It's better to remember everything.'

'Why?'

'Because then you can think about everything over and over. Like a film.'

'Yes, I suppose you're right,' Denis sighed. 'If that's what you want to do.'

*

The traffic crawled on the way home. They had sat motionless at Portobello Bridge for several minutes. Around them, carloads of Sunday shoppers made their exodus from the city.

'Could we turn on the air conditioning?' Jimmy whined.

'Sorry?' Denis said. 'Oh, yes. Sorry.'

Denis fiddled at the controls on the dashboard. Julia looked out the window at the canal. The water was low after a week without rain. A shopping trolley lay half-buried in the colourless ooze.

'Denis,' Julia said.

'Hmm?'

'Catherine. The one we met in town.'

'Yes.'

'Was she in the house too?' she asked.

'No,' he said. 'She had a flat with a few of her chums.'

'But she was part of your gang.'

'Yes,' he said.

'Michael knew her, then.'

'Oh yes. We all knew Catherine.'

'She's quite attractive,' Julia said. 'In an in-your-face kind of way.'

'Yes, I suppose she is.'

'But Michael wasn't involved with her?' Julia said.

'Oh, no,' Denis smiled. 'I don't think so anyway. God, I hate this traffic.'

'So,' she said after a pause. 'I guess we're going to this party after all.'

'Sorry?'

'The reunion,' she said. 'You seem to want to go now. Something seems to have changed your mind.'

'Well, we might as well go up. See the old gang. Relive old times.'

'Yes,' Julia said. 'All those tired clichés.'

Denis pressed the accelerator and the car lurched forward, only to stop suddenly halfway across the junction. They were stalled behind a delivery van, blocking traffic from all directions. Horns started blaring.

'Daddy, you're in the middle of the road,' Jimmy said.

'I know,' Denis said impatiently.

Denis and Julia stared straight ahead as angry horns sounded all around them. Conversation was impossible. The whoosh of the air conditioning filled the empty spaces but the car was still uncomfortably warm.

CHAPTER 3

Anne Smith-O'Donnell woke to the sound of cuckoos calling outside her window. She was alone in bed. Michael was downstairs already, as he was most mornings, busying himself with breakfast long before she woke up.

The morning sun came in through the windows and shone brightly on the naked walls, highlighting the cracks in the ancient pink plaster. It was nearly a year since they had stripped the wallpaper and finally thrown out those mouldy fabric curtains. They were good at tearing down, Anne thought. Good at getting to the roots. But they had yet to start the restoration.

She sat up and looked out the window into the bright green trees that surrounded the house. In the winter, when the room was cold and the trees were bare, they could see for miles, across the fields, over the top of the pine forest, beyond Ballyfinn, all the way to the shadowy Blue Stack Mountains lumbering far off in the distance. On wintry Saturday mornings, they would drink coffee in bed, herself and Michael together, watching the sun spread dawn across the county.

But now the house was enclosed in summer's relentless green. The trees were in full leaf and lush flora encroached upon the drive as if reclaiming its territory, filling the air with rich odours.

The cuckoos. The green. So restful. A summer idyll.

How different it was, she thought, growing up in that tiny house in Trim, County Meath. Seven of them packed into a council cottage. It was a house filled with children, surrounded by activity, inside and out, night and day. Small-town stuff, but there was a buzz all the same: life, people, activity everywhere, always people and voices and life.

Her life in Donegal was so different. Miles from the nearest neighbour. Surrounded by trees that howled like jackals in the winter wind. And a house so big, echoing with such emptiness that at times she felt like a prisoner on a remote, forested island.

She looked at the clock beside the bed: 7.30, time to get up. Another Monday morning. She yawned. Only a few more Mondays left before the summer holidays. There'd be assembly at eleven today, to see the clown troupe from Galway. That should be fun – even if it was the same as last year. And then, after school, two meetings with parents: Billy's mam and dad to discuss whether Billy should stay back a year, and then Ling's mother, again, to talk about Ling's reading, though Ling had improved so much lately that she no longer needed remedial classes.

Anne climbed out of bed. She shuffled across the bare floorboards out into the hall. She passed the room where Mrs O'Donnell used to sleep.

Then she remembered. Denis and Julia were coming on Friday. Must get the house ready, get their room made up. Better make a list.

Downstairs she found Michael sitting in the conservatory, staring into the garden, steam rising from his favourite mug. He looked relaxed, his legs crossed, his slim, sinewy body draped in loose trousers and a cotton top.

'You're a dreamy one this morning.'

'Oh, hi,' he reacted. 'I was just thinking.'

'About what?'

'About Denis, I suppose.'

'We'll have to get the house ready,' she said.

'Ach, we don't need to do much. He grew up here.'

'I know,' she said. 'But still. Can't expect the royal family to lower their standards.'

Michael smiled weakly and drained his mug. 'Your breakfast is ready,' he said.

'Lovely.'

They moved into the kitchen. He had set the table, as he did every morning. Sometimes Anne felt like aristocracy, fallen from grace, surviving in genteel poverty. Their surroundings came straight out of a Victorian novel: the heavy table of indeterminate wood, worn smooth by generations of O'Donnells. High-backed wooden chairs. Grapefruit in cream-coloured Wedgwood bowls, chipped with age. Faded lace serviettes on which sat antique silver spoons. Jam and butter in matching china containers. A rough terracotta vase, a hundred years old, filled with lavender from the garden.

Michael set a cafetière of coffee on the table, followed by a boiled egg in a floral egg cup and two slices of brown soda bread.

'This is lovely,' she said.

He sat across from her and sipped his coffee as she began to eat.

'So,' she said cheerily. 'What's on for you today?'

'Nothing really. I'll go into work, and then I see the consultant.'

'I thought that was next week?' she said.

'No. Next week is the injection. Today it's Mr Harrison.'

'Oh, of course, I forgot. Mr Harrison. God himself.'

'Yes.'

'What time is that?' she asked.

'I'm due in at half-twelve.'

'You'll have to leave work early.'

'Mondays are usually slow.'

'Michael?'

'Yes?'

'Will you be okay?'

'Oh, yes,' he smiled. 'It will be the same old thing. He'll ask a few questions, take my blood pressure, scribble something down on a sheet of paper.'

'You'll tell him, won't you? About the medication? How it makes you feel?'

'Yes, I will. I always do. There's nothing he can do, though.'

She smiled at him. 'You're great, you know. The way you handle this.'

He smiled sadly, sipped his coffee, and stared out the window.

Michael locked his black bicycle in a rack at the edge of the courtyard just off Main Street. The sun was already high and the pavement between the shops gave off an intense heat. He could feel the perspiration across his back. He stood beside the bike for a moment and looked in the windows of the gift shops and boutiques. He stared vaguely at the displays as if he was puzzled by what he saw.

He whistled a few notes quietly to himself, a tune from the

fifties, before taking out a set of keys and opening the door of the small bookshop. Ordinarily, he would have closed the door behind him until he was ready for business, but today he left the door open to let in the warm summer air.

Books arranged by topic lined the walls of the small shop, and three freestanding bookshelves filled with fiction took up most of the floor space. There was room for a few temporary display shelves, usually given over to the latest thriller and a few children's books. Behind the counter were school supplies: copy books, pencils, dictionaries. The shop did well leading up to Christmas and turnover was high when the children headed back to school. A few tourists bought maps and poetry during the summer months and there were a few regular readers in the town who bought books all year round. But, for much of the year, the shop remained impeccably tidy and overly quiet. Michael suspected that, as a business, it barely broke even, but Joan, the owner, had another bookshop in Donegal town that seemed to make a reasonable profit, and she seemed happy enough to keep both shops open.

Michael walked behind the counter and turned on the cash register. There was a parenthetical note from Joan pointing out that three large boxes (sorry!) had arrived on Saturday afternoon (they were due last week!) and could Michael possibly price them and set them out (thanks!) and she'd see him late Monday morning as usual (d.v.).

He walked back to the cramped storeroom and found the three boxes. He lifted the first out and set it beside the cash register, ripping it open and removing the books one by one. There were the usual novels and a new anthology of women's poetry, two new

Donegal histories that Joan got in for the parish priest, eight children's books in English and two in Irish, whimsical and filled with colour, and, finally, at the bottom, an unexpected hardback from a university press: *Survivors' Guilt: A Study in the Irish-American Psyche.* Michael set that one aside, scratching the title and value of the book on a slip of paper and then stowing the note in the cash register. Then he put the rest of the books back in the box.

For a moment, he stopped. He stared out the window into the bright courtyard. He felt so unfocused this morning, had difficulty controlling his thoughts. He was still thinking about Denis, had dreamed about him all night. Nothing definite, no story line, just snatches of images: Denis behind glass, frowning, speaking a few soundless words. Then waving, disappearing again. No explanation, no communication between them.

Michael leaned on the counter and stared into the courtyard for what might have been several minutes. Then Des Geraghty from the hardware shop next door crossed by the door and broke Michael's reverie.

'Lovely morning,' he called out.

'Yes, Des. Lovely morning.'

'You're open early today.'

'Am I? Oh, yes.'

Michael forced himself to smile and then he began making price labels for the new books.

A few minutes later, a dark-haired girl of seventeen in a black-and-white waitress uniform entered the shop. Michael was reaching below the counter and he didn't see her come in. She stopped to examine the paperbacks. And then, a moment later,

Michael was startled to hear a display stand fall over and crash to the floor, spilling books everywhere.

The girl pushed her hair back from her eyes and stared at the pile of books.

'Emma!' he said, rushing from behind the counter. 'Are you all right?'

'Oh, hiya,' she said. 'I'm sorry, Uncle Michael. I just got a bit dizzy.'

'Oh, dear. Look, sit down here.'

He pulled a chair out from the storeroom and set it beside her.

'No, really. I'm all right. I'm so sorry.'

He urged her to sit down. He looked at her with fatherly concern for a moment. Then he righted the stand and began to gather the books from the floor.

'Uncle Michael,' she said. 'You're very patient.'

'Not at all. Are you sure you're all right now?'

'Yes, it was nothing. I just stumbled. I'm a bit wrecked. I've been in the hotel since half-six. I'm not used to Monday mornings.'

'Is this your first day back?' he asked.

'Yes. We got our holidays last week.'

'How are Mam and Dad?'

'Ach, they're grand. Daddy's up to ninety. The inspectors are due in the hotel so he's edgy about the state of the place. Had you a good weekend?'

'Yes, I suppose we did,' he said. 'There's to be a party. This weekend.'

'Really?' Emma said. 'Where? Who's coming?'

'It's Stephen Deane.'

'Oh, him.'

'He's having the party for his friends at the hotel. Your hotel. Our old gang from college, they're all invited. Your mum and dad will be there. And Denis, from Dublin. And his wife, I believe.'

'Really?' Emma's eyes widened. 'This weekend?'

'Yes.'

'Uncle Denis is coming?'

'Yes. They'll be here on Friday.'

'And the boys? The boys are coming as well?'

'Yes. I believe so.'

'My God,' Emma said thoughtfully. 'Uncle Denis hasn't been to Ballyfinn since the funeral.'

'No.'

'That's two years ago now,' she said, biting her finger. 'Why doesn't he ever come and visit you at all?'

'I, I don't know really,' Michael considered.

'Mum says it's bloody rude, so it is.'

'Well, Denis has his life in Dublin . . .'

'But you're brothers!'

'Yes, I suppose we are. I didn't know you felt that strongly about him.'

'Ach, I don't care that much about Uncle Denis. Sure I hardly know the man. I just thought, well, they could bother their arses to drive up and see us. At least once in a blue moon. That's all I meant really.'

'Oh. Right.' He looked at Emma then, as if studying her face. 'Are you sure you're all right?'

'Yes, of course. Why?'

'Your face. You're looking a bit pale.'

'It's nothing,' she said. 'I'm just a wee bit tired.'

'I see.'

'Uncle Michael?'

'Yes?'

'Are you, like, looking forward to the party?'

'Yes and no,' he replied. 'It might be a bit daunting. Seeing the old crowd. We're not the same people we once were.'

'I know what you mean,' Emma said. 'Things can change. Even a year can change things.'

Michael looked at his niece. She was nearly a woman now but for these few moments she looked like a little girl again, staring down as she picked at her fingers in her lap. Then she looked up with innocence in her eyes.

'You know the boys? Jimmy. And Barry. Will they be staying with you?'

'Yes. I don't really know how to deal with boys.'

'But sure, you were boys once yourselves,' Emma laughed.

'Yes, of course we were.'

'And sure, boys are all the same,' Emma said.

'Are they?'

'I don't know,' Emma said thoughtfully. 'Maybe they're not all the same. I hope they're not.'

'Oh?'

'Look, I'd better dash,' Emma said.

'Right. You should go home and get some rest.'

'Okay, I will.'

'Look after yourself, Emma.'

'I will. Don't you be worrying about me.'

He watched her then as she turned to leave the shop. He thought her smile appeared forced as she waved him goodbye.

It was nearly time for his appointment when Michael parked his bicycle at the medical centre on the far side of town. The sun was hidden behind clouds now but the heat had remained, leaving the air heavy and humid, sapping his energy.

He stood outside the brown and white building to catch his breath. He still felt his mind's tendency to wander. His thoughts had meandered through the morning at the bookshop, he had made several mistakes in the pricing, converting sterling to euro. And when Joan finally arrived to relieve him she was all chat, but he couldn't concentrate on what she was saying.

'Good afternoon,' she said, bursting with energy through the door. 'I've had a dreadful morning, a tour bus arrived in Donegal at half-nine, half past nine on a Monday morning, I couldn't believe it! Suddenly I had fifteen Japanese students all trying to buy the same edition of Yeats's poetry, and then didn't the till break down and I had to hand-write fifteen fecking receipts!'

She threw her bag on the counter and placed her hands on her hips. She was thirty-three and worn thin from nervous energy.

'So,' she exhaled. 'How are you? Did you get that pricing done?'

'Yes,' he replied hesitantly. 'Actually, no. Not the books from England.'

'Sorry?'

'Ah, the exchange rate,' Michael said nervously. 'The euro dipped again. The bank wouldn't give me a rate. They were very slow. I only got the rate an hour ago.'

'Oh,' she frowned. 'Well, sure, maybe you could finish it up now?'

'I'm sorry. I have to go. I see the doctor today.'

'Oh, yes, of course. Okay. Listen, not to worry. Are you okay?'

'Oh, yes. I'm grand.'

'Okay. Well, look, good luck. With the doctor.'

'Thanks,' he said weakly.

'I'll see you tomorrow so. I'll try to get caught up with that pricing this afternoon . . .'

Even though Joan had displayed her usual sympathetic concern, he left the shop feeling like a guilty child. He hated these interludes, these patches when he couldn't concentrate. During his hazy times, even the small, simple interactions with people became painful, left him feeling vulnerable and inadequate. He wished she knew what it was like.

He stood with his bicycle outside the health centre staring across the ugly car park. He'd been here six months ago, just before Christmas. Then, last year at this time, in June in the heavy rain. Then again, and again, back across the years. The same visit in a different season. Like levels rising over time. A circular staircase.

He wiped his forehead with a handkerchief. Then he put the handkerchief in his pocket and opened the squeaking door. Inside he gave the receptionist his name. She said there would be a slight delay but that he would be seen shortly and would he like to take a seat inside?

There were eight people on the padded benches lining the walls of the small, sparsely furnished waiting room. Michael looked them over. Two nervous mothers, both slightly overdressed, sitting beside their bored offspring – a teenaged girl with six earrings and shoes with thick high heels, and a puffy-faced boy in baggy clothes, maybe fourteen, angry and detached, stretching his legs across the floor. The other four were adults. Sharing that demeanour, that open stare. The look of resignation. The blank, chemical face.

Michael sat beneath the window, picked up a women's magazine, flicked through a few pages, put it back on the table. Waited.

After a while, he was shown into an examination room. A tall man with silver hair wearing a white medical coat was seated at a desk. His workplace was covered with notepads, pens and brochures bearing the names of pharmaceutical companies.

'Ah, Michael, good afternoon.'

'Hello, Mr Harrison.'

'Take a seat,' Mr Harrison said with a fixed smile. 'Very warm today.'

'Yes, it is.'

'And how have you been since your last visit?' Mr Harrison said as he wrote something onto a note card.

'Grand.'

'And how is Marie?'

'Marie? Oh. It's Anne.'

'Yes,' Mr Harrison said, standing. 'Sorry, it's Anne of course. Right. Now then, can I just check those pupils?'

The doctor bent towards Michael's face and pointed a small light into one of his eyes. Then the other. Then he lifted Michael's wrist while checking his watch, humming to himself. He returned to his desk, scratched a few more notes onto the card. Then he looked at Michael.

'So, that's that. Nothing unusual today. How have you been?'

'I've been fine.'

'How about your energy levels?'

'Energy?' Michael said. 'The same as always.'

'Having any trouble sleeping?'

'Yes. A bit.'

'Anything on your mind?'

'No. Well, my brother. He's coming to visit.'

'I see. And perhaps you're a bit concerned about seeing him?'

'Yes.'

'That's not unusual,' the doctor said. 'Family reunions are never easy. I can give you a tablet to help you sleep . . .'

'No,' Michael said. 'That's all right.'

'Appetite okay?'

'Yes, about normal. I don't really eat very much.'

'No, I can see that,' the doctor said. 'Any other worries? How about the sexual function?'

Michael looked back at him. 'What do you mean?'

'You and your wife. Things all right in that department?'

'Yes. Yes, I suppose things are all right.'

'Good. Now then. You're due to have your injection next week.'

'Yes,' Michael said.

'Right.' The doctor glanced up at the clock. 'Well, unless there's anything else, that should do us for today.'

'Ah, Mr Harrison. Will we ever, you know. Think about quitting.'

'Quitting?'

'Slowing down. Or stopping the dosage. Altogether.'

The doctor sat back in his chair. 'I think we've hit it just about right,' he said carefully. 'You're coping with your life now. The chlorpromazine, well, it keeps everything under control. It controls the confusion. Keeps things clear in your mind.'

'Well, yes. But that was all, well, years ago. After college.'

'Yes,' Mr Harrison said. 'But we've got the balance right now. There's no sense upsetting any apple carts. We're better off proceeding as we have done.'

Michael didn't move.

'Michael, you remember what it was like. You don't want to go there again. With the dosage you're on now, you've put that all behind you. Let's keep things safe and under control. Okay? You have my number at the clinic. If you have any concerns at all, just lift up the phone.'

The doctor stood, smiling stiffly. 'You're doing very well,' he said.

'Thank you.'

'I'll send the instructions to the clinic. And I'll see you here in another six months.'

'Yes. Okay.'

A moment later, Michael was back outside. His eyes hurt from the sunshine. The air was stifling.

He stood for a moment thinking about the conversation he'd just had. It was more or less the same conversation, every six months.

He thought, then, about the day ahead. He'd go home now. Make himself a sandwich. Go for a short nap upstairs, or maybe in the garden, in the shade. Then Anne would come home. Maybe then they would talk about Denis. Make some plans. Start getting the rooms ready.

And next week, then, he'd be back here for his injection. As he did, every month. To keep everything under control.

Right, he thought. Better be off then.

He stood for another moment. Then he inhaled slowly.

Right, he exhaled. Keep those apple carts steady. Much better off.

CHAPTER 4

Denis parked his burgundy Mercedes before the large red-bricked offices of Accent Advertising on Pembroke Road, next to Peter's Jaguar. He saw Henri's bloated new Peugeot gleaming in his mirror. All present, Denis thought. Better dash. Nearly eight.

He climbed out of the car and took his briefcase from the boot. Then he walked back towards the café where, every Monday morning, he met his colleagues for breakfast. He usually looked forward to the ritual. It got the week off to a good start, focused the team, kept everyone in touch. But today he didn't feel up to facing them, couldn't muster any enthusiasm for the week ahead.

He hadn't slept well. He woke several times, unable to settle, trying not to wake Julia as he rolled over and then back. At one point he was going to open the window to let in some air but there was a disturbance on the street, a couple walking by were having some sort of row. Unusual for the quiet road.

When morning finally came he had to force himself out of bed. Downstairs Julia had the routine well under way. Both boys were sitting at the table in front of their cereal. Barry ate mechanically as he scanned the newspaper, and Jimmy stared into the bowl, studying the patterns in his cornflakes. Julia had the school lunches packed and the coffee made. She offered Denis a kiss as he walked into the kitchen.

'Good morning, sweetheart.'

'Hiya.'

'Bad night?'

'Yeah.'

'Oh, sweetheart. That's rotten. Here, have a cup of coffee . . .'

She was an angel, he thought. Always in good form, always on top of everything. So organised.

But he could sense a chill setting in between them. Since yesterday, since they had talked about Michael's phone call, they had fallen out of step with one another. The invitation to the party, the hasty rearrangement of the week so they could travel to Donegal on Friday – it had upset their rhythm, sent them into themselves. And then meeting Catherine on the street after so many years. Denis sensed Julia's curiosity about Catherine, felt her raw jealousy. But he couldn't bring himself to talk to her or calm her fears, or explain why this party was going to be so difficult for him.

He rarely dwelt on the past. He rarely allowed himself to remember, to move back into his memories of his boyhood and college years with Michael. His time with Stephen Deane, his affair with Catherine, that life with the gang that gathered around that famous house – it rarely entered his mind any more.

But now it was unavoidable. Michael's phone call, Stephen Deane, the party, Catherine on the street – it was as if he had walked into a gallery of his past, filled with pictures of himself in compromising positions. Like his photograph in the paper on Sunday, the whole thing promised to be misleading and embarrassing. He didn't want to face them all again. And he certainly didn't want to involve Julia in the whole mess.

And so this divide between them. It seemed like yet another fissure in their relationship, one more problem in a series of problems that had opened up between them in the previous year.

Denis wondered where Julia was right at this minute. Still driving, probably, to some meeting at some school, somewhere in the country. He wondered what she was thinking about as she listened to the radio or looked across the bright green of the countryside.

He thought of her entering the building and the teachers' reactions to her when they saw her for the first time. The men, those earnest types, the guys who gave up their lives to teach, to sit in the staffroom during breaks, seeing no one but children and other teachers like themselves, day in, day out. Then suddenly Julia walks into the school building with her blonde hair and her tall slim body. Denis thought of those men looking at his wife, making eye contact with her as they asked a question or discussed some issue, thinking how lovely she was, how attractive she remained. And yet her husband, the luckiest man in the world, the man who lay beside her in bed every night, hadn't made love to her for months.

As he walked up the busy street, he felt a heaviness come upon him as if he had suddenly aged. He was forty, on his way to forty-one. He was in good shape, he played his tennis and got out for walks in the evening. Kept his weight down. And yet today he felt draggy and decrepit.

It's just the heat, he thought. So humid, already. So early in the day.

Then a memory came to him, a memory from when they had lived in Massachusetts. Barry was eleven, still a boy with a high voice and plenty of energy, and Jimmy was just three, following Barry everywhere like a bouncing puppy. It was a day like today, vibrant with early summer sunshine. Julia had some shopping to do but Denis and the boys didn't want to waste a lovely day inside a shopping mall. So Julia drove them to a wood where they often walked together, with well-tended paths beneath tall deciduous trees. Julia drove off and Denis took the boys into the forest along the familiar paths. They marched down to the river and Denis sat on the rocks while the boys sent sticks on missions through the rapids. They walked further, then, and the boys wandered and explored the cool undergrowth. They found a fallen tree perfect for climbing, and, beyond that, they came to a patch of raised ground ideal for chasing up and running down and playing at King of the Castle.

By then they were off the pathways and Denis realised that he no longer recognised their surroundings. They began to return in the direction that Denis thought was the way, but the path never reappeared, the river seemed to have changed course, and the sounds of distant traffic had died away. Soon they were actually lost. Denis held his feelings within himself because he didn't want to frighten the boys, but it was getting late and he knew that Julia would be waiting for them at the edge of the wood. Now they were five minutes late, now ten, now twenty minutes had passed beyond when they were due to meet. Denis knew she would be annoyed at his irresponsibility, but then her annoyance would change to worry as half an hour passed, and then forty-five minutes. They walked quickly through the forest but Denis still couldn't locate anything that appeared in the least familiar, and he had no way to reach Julia to tell her that they had simply lost their bearings. And it was only after an hour, with Jimmy getting hungry as he rode on Denis's shoulders and Barry going silent with irritation and fatigue, that they finally found their original route and emerged into the sunlight to see Julia standing beside the car.

Denis still remembered Julia's expression. He remembered facing her as she stood in her shorts and sleeveless top as the boys poured forth their stories of the adventure. He remembered that momentary feeling of distance between them as she struggled to contain her emotion. Her eyes were narrowed in the sunshine, searching his face, trying to understand why he had left her there for so long, wavering between relief and anger, and seeking in Denis a clue as to what they were going to do, now, to get themselves back together again.

Denis entered the café. Bare yellow walls of textured plaster, punctuated by black uplighters. Tiny lamps over each booth suspended from the high ceiling on a thread of wire. Black tables, benches of shining black fabric. Tall, thin staff, dressed entirely in black.

He made his way towards the usual booth.

Peter Fagan faced Denis as he approached, an ironic smile playing on his thin lips. His hair was prematurely silver. He wore an expensive suit and a navy silk tie stippled with red fleck. Henri, their Parisian colleague, sat across from Peter wearing his round glasses and an expression of Gallic superiority.

Peter was, as usual, overacting, messing like a schoolboy.

'Ah! Denis, my good friend! I was just explaining to Monsieur Henri here that my good friend Denis is never late, but Monsieur Henri is French and he cannot comprehend these things . . .'

'Good morning, lads,' Denis said as he slid into the booth. 'Hope I haven't missed anything.'

'I believe we should congratulate you,' Henri said with a dour face.

'Congratulations indeed,' Peter said, smiling sweetly. 'Such a dignified portrait in yesterday's newspaper. What shall we call it? Denis and the Dolly Birds. Or how about Denis and the D-cups? I'm sure Julia was pleased.'

'Oh she was delighted,' Denis replied.

'I phoned the paper already,' Peter said. 'They'll have a copy to us in the morning. I'm going to have it blown up. We'll hang it in the reception area.'

'Lovely,' Denis said, rubbing his eye. 'Just what I want to see when I walk into the office.'

A young waitress arrived at the table.

'Good morning, gentlemen.'

'Erika, my dear!' Peter smiled broadly. 'Good morning to you. And aren't you the very picture of health this morning!'

'Ah now,' she replied wearily. 'It's a bit early for that carry-on.'

'In all seriousness,' Peter continued earnestly. 'You're an inspiration to us. An image of the Youth of Today.'

She gave Denis a weary look. 'Sure he'd have you worn out,' she said dryly.

'You should try working with him,' Denis said.

'Now, gentlemen,' she said. 'Can I bring you the usual?'

'Indeed and you can, my love,' Peter said. 'Three large, full-bodied Irish breakfasts. And two black coffees for us, and a double espresso for our French friend here, *ça va?*'

'Right, lads,' she answered. 'Won't be a tick.'

Peter stared openly as she walked away. 'My God,' he said. 'Isn't she a ray of sunshine?'

'He's full of the joys today,' Denis said to Henri.

'He is,' Henri nodded. 'But I'm afraid we have more than sunshine to discuss this morning.'

'Oh?' Denis said. 'Why? What's the news?'

'Yes,' Peter said. 'I'm afraid we have not so good news for you.'

'How can you have bad news already?' Denis said. 'It's only eight o'clock.'

Just then a loud crash came from inside the kitchen. They turned their heads towards the noise, but then focused their attention back to the table.

'Well,' Peter began. 'You were out on Friday afternoon.'

'I was,' Denis said. 'I was at the hotel to run through the launch on Saturday.'

'Yes, yes, yes,' Peter said impatiently. 'And while you were off at your lingerie gig, Henri and I were covering for you back in the office.'

'Okay,' Denis said. 'What's the story?'

'It's our friends at the bank.'

'They phoned at four-thirty,' Henri said.

'We didn't want to ruin your weekend,' Peter said.

'Right, get on with it,' Denis said. 'What do they want?'

'A new approach,' Peter said.

'Oh God,' Denis said. 'Not again.'

'Yes, my little friend,' Peter said. 'I'm afraid our friends at the bank want a spectacularly fresh idea.'

'It's the marketing director,' Henri said. 'He has stopped the campaign. He says times have changed since they agreed the approach. There is less money around. Small investors are too frightened of the markets. So they want a new campaign to focus only on the big fish.'

'So they're canning the "Happy Days" thing?' Denis said. 'But they loved it!'

'It's too glib for the times,' Peter said. 'Too dumbed down, too much mass appeal. They want to redirect the campaign at the ABC1s. Help the rich get richer.'

'But they signed a contract,' Denis protested.

'Yes, they did. But they know we won't force the issue. Their business is worth too much to us. But here's the real problem, poncho – Johnny's threatening to walk out.'

'I can see why,' Denis sighed. 'He bloody killed himself over that "Happy Days" thing. And that was our third go. They keep changing their minds. Right. So what's next?'

'The bank have given us two weeks,' Henri said. 'And apart from Johnny, everyone is busy. There is no one free to work on this project. We are, as you say, in a bind.'

Denis leaned back, stared up at the ceiling, exhaled audibly. 'Look,' he said, slapping the table. 'The first thing we need to do is get Johnny off the case. I don't want him walking. Make it up to him somehow. Give him the week off to recharge the batteries.'

'But who will create the new campaign?' Henri said.

'I will,' Denis said.

'You?' Peter said with exaggerated surprise. 'Mr Denis

O'Donnell, creating a campaign? But my friend, that sounds like real work!'

Denis ignored the sarcasm. 'I'll come up with the pitch myself. Johnny can organise the artwork next week when he comes back. He'll be in better form after a break. I'll get onto the bank straightaway and discuss the new angle.'

'Right,' Peter said sceptically. 'You're sure you can handle this now?'

'We don't have any real alternative,' Denis said. 'Let me remind you, I used to be quite good at this stuff.'

'But what if they don't like your approach?' Henri said.

Just then Erika returned balancing three large plates. 'Now, gentlemen,' she said. 'Three lovely Irish breakfasts for you. And where would you get better?'

'Nowhere, Erika,' Peter smiled. 'Nowhere on God's earth.'

'It's true,' Erika said as she set the plates on the table. 'My sister's in Australia. She says she dreams about Irish breakfasts.'

Peter looked up at her. 'Really now?' he said. 'Dreams? Of Irish breakfasts?'

'Yes,' she replied with a serious look. 'Imagine. Rashers and sausages. The stuff of dreams.'

The three men looked at her, nodding sagely.

'Rashers and sausages and pudding,' she repeated, setting down the plates one by one. 'Stuffed full of dreams.'

CHAPTER 5

Julia had a deep love of harmony and order. She liked arranging things: flowers and outfits and rooms. She liked arranging people: introducing them to one another, watching a conversation begin and sensing that a relationship was about to develop. She indulged her propensity for matchmaking, setting out lists of the singles at the office and inviting them to the house for the Christmas party, the Sunday-afternoon barbecue. She encouraged her students to work in teams, and she glowed when she heard the earnest hum of group endeavour permeate the room. She believed that her love of harmony and co-operation was a core personal quality that had helped her to become an excellent teacher.

And so, two years ago, when she saw the job in the recruitment pages of the *Irish Independent*, she thought it was too good to pass up: 'Academic Advisor on Multiculturalism. Promoting Harmony and Integration in the Classroom. Three-year contract.'

Denis said he worried about her taking on a job in the Department of Education. He couldn't see Julia being happy in that appalling, rundown office building in the centre of town. He said the department was infested with stuffy, self-important, overly ambitious ex-teachers. He predicted, quite inaccurately, that they would all wear threadbare jumpers and smoke in the corridors. He exaggerated the absurdity of her situation: Julia O'Kelly, the beautiful Chicago blonde, stuck in an office filled with frustrated tyrants where the very walls stared and schemed and whispered as she walked past . . .

'Oh, Denis!' she laughed as she signed the application form. 'It won't be that bad.'

Her interview for the job took place on a bitterly windy morning in March. She faced the panel of four in a sombre wool suit and cheerily rehearsed her life story. Yes, she grew up in Chicago, the eldest daughter of staunchly Irish-American parents. She came to Ireland for a working holiday straight after college and took a temporary job teaching geography at a private school. She fell in love with Dublin and decided to extend her one-year stay. She studied for her Higher Diploma to teach full-time in the Irish system, and she nearly killed herself preparing for the Irish-language exam. She met Denis during one of his visits home and, after a long-distance romance, she moved to Boston, they married and soon had their first son. In Boston, Julia found herself teaching in a primary school where many of the children were Hispanic. She loved the challenge of bringing together children from diverse backgrounds, watching them grow and develop trust and form friendships. She pursued a Master's degree in educating immigrant children and, once again, crammed hard to pass her Spanish exam. She served for two years on a state board dedicated to issues affecting multicultural schools. Within a short time, she had developed a reputation as an advisor, making presentations to school boards and lecturing teachers on in-service days. But then, after she and Denis had been in Boston nearly fifteen years, Denis's company set up an office in Dublin and offered him a senior position. And so they returned to Ireland once again.

The members of the panel listened carefully, nodded sagely and hired her that afternoon.

From the start, Julia determined to make a success of this job. She decided to ignore the greyness, the stuffiness, the petty ambitions within the department. She focused on the good things, especially the good qualities of her peers, who, despite an initial coldness, proved to be bright and funny and dedicated to their work. And before long she absolutely loved it.

She was largely her own boss. She visited schools across Ireland and advised teachers how to cope with the large number of immigrant children coming into the country. Up until recently, foreigners in Irish schools had been a relative rarity. Teachers were used to dealing with the needs of round-faced Catholic children and, as far as Julia could see, they did their jobs very well. But suddenly, in the past five years, schools were faced with children from China, Eastern Europe and Africa, not to mention the Irish children who had returned from abroad with little sense of their Irishness. Many of the newcomers spoke only basic English, never mind that the Irish language was still compulsory. They came with no experience of Irish life and yet their teachers were expected to attend to all their needs – academic, social, emotional – with little or no training. And, as a result, schools were crying out for help.

Julia remembered fondly her first official visit. It was a busy little school in Wicklow where, in the space of one term, students from six different countries had entered a single class of nine-year-olds. The teacher was Mrs Delaney, a short, elderly but sparkling woman whose glasses hung down on an antique brass chain. She was very committed to the children's happiness and she was coping as well as she could, but she found the new situation quite distressing.

'I don't know what to do,' she confided to Julia as the children filed out of the room. 'They're well behaved for the most part, thank God, and I can just about deal with the ones who speak English. But the rest of them, Julia, the rest of them! All they can do is draw pictures. I keep rewarding them with sweets. But, Julia, that's not really teaching, sure it's not?'

Julia talked with Mrs Delaney during the break. She recommended a language game that she used to use, a series of role-plays that engaged the entire class while providing useful communications skills for the foreign students. Mrs Delaney decided to give it a go. Julia watched then as the children began mouthing the script, slowly, then a little faster, with corresponding movements, exaggerated and silly but great fun. And then the whole thing again, but this time in Chinese, coached by a new girl who had never before spoken in class!

Julia drove away from the school feeling very fond of Mrs Delaney and hoping that their efforts together would pay off. Two weeks later Julia received the sweetest letter, written on old-fashioned vellum stationery, thanking her kindly and enthusing over the progress that the children, and their teacher, were making.

So Julia thought she was off to a good start. She worked with new teachers every week, sometimes in Dublin, sometimes out in rural communities. Most of her visits were successful. Thanks poured in from villages in Kerry and inner-city schools in Dublin and new suburban schools in Kildare and Meath: cards and phone messages and invitations to come back any time to see the class.

But it wasn't always easy. Julia set high standards for herself. She wanted to be good at this job, and to make it happen she had to make some changes. She overhauled her wardrobe for starters. She set aside her collection of tight skirts and low-cut blouses and replaced them with dark trousers and sensible warm tops. She learned to swallow instant coffee without choking. She listened hard to the way teachers talked, especially those from the country, trying to get into the lingo. She practised saying 'Grand' and 'You know the way' and 'Sure, give it a lash'. She tried to soften her accent when she entered a school so that it took them a few sentences to catch the fact that she was American. And she softened her approach as well. She believed she had become more diplomatic and had learned to avoid confrontation. She perfected the subtle Irish art of circumlocution.

'It's nice,' she explained to Denis. 'The way people talk to one another here. Very polite. They never actually say what they really feel.'

'Yes dear,' he responded blandly.

'Infuriating,' she said. 'But nice.'

And so, most days, she loved her job. She loved meeting teachers and discussing their problems. She loved the fact that, most of the time, she knew what she was doing. She enjoyed making presentations in staffrooms or school halls. She rehearsed everything well in advance, practised delivering her facts, her statistics and her methodologies, fine-tuned her arguments and prepared her refutations. She loved the question-and-answer sessions, really enjoyed a lively debate about the rights and wrongs of cultural integration.

She believed that, after a year in the job, she was pretty much in control. Her image was right: she wasn't frumpy but she wasn't too glam either. She kept her American energy and positive attitude but she did her best to stick to the Irish way of doing things. She never tried to become anyone's friend, but she got close enough to the teachers in the schools she visited to enable her to relate to their problems. She supported their work, and she helped make a positive difference in the way they ran their classrooms.

But all her efforts had not come without cost. There were days when she felt very alone. Despite all the satisfaction she received from her work, she had no workmates with whom to share her successes. Her colleagues had their own schedules in their own schools, and often weeks would pass without their paths crossing. Her supervisor – a balding administrator awaiting retirement – praised her warmly but knew nothing about multiculturalism and cared little about Julia's day-to-day activities. The headteachers she met, while valuing Julia's input, remained mistrustful of anyone from 'The Department'. And she could never say to any teacher, in any school, what she thought of any other teacher, in any other school. Her position made it impossible to open up, to share her experiences, or to make friends on the inside.

And that was the problem, really. She showed them the outside, the practised, professional Julia. She had that down to a T. But the inside. What she really thought. That was harder for her to share.

And for the past year it had been getting more difficult. She and Denis had become more remote. They didn't talk the way they used to do at the end of the day. She couldn't seem to tell Denis

the little things any more. What that six-year-old had said about
her shoes. Or what Sister Majella had said about the rats that had
infested the playground.

This was the hardest aspect of all, knowing that there was no
one to share her stories with. Sometimes it got so bad that Julia
stayed in the car, outside the house, before going inside. She
stayed in the car, where it was quiet, and she gathered all her
frustrations into a single knot in her head. And then she cried.
Sometimes it took a while, because she had to wait till she'd
stopped crying and then re-do her make-up so the boys wouldn't
know. And then she'd go inside, and try to be the mother they
needed, and the confident wife she used to be.

But now this reunion in Ballyfinn would bring its own
particular challenges. Because, in Julia's mind, Ballyfinn was
where all her problems had started, a little over one year ago.

Early in March of last year, Julia had looked at the roster in the
office and discovered that she was due to visit St Mary's National
School in Ballyfinn, County Donegal.

'Denis,' she had said over dinner. 'St Mary's. Isn't that where
Anne teaches?'

'I don't know,' Denis said. 'Yes, it probably is. Why?'

'I'm going there. For a visit. Next week.'

'You should probably give Anne a bit of warning,' he said.

'Yes, I suppose I should. Maybe I could visit them, spend the
night?'

'Be careful. You don't know what you'll find up there. You're
the supervisor now. It might be a lousy school. And Anne
mightn't be the greatest teacher . . .'

'Oh, Denis. I'm sure she's very good.'

At that time Julia had felt pleased to have an opportunity to visit Anne. Ever since they had moved back to Dublin, she had been uncomfortable with the distance between Denis and his brother. They never visited one another and rarely even spoke on the telephone. Denis didn't seem to mind the situation, but Julia wondered how he could be so insensitive. It never seemed to occur to Denis that Michael might need some support from his family. And it had bothered Julia increasingly as time passed.

So Julia had thought that this visit to Anne's school might be her chance to strike up a relationship and to build some bridges between them. Besides, she'd always wanted to get to know Donegal. Maybe if this worked out they could all go up and spend some time there. Unite the two brothers once again. Become a family. It could turn out to be really nice.

After dinner, Julia had rung Anne. Anne seemed delighted to hear from her, invited her to stay over after the visit. And so it was settled. Julia walked into the sitting room. Denis had parked himself on the sofa with a magazine on his lap and a western on the telly.

'So are you staying with them?' he asked.

'Yep.'

'And are you okay with that?'

'Of course I'm okay. I'm really looking forward to it.'

'Are you? Why?'

'What do you mean, why?' she said, sitting beside him. 'I want to get to know Anne.'

'Why would you want to do that?'

'Why not?' Julia said. 'You never talk to Michael. So maybe I'll be your little ambassador. Where are the boys?'

'Upstairs,' Denis said. 'I think Barry is studying . . .'

Julia had moved closer, then, and straddled Denis on the sofa, knocking his magazine to the floor. She put her arms around his neck.

'Do you want to come with me?' she teased. 'We could have fun in your old bedroom.'

'Damp old house,' he said, looking directly into her eyes.

'I'd love you to show me,' she said softly.

And then she had kissed him, there on the sofa, as the television shouted and shot and screeched behind them.

Of course Julia was in good form generally at that time. It was just over twelve weeks now. No morning sickness, no problems whatsoever. And she was certain it was going to be a girl.

She had planned to drive to Donegal on Wednesday after work. She was spending that first night in a hotel and, after the school visit on Thursday, she'd go home with Anne. Denis was able to be home early and the boys were used to her travelling, so everything was sorted out at home. She had packed that morning and brought her suitcase with her into the office, and she planned to leave early and avoid rush-hour traffic. But, as it happened, a meeting in the afternoon ran over and then, just as she was making her escape, she received a phone call from a teacher in Thurles who wondered why her Chinese children were so much quicker than her Irish students, especially at maths, and sure if we could only find out how they learned their sums wouldn't we all be better off, and could Julia recommend something on Oriental culture that might offer a key to how these Chinese children all seemed to be so quick off the mark?

As a result Julia didn't leave the office until after five. It was raining heavily and the rush hour had slowed to a crawl. By the time she reached Finglas it was nearly six and she still had a four-hour drive ahead of her. She phoned the hotel from the car to tell them she'd be late and to ask them to hold her room.

To make matters worse, she didn't feel well. For the past two weeks her schedule at the office had been more demanding than usual. There were quite a few school visits to get through before the Easter holidays, including several over-nights. She hadn't yet informed her colleagues that she was expecting and she was tired from her nights away from home. Then Jimmy had been out sick for a few days from school and she and Denis had to shuffle their work to be with him, leaving both of them behind and trying to catch up all the following week.

She had been fine up to now but, suddenly, she began to feel quite drained as she drove north through the heavy rain. She didn't arrive at the hotel until after ten and she was hungry after the long drive. She got soaked as she walked from the car to the hotel lobby. Then there was no porter to carry her suitcase, so she dragged it herself down the hall to her room. She ordered room service as soon as she checked in but the meal took nearly an hour to be delivered and by then she was so tired she could manage to eat only half her fish and a few tepid potatoes.

Still, she tried to maintain a positive attitude about the visit. When she finally climbed between the fresh sheets, she felt all right. She looked forward to seeing Anne teach and to chatting with her and Michael over dinner.

But when she woke the next morning she still felt ill. She wondered whether her meal of the night before had been properly cooked. She felt shaky in the shower and then she sat on the bed to catch her breath as she dried her hair.

Downstairs a friendly waitress greeted her, offering a cooked breakfast, but Julia only wanted tea and toast.

An hour later, she arrived at the school. It was a cold morning, still damp and gusty. She didn't feel at all well as she walked down the school's sea-green corridors. She was scheduled to meet the headmistress first thing. Then, after coffee, she was to observe a few teachers in action in their classrooms.

Julia's first impressions were not inspiring. Mrs Fowles was a crisp, business-like woman in her early fifties. She made it clear that she considered Julia's visit to be an empty formality. There were a few children from Nigeria, South Africa, and China in the school, but she seemed reluctant to recognise that they were here to stay – and she had little to offer in terms of support for her staff.

'You must realise,' she said with her chin slightly raised, 'that our first priority must be the children who live, and who will continue to live, in this community. For a small school in a small Irish town, we at St Mary's have maintained a very fine academic record. If we have short-term visitors passing through, we'll do our best to give them whatever attention they require. But I do not expect my teachers to change their approach to teaching, an approach that has produced hundreds of happy, well-educated children, in order to cater for a few newcomers who might only be here for a year or two at most.'

Julia was going to counter the argument, but she felt she lacked the energy to take this woman on in debate. She set down her coffee and said that she knew St Mary's had a very strong academic reputation indeed.

During the morning, Julia observed two classes, each of which had only one well-adjusted foreign pupil, and she began to feel that the visit was a waste of her time. But then, just before lunch, she was scheduled to visit Anne's class. She scanned the corridor as she approached, finally spotting Anne, small and wiry, in her navy jumper and skirt.

'Hello, Anne,' Julia smiled and extended her hand.

'Oh, hello,' Anne whispered quickly with a half-smile. 'Lovely to see you. The children won't be used to visitors – they'll find it a bit hard to settle.'

'Don't worry,' Julia said, touching Anne's arm. 'I'm used to antsy kids. They'll be okay after a few minutes. I'm looking forward to seeing you in action!'

Julia squeezed into a small chair at the back of the room and surveyed the ranks of eight-year-old heads. She checked her notes – yes, they appeared to be here: two Africans and two Chinese. She crossed her fingers and tried to ignore the nausea that was becoming more persistent as the morning wore on.

She was not disappointed. Anne kept a steady pace in the class, moving around the room, constantly asking questions and calling on every student in turn. At one point she asked the children to read out passages from their books. She called on a Nigerian boy to go first. He stood up proudly and began to read, haltingly and with a heavy accent.

'An' den Sain' Brigid took de reeds from de water, and she ben' dem into a cross. Den she took de cross an' she carried it up to de chieftain of de village. De chieftain did not believe in Jesus. But he took de cross from her, and den his eyes began to glow . . .'

And as he read, his eyes widened with the surprise of the story.

Julia watched as Anne worked with him, correcting his pronunciation quickly and quietly and without belittling his efforts. And when he was finished reading, Anne sighed a sigh of contentment:

'Well, class! I think Ngezi did a lovely job, don't you?'

And the class broke into hearty applause. Ngezi sat down then, obviously proud of his efforts.

But what had impressed Julia even more was when Anne had an Irish girl go next, a bright little thing with freckles and a long red ponytail. She read the passage beautifully, and in a clear effort to ensure that no one was singled out, Anne got the class to applaud her too.

Julia smiled broadly as she made notes on her pad.

At the end of the hour, Julia winked at Anne as the children filed out of the room. But Anne was busy with a boy who had popped a button, so she didn't see Julia's sign of support, and Mrs Fowles was waiting impatiently to herd her off to lunch with the rest of the staff.

As the afternoon wore on, Julia's condition deteriorated. She made several visits to the ladies and finished the day back in the headteacher's office. Mrs Fowles made it clear, speaking over her lowered half-glasses, that she looked forward to reading Julia's report. But she also made it clear that any feedback would be reviewed in the context of the exemplary standards that she and her staff had maintained over many years. And then she thanked Julia for her time and attention, and showed her to the door.

Julia phoned Denis from the car.

'How'd you get on?' he said. 'Can she teach?'

'Oh, yes, she's excellent. But this woman, the headmistress. She runs the place like a labour camp.'

'Bit of a crow, is she?'

'She's really bad. No one seems to mind her but I thought she was awful.'

'So what are you doing now?' Denis said.

'I don't know. I'm not feeling great.'

'Oh, dear,' Denis said. 'Do you want to come home?'

'No, I'd better go through with this.'

'Okay. Well, listen, have a good time. See you tomorrow.'

Julia was just putting her phone away when a wave of nausea much worse than any she'd experienced all day hit her. After the worst of it had passed, she dialled Anne and Michael's number. She got their answering machine. She stalled.

'Hi, Anne, hi, Michael, this is Julia. I'm sorry, but I can't see you tonight after all. It's, it's Jimmy again. He's not feeling well, and Denis has a meeting tonight, so I have to get back to Dublin. I'm sorry about this, I'll phone you soon. And you were great today, Anne, really great.'

Then she rang off. Perspiring freely, she started the car and drove north over the hills to Letterkenny, following the signs to the hospital. She was admitted at half-past four. By seven-thirty she was told that she had miscarried.

She spent the night in hospital, and in the morning she drove back to Dublin. She phoned Denis at the office to say she wasn't well and asked him if he could come home. She was crying when he met her at the door. He sent her upstairs to bed, made her a cup of tea and brought her a hot-water bottle. She slept that afternoon, and all night long, troubled by menacing dreams.

She couldn't bring herself to phone Anne afterwards. She wasn't close enough to her to expect sympathy and she didn't see the point in telling her useless lies.

In the beginning, Denis was very supportive. They talked about it several times late into the evenings, and he shared her sadness about losing the baby. They hadn't planned the pregnancy but for both of them it would have been a happy accident. Denis loved the boys, and had always been a good father, and it seemed a good time for them to have another child. Whether it was another boy, or especially if it had been a girl, it would have been lovely.

But Denis's support in some ways made it worse. She blamed herself for losing the baby. She felt that she should have shared her news, she should not have allowed herself to become over-tired, she should have taken the care that was needed to get the baby off to a proper, healthy start within her. Even now she couldn't forgive herself for what had happened. She felt guilty before Denis, and guilty before the baby, and guilty before her own conscience.

And now her opportunity had passed. She was still physically capable of having another pregnancy, but she felt that her natural time was over. She had squandered her last chance to have a daughter.

The whole episode had come between her and Denis. She still wanted to talk about it but he seemed to have tired of the subject. She felt inhibited sexually in a way that she had never been before.

When Denis was with her in bed, and she could feel his body beside her, and the time should have been right to make love, she found herself quite often – not always, but often – uninterested, and she turned away. Since the miscarriage, she had begun to feel older and less desirable to Denis. She had also begun to feel jealous of him in a way that was new and uncomfortable. As the year passed, they spoke less, they made love less and they were less happy with one another than any time in their lives together.

Now, as the week progressed, she began to panic about the reunion in Ballyfinn. She imagined, quite irrationally, dreadful scenes at the party, unfolding before her like a slow horror film: Denis seeing Catherine again, talking to her with their heads bent low, drinking wine, laughing, that look appearing in Denis's eyes as he drew Catherine towards him. Julia imagined it like a slow-playing film, over and over.

Though she'd been enthusiastic at first, she had come to fear the reunion. She feared that the whole thing – their life together, their love for each other, their lovely home, their marriage –might just come tumbling down around them, this weekend, at this stupid bloody party.

The sun hung on in the sky and late-evening heat still filtered through the windows in the front of the house. Across the road, woodpigeons settled into the tall trees surrounding Kenilworth Square.

Julia walked upstairs with a bundle of freshly ironed clothes. She knocked gently on Barry's door. He grunted for her to come in. She opened the door a peep. He was lying on top of his bed reading a novel, listening to his Walkman.

'Hi,' she said, opening the wardrobe to put away the clothes.

'Hi,' he said, pulling off his earphones.

'How are you?' she asked.

'Mph.'

'Tired?'

'Yeah.'

'Your exams are nearly over. I bet you can't believe it.'

'No,' he stretched. 'It's great.'

'So. School tomorrow and Wednesday. And then you're off for the summer.'

'Yeah.'

'You seem really tired.'

'I'm okay.'

'Did you run today?' she asked.

'No. There wasn't time.'

'Are you okay with the trip this weekend? To Donegal?'

'Sure,' he said. 'Why?'

'I just wondered. Because if you're not into it, I wouldn't mind staying here.'

'Oh no. I'm okay. We might as well go.'

'Okay,' she smiled. 'I guess we'll go then.'

'Good.'

She started to straighten the books on his desk, setting them into neat piles.

'Mom,' he cautioned.

'Sorry, okay, I'll stop cleaning. Good night.'

'Good night.'

Downstairs she found Jimmy and Denis at the kitchen table, a deck of cards between them.

'Maybe if we used books, you know?' Denis asked. 'To prop it up?'

'No, Dad,' Jimmy objected.

'But look,' Denis said. 'We could make levels. We could put different cards on different books. It would be like a block of flats.'

'It's not a card house if you prop it up,' Jimmy explained. 'It has to stand on its own.'

'But cathedrals,' Denis said. 'They used flying buttresses.'

'They still stand by themselves,' Jimmy argued. 'Anyway, the guy on telly just used cards. No books.'

'Okay, okay. Look, how about if I hold the bottom ones and you balance the roof on top?'

'Guys,' Julia said. 'Isn't it about time Jimmy went to bed?'

'Yes,' Denis said. 'Soon. But look, what if we place a pile of cards here . . .'

Julia settled into the sofa and paged through a gardening magazine. She sighed, told herself not to get involved. But soon, as expected, she heard Denis cursing, and Jimmy shouting, as the cards fell and scattered across the table and down onto the floor.

CHAPTER 6

Anne curled up on the sofa in her blue satin dressing gown, holding a glass of white wine. A Scrabble board rested on a small table and Michael sat across from her, cross-legged on a large cushion on the floor, sipping tea from a cream-coloured mug. Even on bright summer evenings such as this, the room remained dark, the trees outside blocking the light from the bay window.

Anne looked past Michael across the large room. The old fireplace was filled with logs, resting for the summer, as if waiting for the heat to lift so it could return to its cold-weather routine. Above the fireplace was a heavy oak mantelpiece, empty save for a photograph of their wedding: Anne in her demure, knee-length dress, and Michael in a dark suit and that colourful floppy bow tie.

Flanking the fireplace was a set of tall, white bookshelves. Michael kept them neatly ordered, leaving spaces for a few small ceramic sculptures, things he had made at art college: a metallic-blue laughing dog, its teeth shining with menace. A drab green willow, wilted, bowed down with sadness. His books were on the shelves to the left, a collection of biographies, several oversized art books, a shelf of paperback novels and a few books about music. Anne's books were on the right, mostly plays and recent hardback novels, with a few thick histories arranged along the top.

Beside Anne's books was the stereo system in its ebony cabinet
– black and chrome, with an array of lights and knobs – flanked
by two narrow, six-foot-tall shelves filled with Michael's CDs.
Then the old upright piano, a massive cherry-wood piece of
furniture with brass candle holders. Anne wondered how it ever
found its way to this remote hillside house. Michael had it tuned
every year by an elderly man from Donegal town who stayed for
dinner, spent the evening talking with Michael about music, and
treated Anne with excessive old-world courtesy.

At the end of the room, French doors led into the kitchen.
Inside was the dining table with its heavy, high-backed chairs.
Through the rear window the trees at the back of the house, dark
and ivied, could be seen. The windows were open but there was
no movement in the air and the atmosphere was hot and stifling.

'Is it my go?' she asked.

'Yes,' Michael replied, studying the board.

'Sorry,' she said.

She looked down at her tiles and then began setting letters
down one by one.

'Lovely,' he said.

Anne looked across the table at Michael as he pencilled her
score onto a sheet. He wore a new T-shirt that hung loose over his
sinewy torso. At least we've got enough money, she thought, as
she glanced around the room. Enough for clothes and books and
CDs. The occasional holiday. And we eat well. And the house: no
mortgage to worry about. That was a blessing. Even if she
occasionally wanted to burn it down.

She felt restless. She shifted, stretched her legs, sipped her wine.
Tried to relax.

The O'Donnell house, she thought. Such a family of men. Michael's grandfather, a big noise in these parts. A builder-turned-politician, back when Ireland was still a new nation. Worked to have new houses built to get people out of their run-down cottages. Modernised the hospital in Letterkenny. Supported the fishing and farming co-operatives, worked to improve the roads. A bit of a visionary.

Of course he looked after himself. Bought this old house and the lands around it from the Binghams when they fell on hard times. A Catholic man buying a big Protestant house, back when no one in the area had two shillings to rub together.

And then Michael's father, the eldest son. He went off to Africa after the war, got involved in shipping during Nigeria's boom time. Had hundreds of natives working for him. Retired young, acted the country gentleman, married, took his father's seat in the Dáil. He had died by the time Anne came on the scene. Michael's mother had been such a dignified woman, playing the beauty to her husband's beast, locked away up here in the middle of nowhere with her boys.

Such a blow it must have been to them, Anne thought. When Michael broke down. Such a frustrating disappointment.

Michael had told her the basic facts about that time, the onset of his condition, when everything seemed to fall apart. But she suspected that she didn't know the full story. She knew there were problems towards the end of his time at college in Dublin. She knew that there were some wild parties, maybe some drugs involved. She knew that Michael had gone missing at one stage and that Denis had had to go looking for him. He was only twenty when it hit him, that first incident, but it was the start of a long struggle to control the errant impulses of his mind. He didn't speak about it any more but she knew there had been long patches of strangeness, when he heard things and had desires and delusions that were well beyond the pale. He had been admitted back into hospital three times in those early years, at his own request, feeling he needed time to himself, time to calm down and rid himself of the voices that plagued him, the voices that confused his thoughts and kept telling him to seek the impossible and resolve what could never be resolved.

But then he learned to manage his condition. He left hospital for good and got into a routine at home. A quiet life. He took the job in the bookshop, which left him time to rest in the afternoon. He stopped drinking, stopped smoking, slowed down on the coffee. Kept everything at a low, steady boil. Received his medication once each month. And for the past fifteen years, nothing. No confusion. No incidents. Just a calm, steady life.

Of course Anne wanted to know more. She wanted to know what he had experienced at the onset, how he managed to get over it and become the person he was now. But she suspected that he was actually embarrassed by the whole thing. Now that it was past, he wanted to deny that it had happened, that he had ever lost control in that way.

For the past few years, it had been relatively easy for Michael to forget that time and to exist entirely in their present lives. There was no one around to remind him of those events. His parents were both dead. His brother Denis had, as far as Anne could see, disowned him entirely. Denis and Julia rarely phoned except at Christmas, and they certainly never bothered to visit. In fact, Julia didn't condescend to call, even when she was here, in town, visiting the school, just up the road. Instead she backed out at the last minute, dreaming up some lame excuse about Jimmy being sick.

And, to a certain extent, this state of affairs suited Anne. They could lead their lives without being reminded of the past, without competing with Michael's more successful brother. Because for no good reason, Anne was intimidated by Denis and Julia. And she envied them. Denis had money, he had charm and wit and a successful business. Julia was confident, a pretty American blonde with a supervisor's job that most teachers would kill for. And the boys, well, the boys were lovely, well reared and polite, she had no grudge against them. Except, of course, that the boys threw a spotlight on the fact that she and Michael had no children of their own.

She looked at Michael now, so relaxed as he placed his tiles on the board. All seven letters. An excessively high score.

'Well done,' she sighed as he noted his score on the sheet.

He did this every night. He was a wicked Scrabble player. So frustrating, she thought. He's so damn good, at everything. Except at being, well, a normal sort of man.

He read all the time. He regularly cleared out the bookshelves, brought his old books down to the school or to the public library and gave them away to make room for more. Books by the boxload. And he knew his music. He listened to the radio in the afternoons and evenings, was always bringing home the latest CDs, knew the up-and-coming performers. He sat at the piano and played his old Mozart pieces and his bit of Beethoven, learned so long ago. And then he improvised, did his Keith Jarrett thing, hummed along to himself while his right hand tinkled up and down the keys.

Before his illness, of course, there had been his sculptures at college. He had described to her his gnomes and grotesque characters, the mobiles that had hung from the ceiling, floating like ships through the air. It was all lost now, or destroyed, apart from the few pieces on the shelves. She wished he had kept it up. He could get back into it, set up a workshop here, sell his work in the local shops. Maybe get his own premises. The problem was, though, that art was too painful for him now. Too many memories. He needed his routine, the quiet life. So she didn't push it.

Michael was a lovely man, of course, very charming. Her colleagues at school loved him, always insisted that she bring him to the staff parties. They were the teachers, considered to be the town intellectuals, but he could talk rings round them if he had the energy. She never forgot that night when Dick Molloy had a few jars on him and started quoting poetry, so full of himself, and then Michael stood up and did his rendition of 'The Wild Swans at Coole' and there were tears in everyone's eyes.

Anne's family didn't get it at all. They didn't understand why she had chosen to dedicate her life to a man like that. Dreamy. Impractical. Harmless, maybe, but feckless, too, gormless even, in their eyes. Her brother Donal, at his mechanic's shop. He never said anything when she brought Michael down to visit, but she knew what he thought. From the minute she watched Donal shake Michael's hand, she knew what he thought. He never even invited Michael down to the pub.

Her mother did her best, Anne knew, but her mother really couldn't understand Michael's lack of career. She didn't know how a girl like Anne – a teacher, so organised, so in control – could be interested in a fellow who did nothing only sit behind a counter in a quiet bookshop for a few hours a week. Anne tried to explain but she simply couldn't use the medical terms, couldn't bring herself to label Michael as *schizophrenic* to her family.

'He's got medical problems,' Anne said in her mother's kitchen. 'It's like a disability.'

'I see,' her mother replied as she peeled potatoes at the sink. 'He certainly looks healthy enough.'

'No,' Anne explained. 'It's not that sort of thing. It's a sort of handicap. He gets tired.'

'Your father had a dose of that once. It lasted seventeen years.'

'Mammy!'

'Sorry, pet,' she said to the potatoes. 'Maybe I'm just too old to understand these things. Does he expect to get better?'

'Well, he is better. I mean, he's doing very well.'

'I see,' her mother sighed. 'Well, that's great, anyway.'

She lifted the potato peelings from the sink and dumped them into the bin. 'It's great that he's doing so well,' she repeated sadly.

Since the wedding, Anne tended to visit home on her own, reassuring her parents that, despite the lack of grandchildren, everything was grand.

But was it? she asked herself. Was it really grand between herself and Michael? Was this quiet friendship of theirs, this close companionship, enough to keep a marriage alive? As much as she detested male machismo, could she really survive without the occasional bit of red-blooded life?

Ah now, let's be fair, she told herself. Most of this was your decision. *You* asked him to marry you, remember? You knew about his handicap, you knew he would never take on a proper job. And as for children, well, that was your decision too. But it was a decision taken some time ago, and a decision that was getting more and more difficult to stand by.

She looked around the room. Such a big house, with so much garden out the back. The perfect house to raise a family. And she looked at Michael again. In some ways he would make the ideal father. He was interested in everything, he loved explaining things. He had excessive patience, rarely got angry or upset or flustered. He had time on his hands. The bookshop paid so little that if he gave it up they wouldn't miss the money. Anne was home most days by three and she had the summers off. It was the perfect situation in which to raise a child.

Except that she just didn't know how Michael would cope. He needed his sleep, his routine. And she didn't want to impose her urges or needs on him when he was doing his best to live with a handicap, a handicap that prevented many people from leading any sort of normal life themselves, never mind raising children as well.

She sighed. The weekend would be upon them soon. Denis and Julia and the boys would be here, like a picture of how it should have been, challenging her to assess her life and maybe even defend what she had. She felt sorry for Michael because she knew that, in a few short days, the past would return to challenge him as well.

She glanced down at the board, set down her word. Double word score.

'Well done,' Michael said, entering her score onto the pad.

'Thanks,' she mumbled. 'Michael?'

'Yes?'

Michael's blue eyes shone like a child's. She smiled at him.

'Nothing.'

'Are you sure?'

'Yes, love, I'm sure. Your go.'

She looked over at him again, sitting on the floor below her. Then she sank back on the sofa and sipped her wine.

But why? she thought. Why did she have to defend herself, her situation, her life with Michael? It was good overall. They had time. They had a few friends. They lived in a beautiful part of the world. And, despite its drawbacks, hadn't she chosen this lifestyle for herself?

She thought back to that strange and wonderful period in her life, eight years ago, that had led her to Donegal and to Michael.

She had been teaching in Dublin for several years and had recently ended a long and difficult relationship with a man who worked at the bank. He was separated from his wife and his son was one of Anne's pupils. For the first six months, Anne had enjoyed his charm and his inordinate affection. Then, for the next two years, she had endured his drinking, his jealousy, his penny-pinching meanness, his excessive control. She was tired when it was finally over. She wanted to start again and to approach life afresh: from a new angle, in a new place, far away from him and Dublin and everything in her life at that time.

She had read a notice regarding a temporary teaching job in Ballyfinn, starting in January, to fill in for a woman on maternity leave, and she turned out to be the only applicant for the position. Over Christmas she packed her things and moved into a rented cottage two miles outside town. On her first day at work, a bitterly cold Monday morning, she trudged her way through the snow and entered a room filled with red-cheeked children with the loveliest accents she had ever heard.

That first term raced by. She liked the staff, adored the children and settled nicely into small-town life. Summer approached and, just as she was about to pack her bags to return to Dublin, they offered her a permanent job, and she gladly accepted. Apart from the headmistress, she found her new colleagues to be good fun and good company. She joined them on their outings to the cinema in Letterkenny or the theatre in Derry. She grew fond of the beach at Rathmullan, went for long solitary walks on the miles of clean, deserted strand. She joined the local drama club, took over the director's chair, rehearsed her amateurs Tuesday and Thursday nights at the local theatre and won great recognition in the town for her production of 'A Doll's House'.

She embraced the soft countryside, the friendly people and their cheerful resilience. She came to know the local craft shops run by efficient, hard-working women – pottery and landscapes and coffee and fruit scones with home-made jam. Colourful road-side pubs, Biddy's and Rosie's and Jimi's, so welcoming on a cold, wet evening, and you could chat to anyone there, you could actually have a conversation with the old men at the bar or the people at the next table, and it was all so friendly and so easy. And in the summer, those fairs and festivals they had – bunting stretched across the streets, country-and-western music, awful beauty contests, car-reversing competitions. Drinkers spilling out of the pubs, raucous and good-humoured as summer evenings stretched late into the night.

As time passed, though, her weekly conversations with her mother began to have a predictable edge.

'So Annie, how's the form?'

'Grand, Mam. And yourself?'

'Sure we couldn't be better. Any men on the scene?'

'No, nothing to report. I went to the cinema with Thomas last night.'

'Ah, Thomas. But I thought you told me he was . . .'

'He is. But he's great company.'

'Sure maybe you should go back to Dublin. There's plenty of fellas about in Dublin.'

'Mam . . .'

'Might as well face facts, Annie. You're not getting any younger.'

'I know, Mammy.'

Anne said goodbye every week trying to keep the annoyance from her voice. The problem was, of course, that her mother was right. Anne had analysed the situation carefully within weeks of moving to town and determined that it was going to be slim pickings. The few men at school were well married and smothered with children. She met Thomas through the theatre and they became good mates, but never in the animal sense of the word. Most of the young men had gone to Dublin to find work, only coming home at the weekends for pints. She'd had a few approaches, of course – middle-aged farmers or strong-looking lads in black T-shirts with silver belt buckles. She frightened most of them off by telling them she was a teacher.

That first summer, she did have a go at Jason, who owned the shoe shop. He was attractive in an untamed sort of way, a high-energy type, dexterous and quick-witted. They went out twice before Thomas gave her the inside story, revealing to Anne that she was the only eligible female between seventeen and thirty-five in the whole of the town that Jason hadn't already shagged. Something about his way with shoes, Thomas explained. Anne decided to remain the trophy that got away and promptly dropped Jason.

And so, as the weeks wore on, Saturday nights became nights for washing her hair and catching up on her reading. And dreading the phone call from her mother.

Midway through her second term of teaching on a bright October day, when school was out for the afternoon, she went to church to pray, as she did every year on the anniversary of her father's death.

Just outside town there was a lovely small church high on a hill that Anne visited when she felt the need. It was quiet there and she could always get the key from the curate, a gentle elderly man who always said hello and chatted about the weather but never interfered.

The air was bright and when she walked into the church the cool interior glowed with the colours of stained glass. She thought it was empty. She walked up the aisle, slid into a pew and knelt down. For a few moments, she recalled her father. She spoke to him silently. She asked him how he was and assured him that she was okay. And then, as she did every year, she sought his blessing on her life.

As she finished her prayer, she became aware of a sound at the back of the church, a sort of delicate scraping. And there, in the shadows beneath the tiny choir loft, was a man with sandy hair wearing white coveralls, kneeling on the floor. There was a cloth on the ground and, in the centre, a small painting in an elaborate gilt frame surrounded by tiny pots of paint and thin brushes.

Anne blessed herself, stood, and walked back to him.

'Oh, hello,' he said as she approached. 'I'm sorry. I hope I didn't disturb you.'

'Not at all,' Anne said. 'On the contrary. Perhaps I'm the one who's disturbing you.'

He seemed nervous and his eyes didn't meet hers as he spoke.

'I'm just finishing here,' he said in a soft Donegal accent, gesturing to the floor. 'It's a station of the cross. The sixth. The plaster, it seems to have got a bit damp, and the old hook fell out. Crashed to the floor in the middle of Mass. This corner of the frame was damaged.'

'I see,' she said, finally catching his eye. 'And you're repairing it?'

'Yes, well, I'm doing my best. I patched the frame at home, but the painting was also a bit damaged. I wanted to get the colours right, so I'm doing the finishing touches, you know, here. In the natural light, where it will hang.'

'It's lovely,' Anne said, bending down. 'I can't see where it was damaged at all. By the way, I'm Anne.'

'Oh, yes. Hello, Anne. I'm Michael. I'd shake your hand but, well, I've got paint. On my fingers.'

'That's quite all right.'

'I wonder, though,' he said, looking again at the floor. 'I

wonder if you could give me a bit of a hand? I need to hang it, to centre it properly.'

'Sure. Of course.'

For the next few minutes, Michael tried to position the icon on the wall while Anne gave instructions: raise the left side, okay, now back down just a bit . . .

Then they circled the space, walking around the church, viewing it from all angles to see if it was straight. They finally decided that, while their number six was right, perhaps the rest of the stations were a bit crooked. So they repositioned them with care, feeling quite proud of themselves.

When they had finished, Michael thanked her and apologised once again for not shaking hands. And then, silently, he began to gather his things, and Anne turned to go. But when she reached the door, she looked back once again. She studied him for a moment as he packed his materials into a canvas bag and prepared to leave.

'Michael?'

'Yes?'

'Forgive me for asking, but are you married?'

'Me? No, I'm not.'

'Right. And are you, well, seeing anyone?'

'No. No, I'm not seeing anyone.'

'I see,' she said. 'There's a film, in Letterkenny. On Friday. It's a new Woody Allen. Would you like to go?'

'Well, yes. Yes, I think that would be, well, very nice.'

'Right,' she said, suddenly unsure where to go next. 'So. Would you like me to collect you?'

'Ah, no. Sure I'll drive.'

'Are you sure?'

'Yes,' he said, more confidently. 'Yes, I'll drive. I'll collect you. I can collect you.'

And he did. He arrived ten minutes early. He drove a bit slowly for her liking, but his ageing Peugeot saloon was very clean and comfortable. They talked about Donegal on the way, and Michael told her things about the countryside and how the ancient townlands in the area had got their names.

When they left the cinema, Anne felt like a character from the movie, strolling through the town relaxed and urbane as if she was in New York. He drove her home and she was in bed by half past ten.

He was very nice, she thought, and very attentive. A bit quiet. She knew he hadn't been out with a woman for some time. A gentlemanly sort, perhaps a bit lonely. But she liked his hands, she liked the way he spoke about the film. She even liked the way he repeated himself when he got nervous. She felt she could trust him. But, at the same time, she felt there was a story here, and she wasn't sure what it was or how to get at it.

They met again a week later, on Sunday afternoon. Michael drove her to a spot with a wooded path along the River Finn several miles east of town. They walked through the forest over the rocks beside the river. They stood and watched the salmon leap and soar, flying like muscular, silvery rainbows over the violently rushing water. He took her hand as they walked, so naturally, to help her over the gaps in the path. And she felt the strength in his arms as she stepped up beside him on those massive, ancient rocks, watching the salmon in their quest upriver to the waters where they had been born.

That afternoon he told her that, in the past, he had been through a bad patch. He hadn't been stable for a period when he was younger. He had lost control of his thoughts for a short time. He explained that he had to take medication and that the medication sometimes made him tired, but it kept things in his head in reasonably good running order. He looked out over the water as he told her, not meeting her gaze until the end when he had finished talking. And then he turned to her and studied her face, as if gauging her reaction to him, to the river, to the whole scene.

'Well,' Anne said, with the sound of rushing water all around. 'I didn't realise . . .'

'No,' he said. 'I thought perhaps you didn't.'

'So. What am I supposed to say?'

'I'm not sure,' he said. 'But I want you to know that, if this makes a difference to you, I understand.'

'Michael?'

'Yes?'

'Thank you for telling me.'

'You're welcome.'

'It does make you more clear to my mind.'

'Yes,' he said. 'Perhaps that's what I was afraid of.'

They spoke little on the way home. As she was about to get out of the car, she turned to him and thanked him for the day, and kissed his cheek. Then she left him and let herself into the house, and he drove away.

She thought hard about Michael that night. She thought about his condition, and how difficult it must have been for him to explain it to her. She thought about his strength, but also about his vulnerability. On Monday, she found that she missed him, that she wanted to see him again. And so she phoned him and invited him to a staff party that was happening Saturday at one of the girls' houses.

As the weekend approached, though, she wasn't sure if she'd made the right decision. She wasn't sure if they would ever be an item. It was too early to introduce him to her colleagues, she thought, and she was feeling none too well, either, trying to ward off a dose of the flu all week. And so, on Saturday afternoon, she phoned him, said she wasn't feeling well, said she was going to wash her hair and have an early night. She apologised and said that maybe they could get together another time. When she put down the phone she felt relieved but saddened as well.

And then, on what turned out to be a grim, wet, unpromising Saturday night, when she was wrapped in her cotton pyjamas and her blue satin dressing gown and her furry blue slippers thinking she was set for a quiet night in, the doorbell rang.

'Michael!'

'Hi.'

'I, I didn't expect you.'

'No, I know. I'm sorry. I just thought that, maybe, if you were washing your hair, you might like these things. You know. To help.'

In his arms was a large bundle, a new fluffy white towel. He opened the package with one hand to reveal a bottle of French shampoo and a bottle of conditioner and a new wooden-handled hairbrush. He looked awkward standing there behind his pile of gifts, like a nervous delivery boy waiting for a tip.

She smiled. She was about to say 'You're mad' but she bit her tongue.

'How lovely,' she blurted. 'How nice.'

She took the bundle from him and then they faced one another for a moment with the door still open and the rain seeping into the front hall.

'Would you, well, like to come in?'

'Well, yes, actually, I would. I would like to. Yes.'

Ten minutes later she sat on a kitchen chair in her (thankfully tidy) bathroom with her back to the sink. Michael stood beside her and ran the taps, swirling the water, testing the temperature to get it just right. Then, with both hands, he lowered her head gently back into the steaming water. She closed her eyes then, and she could feel his fingers running through her hair. She had let it grow since coming to Donegal, not trusting any of the local hairdressers to do much of a job, and she could feel his hands massaging her scalp slowly in the hot water. He worked the rose-scented shampoo into a thick lather, slowly, thoroughly, almost scientifically running his hands through her hair. She looked up momentarily at his chest as he stood over her, seeing his arms and shoulders flex beneath his T-shirt, hearing him breathe as he worked. In the background the music from the stereo wafted from the living room, kd lang crooning with longing, as he tenderly squeezed the water from her hair, and then pulled the plug in the sink, and then used the spray to rinse her hair, so gently, so fresh and clear and clean.

He draped a fresh towel over her forehead, lifted her upright and wrapped the towel around her hair. Then he knelt beside her, looking up into her face like a father looking at his little girl.

'Now,' he said. 'How was that?'

Later they sat on the sofa. Anne had a glass of wine and Michael had a cup of tea. They watched most of a video together – *Rebecca*, the old Hitchcock film. Anne must have fallen asleep. She woke the next day alone on the sofa to find that he had, some time during the night, tidied away their dishes, covered her with a duvet from her bed, and then slipped quietly away.

She knew from that night that Michael had an attraction for her that no other man had ever had. He was quiet, but his silence was expressive and comfortable and comforting. He could speak when he needed to but he was very keen to listen and to respond to her, and just to be there. She felt he had a quality that was deeply spiritual but somehow deeply sexual at the same time, a total acceptance of what she was, a deep, satisfying acceptance.

She desired him from that night, desired him for the week that followed. She phoned him but he didn't want to see her during the week, said he preferred going out at weekends, so she invited him to a restaurant for Saturday night. But then, when he arrived at her cottage, she wouldn't let him go. They were together in bed, awake, all night, so long, so slow, so intense it was, a slow burning, hot and strong and beautiful. He left her at dawn to return to his mother's house. Anne smiled to herself as she listened to the sound of his car driving away, laughing at herself and Ballyfinn and her dire memories of Dublin and her new, happy life.

Now, after four years of marriage, she looked at him sitting across from her on the floor. She could never read his thoughts, even now. Sometimes she was frightened at what might be happening in his mind. And yet, when he looked up at her, even after all these years together, he always looked as if he was seeing her for the first time. Discovering her. She loved him and she desired him, now — even now — she desired him, on this uneventful Monday night, when nothing was happening, and the air was warm and still.

CHAPTER 7

On Tuesday morning Emma Gallagher stood at the top of the stairs. The magnolia-coloured walls still appeared clean and new, the green carpet showed no signs of wear. Above her hung a brass, glass-plated light fitting from which hovered a weightless cobweb suspended gently in the warm air, the only imperfection in the immaculate, still-new interior. She descended the stairs. She was in rotten form.

A few moments later she sat at the kitchen table cradling her head in her hands. All was quiet, a midday lull permeating the air. No noise issued from the neighbouring houses, no birds sang from the wispy ash trees that emerged over the tops of the surrounding garden walls.

Emma glanced around the bright kitchen. Clean maple-wood presses; clean green tiles over the sink; a tall white fridge with a calendar held on by a magnet in the shape of the Eiffel Tower. She yawned. She found it hard to wake up, stifled by the heatwave that had settled over the town.

Her mother was bent down, pulling a load of clothes out of the washer and into a pile on the immaculately clean kitchen floor.

'Good morning, love,' she smiled. 'Had you a good sleep?'

'Aye.'

'It's another lovely day,' she said, gathering the clothes off the floor. 'I'll just hang these out to dry, and then I'll be back in to you.'

Emma stood and walked to the sink. She pulled a tissue from a green box and blew her nose. She filled the kettle and shuffled back to the table, rubbing sleep from her eyes. She watched her mother through the glass doors as she hung the clothes out on the line, ding ding ding, quick as lightning. First her mother's underwear, catching the light breeze, then her bras with their white straps and thick, protective padded cups. And then her father's broad, black cotton underpants, designer labels on the waist. Funny, she thought. Daddy has the arse of a bear. You'd never know he was so fit, dashing from room to room at the hotel, barking at everyone.

Then Emma watched as her own underwear appeared on the line, a colourful row of knickers bobbing up and down like festive bunting.

'There now,' her mother said, returning to the kitchen. 'They'll be right in no time. There's great drying in that sun.'

She hung her housecoat on the back of the door and then dried her hands on the tea towel hanging from the oven. Emma watched as her mother performed these simple actions. She noticed that her mother had been putting on weight. She was starting to look more and more like the other women in Ballyfinn: shapeless, getting on in years, with that convenient haircut and, lately, worst of all, a grey housecoat. And her skin, so dry and cracked, with little veins crossing her cheeks. So old, Emma thought, so worn out, for a woman just thirty-nine.

Emma yawned from her seat at the table, pushed her hair off her face.

'So,' her mother said brightly. 'Can I make you a cup of coffee?'

'That would be lovely,' Emma said.

'Do you have your timetable for the week?' her mother asked as she checked the kettle. 'We should write it up on the calendar. So I know when to wake you.'

'Aye.'

'Would you like some toast?'

'No, thanks. I'm grand for the minute.'

'Are you all right?'

'Aye. Aye, I'm grand. Just a bit tired.'

'You weren't out late.'

'Ach no, I was home by eleven. Lorna had to work this morning so we left early.'

'Then what is it?' her mother asked. 'You look very pale.'

'It's nothing, Mum. I'm grand.'

Her mother spooned instant coffee into a new green ceramic mug and then filled it with boiling water. She set the mug on the table along with a small green jug of milk. Then she stood beside the table with a nervous smile.

'There you are now.'

'Mum?'

'Yes, love?'

'I called in to see Uncle Michael. Yesterday, in the bookshop.'

'Did you now?'

'He was on about this party,' Emma said. 'In the hotel, Saturday night.'

'Yes,' her mother said proudly. 'Daddy and I are on the guest list.'

'He said Uncle Denis is driving up. With Aunt Julia. And the boys.'

'Oh, was Michael speaking to them?'

'Aye,' Emma said. 'On Sunday. He said they're all going to be here.'

'Well that's one for the books. They haven't been up since . . .'

'Two years ago,' Emma said. 'For Auntie Jennie's funeral.'

'That's right. Two years ago. Sure you've a great memory.'

'It was just after we moved into this house,' Emma said.

'Aye,' her mother said as she filled the sink with hot water. 'But Julia wasn't here then, sure she wasn't?'

'Yes she was,' Emma insisted. 'She arrived with them all, don't you remember? But then she had to go back to Dublin. Some sort of interview. She didn't stay for the funeral. Just Uncle Denis and the boys stayed.'

'Oh, aye. I remember now. And Denis wasn't at his best, sure he wasn't?'

'Ach no,' Emma said. 'Back at the house, after the funeral, he was scuttered. Langers so he was. Mind you everyone else was drunk as well. Except Uncle Michael, of course.'

'No,' her mother said, washing the dishes. 'Michael wouldn't touch a drop at all. He says drink doesn't agree with him.'

Emma watched her mother at the sink, rinsing the breakfast dishes one by one, setting them on the draining board to dry. The sun shone brightly into the kitchen and Emma could see steam rising from her mother's hands. Her mother stared into the back garden for a moment as if considering a difficult proposition.

'So strange for your Uncle Michael,' she said dreamily. 'Cut off from drink. And from other things as well. Things that people take for granted.'

'Aye,' Emma said. 'But sure Uncle Denis makes up for it. Shouting and roaring.'

'Ach, he wasn't that bad now.'

'He was! I was there. You fell asleep, remember? I had to wake you at the end of the night. I don't know how you fell asleep. So much noise. Like children, so they were.'

'Aye,' she sighed. 'But sure it's not easy to lose your mother.'

'She was like a mother to you as well,' Emma protested.

'Aye, she was, in some ways. Sure we were all very close back then. My God, when I think back. Denis and Michael. What a pair they were.'

'Oh?' Emma said. 'Used they be close?'

'Oh aye. They were a great team long ago. The girls in the town, now, they were fascinated by the O'Donnell boys. When it got out that I was their cousin, I became the most popular girl in the school. I had loads of friends all of a sudden, everyone wanted to be invited up to meet them.'

'Auntie Jennie was a lovely woman,' Emma smiled. 'I used to love going up there.'

'Aye.'

'I used to love to visit them. Uncle Michael and Auntie Anne and Auntie Jennie.'

'Why don't you go up there now any more?'

'Ach, no reason really,' Emma said. 'It's a wee bit too far, since we moved house.'

'But I could drive you . . .'

'But maybe, I don't know. It's not the same when you're older.'

'Oh?'

'They treated me like I was their own, back when I was younger. But I'm not a kid any more. I feel like an intruder now.'

'Aye. I know what you're saying.'

'Why don't they have their own children?' Emma asked.

'I think it's, well, Michael.'

'Oh, aye,' Emma said, suddenly embarrassed. 'Sure won't it be great to see them all on Saturday?'

'You know you'll be working at the party . . .'

'Working?' Emma protested.

'Aye, did Daddy not tell you? You'll have to help out in the kitchen. There's a wedding on in the other function room. Daddy says they're desperate for staff.'

'But Mum! They're my relations too!'

'You'll be paid a wee bonus,' her mother said, drying the dishes. 'Stephen Deane is paying for everything and he's put in something extra for the staff. Sure wouldn't it be lovely to be married to a film star, someone to put on a grand party any time he liked?'

'But everyone will be there,' Emma protested. 'Uncle Michael says even the boys are invited to the party, Jimmy and Barry as well. So why am I working?'

'Because you just are. There'll be a photographer there. You'll get your photograph taken with Stephen Deane.'

'I don't give a shite about Stephen Deane.'

'Emma!'

'Sure his picture's everywhere in this town. There's a million photographs of him at school standing with Mr Johnson and with

Martha at the front desk. It's pathetic, so it is. He's not a fecking God.'

'Ach, all right now, calm down.'

'But Uncle Denis, Auntie Julia and the boys . . . sure if I'm working I'll hardly get to see them at all!'

'Maybe you could see them on Sunday.'

'Sunday? They'll be gone on Sunday. Couldn't we see them Saturday? For lunch, here?'

'No, lovey, we'll all be preparing for the party on Saturday. Maybe they'll call to the house on Friday night.'

'But they'll only be arriving then,' Emma said.

'But there'll be other times . . .'

'Other times!' Emma erupted. 'But they're never here!'

'Aye, it's true. Sure we're not as close as we used to be, not since Denis went away. But I didn't think you'd want to see them that badly.'

Emma stared down into her mug, colour rising to her cheeks.

'Look,' her mother continued. 'Maybe we could have a chat with Daddy and see . . .'

'No. It's all right.'

'But if you really want to see them . . .'

'No. Just leave it. I'll be grand.'

Her mother looked at her with a sympathetic face. 'I'll make sure Daddy lets you out early when the work in the kitchen is finished. You can sit with us then and chat with everyone. Would that be okay?'

Emma was considering this when the phone rang. Her mother dashed out to the hall to answer it. Emma could hear her outside, saying something about some curtains. She finished her coffee and stared out the window at the clothes drying on the line.

'Barry,' she thought. 'Here. After two years. And I have to fecking work.'

She leaned back in her chair, resting her hands on her lap.

'Sure, maybe it's all for the best.'

Emma walked slowly up the stairs. Despite the heat, she shivered as she entered her room, closing the door behind her. She sat on the white chair at her desk and picked up her diary. She checked back into May, counted the days until today.

Forty-two days. Two weeks overdue.

She sat for a moment and gazed at the print hanging above her desk. Anne and Michael had given it to her on her twelfth birthday. She'd thought it was lovely then: a French farming scene of lavender in bloom, vibrant greens and soft purples. So calming.

She opened the bottom drawer of her desk and lifted out a shoe box which had once held a pair of summer sandals. She pulled a green ribbon from around the box and took off the cover.

Inside were the letters from Barry, from that time, two years ago. She took them out one by one, still in their original envelopes, and arranged them on her desk according to the date on the postmark. The earliest was April, with its neat address in an overly careful hand, and the last was late September in an almost illegible scrawl.

Emma looked at the envelopes laid out on her desk as she had done so many times before. She didn't remove the letters from the envelopes. She hardly needed to read them any more. None of them was very long and she knew most of them off by heart.

I can't seem to talk to anyone else the way I write to you . . .

That was the phrase, the one that stuck out in her mind, the phrase from the penultimate letter. It made her feel so sad at the time, knowing Barry was so lonely down in Dublin. But she was happy too, happy that he thought so much of her, that she was the one to whom he could tell all the things he couldn't say, to anyone, except to her.

And she knew what that felt like. Seclusion. Even now she knew what it felt like to have things bottled up in you, and to feel that no one could really understand what you were going through, and there was no one there to tell.

CHAPTER 8

On Wednesday morning Barry woke early, having dreamt, once again, of the lake.

As always in his dream it was night and the water was smooth and inky black. Sometimes the lake was threatening and accusatory but this time the aura was calm and serene, the black water suspended like glass within the gentle curvature of the bank. The air was heavy and still and the hills around were as black as the night but, once and again, they were lit up by flashes of hot summer lightning, a sudden whiteness exposing the desolate, mountainous terrain.

Barry stood alone on the shore but he felt Emma's presence all around him. He turned from the water to look for her, scrambled along the undulating shoreline. He discovered a path through the gorse and heather and made his way through the darkness, his skin scratched by the spiky undergrowth, expecting to find her at every bend. He held an envelope in his hand and he felt an urgency to find Emma, to give her that one last letter there in the black night.

Then he stood again at the lake, feeling her all around him as the foxes darted beneath his feet, little fox kits running quick like the lightning, dashing in and out of cover, fuzzy copper-coloured pups weaving patterns beneath the prickly gorse.

And then suddenly he knew that the lake was Emma and Emma was the lake, there, laid out like a benevolent force before him. He felt alive and electric, then finally, with her, as the water lapped against his bare feet and he walked in, deeper and closer, the cool water lapping in wavelets against his body as he swam into her, feeling her skin in the water, seeing her face in glimpses lit by lightning, with her, together with her, in the water that was the lake, that was Emma.

The bell rang out through the corridors with ear-splitting urgency, signalling the end of the school year.

Suddenly the halls were wild with boys, laughing, shouting, banging the doors of steel lockers, flinging paper missiles through the passageways, letting them fly through the air like spirits set free. Younger boys chased each other and knocked themselves about, dropping books on the floor and scattering papers across the corridors while the older boys called to each other with their deepened voices.

'Decko!'

'Johnny!'

'We're outa here, right? Catch you later!'

'Fuckin' brillo!'

Barry threaded his way through the melee.

'Oy! Barry O'Donnell!' someone called out. 'Would you ever quiet down? I can't fuckin' hear meself think!'

Boys laughed and Barry smiled sheepishly. He stood before his locker and removed the last few books, sliding them into his school rucksack. He had a heavy sports bag hung over his shoulder.

'So, big man. Are you racing Saturday?'

Barry looked down the row of lockers to see Pat Devany, lanky and mischievous, his arms folded over his chest.

'Racing?' Barry said. 'Where?'

'Rathfarnham. Five thousand metres.'

'I can't. We're going to Donegal.'

'Thanks be to God. Now the rest of us have a chance.'

Barry smiled. 'Are you going to run?'

'Don't know,' Pat said, stretching his arm over his head. 'I'm still sore after sports day.'

'Really?'

'Yeah, you fucker,' Pat said. 'You knackered me. I would've had you in the mile if it weren't for my shoulder.'

'You should see a doctor.'

'Pah. Fucking nancy boy doctors know fuck-all about sport.'

'Yeah.'

'So you're off to Donegal? What's up there?'

'It's a party. My dad. He's from Donegal.'

'Oh right. Any women up there?'

'Maybe,' Barry said nonchalantly.

'Really?' Pat said, surprised. 'Oh, here, lads! The Quiet Man's going to get his bit in Donegal! Who is she?'

'No one,' Barry said. 'She's my cousin.'

'Cousin? You can't shag your cousin.'

'She's not really my cousin. She's Dad's cousin. Her daughter, like.'

'Ah sure, you're grand then,' Pat swaggered. 'Happy days, you can shag her all you like!'

Barry laughed.

'Is she nice anyway?' Pat asked.

'Look, she's just a girl. I met her two years ago.'

'Okay, okay. So she is nice?'

'Well, yeah.'

'Right,' Pat grunted as he stretched sideways. 'Jolly fucking good. I'll be thinking of you Saturday, then, when I'm crossing the finish line, a hundred yards ahead of the pack.'

'Thanks.'

'Righty-o, big man,' Pat said, turning away. 'Hey, enjoy the summer.'

'Thanks. You too.'

'And enjoy shagging your Donegal cousin!' Pat taunted, his laughter ringing through the corridor as he walked away.

The afternoon sky was awash in hazy sunshine and the air was close and balmy. Barry entered the gate of Bushy Park, leaned his mountain bike against the railings and locked it firmly. He paused to look across the playing fields. The park was nearly empty: a vast, tree-fringed, summer-green space. Two women played tennis on the courts, the sound of their play dividing the air like a metronome.

He breathed in deeply, inhaling the sweet smell of freshly cut grass. Then he walked over to a large beech, peeled off his tracksuit and tossed it at the base of the tree. He tucked his singlet into his running shorts. Looking down he remembered that he was wearing his new running shoes, bought last Sunday. This would be their maiden voyage. They felt snug but light and comfortable.

He began to stretch: bending, reaching, feeling for tightness in his legs, shifting his weight back and forth to flex and then loosen his muscles. He paused to take stock of his body. He felt good, full of energy, freed from school. He checked his stopwatch, adjusted the strap and squeezed the timer on. And then he began to run.

He ran on the grass around the perimeter of the park. His shoes felt good, his legs were a little tight but not sore. He breathed deeply and slowly, felt the sunshine and the clean air playing across his skin.

The first mile was a bit stiff and awkward. His body took a few minutes to adjust. His breathing increased, he had to concentrate on his pace. A piece of music ran in his head, U2 singing about a beautiful day. The music gave him an early rhythm but it wasn't right, it didn't match his step, so he put it out of his mind.

After a few minutes his pace settled. His breathing fell into harmony with his arms and with his steps. He still felt good, very strong. He had circled the entire park, a mile was gone, he ran well and breathed easier. The sun was bright in his face. Perspiration began to run down his forehead and sting his eyes, but he felt good. As he ran he began to slip into himself, his mind wandering into a space filled with memories, voices from the past, inner voices suddenly more real than the sounds around him.

Soon he had completed his fifth circuit of the park. He forced himself to break his steady pace and to increase his speed, turning up the beat of his legs as he entered the final lap.

He ran down the straight path to the far corner of the park, rounding the bend behind the three benches. He began to cross the football pitches then, breathing harder as he crossed the open space. The sun glinted through beads of sweat in his eyelashes. He reached the end of the pitches and entered the shady path through the trees, the sun again piercing his eyes as it shone between the branches overhead. Then he came out near the playground, glancing at a pair of young mothers smoking as their toddlers slipped down the slide, laughing and shouting. He took the wide bend behind the playground and then ran down the gentle slope to the duck pond where the sun played gold off the water and the swans were feeding, dipping their necks gracefully into the water then up again as he ran past. He was running fast now, he could feel his heart pumping as his breathing increased, his movements perfectly in tune as he ran up the short hill to the last stretch. Now he ran hard, pushing himself for the final straight, focusing on the tree where he had thrown his tracksuit, now coming into view as he began to feel pain through his body. He ran, pushing himself as he sprinted at full speed with his body throbbing as he neared the end, running faster, as fast as he could push himself, all the way, all the way over the line, grasping his wrist to stop his watch with his final stride.

Then he let his arms loosen and his strides grow longer, slower, then slowing to a walk as the sound of his heavy breathing came into his consciousness, feeling the wetness of his jersey as it slackened and stuck to his heaving body. He ran his hand back through his curly hair, pushing the perspiration back, smoothing his hair, now glistening golden in the bright summer sunshine.

And then he looked down at his watch and smiled, smiled as he breathed, smiled with a satisfaction at his time, a good time, strong and fast. And his mind flooded with confidence, knowing that he was strong and fast this week, the week when he would see Emma again.

Two and a half years ago in the depths of December, Barry had left Boston and flown to Dublin with his family. Although he knew something of Ireland from his father and from a few holidays, he had lived in the US for his entire life. His favourite impression of Dublin remained rows of sweets at the newsagents. When they moved he was fourteen, slender and tall for his age, a budding track star. He considered himself an American through and through, and he believed the Irish liked Americans, and so, although he was nervous about changing schools, he tried to be optimistic about the move.

When he started school he soon learned the real story. The boys mocked his accent and criticised America relentlessly. He had been a good student in Boston, but in the Irish system he was way behind. He worked hard to catch up and his teachers gave him extra lessons. But then he developed bronchitis, missed a whole week of school and seemed to be further behind than ever. He made no friends. His parents, busy settling into their own jobs and readjusting to Ireland, seemed distant, too caught up in their own problems to care about his experiences. Jimmy alone, six years old, seemed to sail through the changes in their lives: each weekend brought another birthday party or an invitation to a new friend's house.

In Barry's memory those first months were covered in a pall of depression and frustration. Nothing seemed to be falling into place. He hated school, hated the weather, hated everything about their new life.

Then, just as spring was arriving, Barry's grandmother died. He had met her only a few times – once or twice when he was a little boy, and then recently when she paid a short visit to Dublin with Uncle Michael, to welcome them home to Ireland – so Barry was not especially saddened by her death. When they got the news, his dad was in New York on business. Barry remembered helping his mother pack the car, settling Jimmy into the back seat and then collecting his dad at the airport. His father was clearly distraught, his face looking worn and washed out.

They drove up to Donegal straight from the airport, a long, silent journey on a dismal Wednesday night through an endless series of bleak Irish midland towns. Aunt Anne was not home when they arrived and Uncle Michael was friendly but a bit nervous and preoccupied. Barry and Jimmy were shown to a draughty, damp bedroom, and Barry couldn't get to sleep in the undersized twin bed. Then his mother got a call on her mobile phone. She'd got a job interview in Dublin. She would have to leave Donegal the next day, even before the funeral took place. So Barry was left there, surrounded by droves of visitors whose accents he couldn't understand, while his father grieved and drank to excess, and Jimmy charmed everyone, and the rain fell continuously.

Barry had tried to get outside to run in the hills but the severe wind and rain sent him back after only a few hundred yards. He was tired, frustrated and unable to relax. It was especially bad the day of the funeral. The rain fell without a break and Barry still remembered the scene at the graveyard, the muddy hillside ground, people in black clothes, mostly quite elderly, dripping silently as the priest hurried through his prayers and the coffin was lowered into the cold, sodden earth.

A crowd of relatives and hangers-on went back to a hotel for dinner. Barry was placed next to an old woman with loose false teeth who claimed to have been the O'Donnell housekeeper of old. She told long, rambling stories of his father's younger days, but Barry missed much of what she was saying, catching only glimpses of English through her heavy Donegal accent. The afternoon wore on interminably. Barry felt trapped with nothing to do as his father drank steadily and Jimmy gathered more and more fans. At least Uncle Michael seemed to care. He sat next to Barry for a while and, though he said very little, he did bring some comfort to an uncomfortable day.

Finally evening came and they left the hotel. A crowd followed the O'Donnells back to the family home, and soon the sitting room was filled with smoke, drink and the noise of laughter and conversation. Jimmy went to bed early, exhausted from the day's activities. Barry wasn't tired but he couldn't face the party, hating all the noise and smoke. He wandered into the kitchen, found a deck of cards and sat down in the conservatory overlooking the back garden, now hidden in darkness. Enough light filtered through from the kitchen to enable him to play patience on a low table. He had played three games and was sinking into a sense of hopelessness when a figure appeared silhouetted in the doorway.

It was a girl dressed in a loose jumper and a long skirt. She didn't notice Barry sitting in the shadows. She looked out into the blackness that engulfed the garden beyond the windows. He could see that she had long hair which, every so often, she pushed behind her ear.

She crossed the floor and flicked a switch on the wall, casting a red glow across the garden.

'Oh Jesus!' she whispered. 'I didn't see you there.'

'I'm sorry,' Barry said. 'I didn't mean to scare you.'

'No, I'm sorry,' she said, catching her breath. 'I didn't mean to scare you either.'

She looked back outside. Neither of them spoke for a moment.

'Right, so,' she said finally. 'You're Barry, then.'

'Yes. I am.'

'I'm pleased to meet you,' she said.

'Um,' he muttered, 'what's your name?'

'Oh, sorry. I'm Emma. Gallagher. We're cousins, like.'

'We are?'

'Well no, not really. You see, my mum is your dad's cousin. They all grew up together. Here, in Ballyfinn.'

'Oh. I see.'

'I think that makes us second cousins,' she said.

'Oh. Yes.'

'And you're American.'

'Yeah. Well, half-American, I guess.'

'You sound like the full thing to me,' she laughed.

'Yeah. Everyone says so.'

There was silence then as they looked out across the garden.

'I'm sorry about your aunt,' he said.

'She was your grandmother,' Emma replied.

'I know. But I didn't really know her.'

'She was a lovely woman,' Emma said.

'Was she?'

'Aye. She was wise, like. And she really cared. About the people around her.'

'Oh.'

'Uncle Michael,' she said. 'You know about him, do you?'

'No, not really,' Barry said. 'He seems nice enough. But Dad says he's not all there.'

'Oh, he's there all right,' Emma corrected. 'It just takes a while to get to know him.'

'Oh.'

'It's a big change for us here,' Emma said thoughtfully. 'With Auntie Jennie gone. I'm going to miss her. But it's worse for Auntie Anne and Uncle Michael. They will be all on their own.'

Barry studied Emma then. She was looking down at the floor and he could see that there were tears welling up in her eyes. And for a moment he felt that she was caught in private feelings far beyond his understanding. But then she pushed back her hair and her face changed as she turned towards him.

'So,' she said. 'Do you like foxes?'

'Foxes?'

'Yes, foxes. You know. Foxes, like.'

'Vulpes vulpes,' he said.

'Oh, very good,' she said. 'You must know something about them so.'

'Not really. Latin class, in the States. Why?'

'There's a family of them living here, in this garden.'

'No kidding?'

'No, no kidding at all,' she said. 'They may come out, if we wait a bit.'

Emma sat down on the settee. Barry pulled his chair over closer to the window. Neither spoke for a few minutes.

'You don't say much, do you?' Emma said finally.

'No,' he replied. 'I guess I don't.'

'And why's that then?'

'I, I don't know.'

She looked at him. 'I don't believe it. A quiet Yank. Sounds like something from a film!'

He smiled and looked down at the floor, rubbing his hands together nervously.

'But look,' she whispered, 'there she is!'

At the end of the garden the fox appeared, silent and ghost-like, sleek and ethereal. The copper in her coat shone in the artificial light and they could see her jet-black eyes and her full brush. She took a few steps towards the house, sniffing the air cautiously. Every few moments she perked up her ears as if made nervous by the noise within the house. Then, responding to some silent stimulus, three small kits followed her into the garden, barely visible in the overgrown grass. Their little heads bounced as they padded into view. Then they began to snarl and nip at one another. After a few steps, the mother sat down and they played around her, attacking her tail, wandering off and then bounding back to her protective presence.

'She's lovely, so she is,' Emma whispered.

'Yes. She's beautiful.'

Barry watched the foxes, fascinated with the rough-and-tumble, with their wild but intimate play. But then he looked at Emma as she sat, leaning forward, mesmerised by the animals. She focused on the scene before them: so rapt, so passionate she looked, the sadness of a moment ago now gone from her expression. Her face was pale and her cheeks were still red from the heat of the party inside. She looked very awake and alert. She wore a baggy black sweater which hung loosely from her thin shoulders. She folded her legs beneath her in her long black skirt.

She looked like a postcard, he thought. A postcard of an Irish girl.

She turned to face him, then, and for an awkward moment they looked at one another fully. And then they turned away, back to the foxes still frolicking in the glow cast by the dim light. They stared into that space with suspended breath, suddenly aware that they were near to one another.

But then a white light flashed across the garden and noise burst from within the house. Barry could see his father letting a window fly open and shouting into the night: 'Christ almighty, Michael! Are you trying to roast us alive?'

The fox bounded and the kits scampered back beneath the blackness of the tree, gone from sight in an instant. Barry stood abruptly.

'Idiot!' he cursed.

'That's your father,' Emma said softly.

'I know. He's not usually this loud.'

'His mother has died,' Emma said. 'He's upset. He's trying to cover up.'

'He's been so stupid this week,' Barry said. 'I've never seen him like this before.'

He stood at the window, staring into the empty space.

'Barry,' Emma said softly. 'He's just trying to adjust. He's home for his mother's funeral. His world has changed now. It's all strange for him, too.'

He turned towards her. 'I'm sorry,' he said. 'It's just, well. I'm just tired of all this. I've only been here a few days but it feels like forever. I feel trapped.'

'It's not easy,' she said. 'When they're in control the whole time.'

'Yeah. Listen to them in there. They're like kids. They're worse than kids.'

'I know,' Emma said. 'Sometimes I just want to get away, to live my life without them.'

'Do you?'

'Aye. Just to be far away, where they can't get at you. Where you can be what you want to be.'

They looked again into the back garden but they knew that the foxes were gone, there was nothing there to see.

'Look,' Emma said. 'Would you like to, like, go out?'

'Out?'

'There's a lake,' she said. 'It's over Trooper's Hill. It's one of my favourite places. It's a bit of a walk. But the rain has stopped. It would be lovely there tonight.'

Barry looked at her face. He saw that expression once again, the same look of concentration that she wore when she was watching the foxes. He hesitated, listening to the noise of the party within swell and recede like the wind.

'We can go out this door,' Emma urged. 'No one will see us.'

'Okay,' he whispered. 'Sure. Let's go.'

They found jackets hanging in the kitchen and then they slipped out the back door. They walked through the darkness around the side of the house, finally reaching the overgrown drive. As they turned up the narrow road towards Trooper's Hill their eyes began to adjust to the dark. It felt strange and exciting to be outside, away from the noise of the party, suddenly alone on a country road in the black night.

'Can you see?' Emma asked.

'Sort of. It feels like we're in the middle of nowhere.'

'Aye.'

'Are you cold?' he asked.

'A bit. But the walk will warm us up.'

The narrow road was surrounded by high, unkempt hedges that looked like black walls against the night sky. There were thick clouds overhead but the moonlight broke through now and again, turning the sky into a heaving sea, grey and smooth. There was no sound except the crunch of their feet on the gravelly tarmac. They walked for a few minutes in silence.

'Here's our path,' she said.

In the moonlight they climbed over a rusty gate through the hedgerow. They found themselves walking uphill on a path through a disused field. The path was just visible in the grey light, two ruts used by a farmer to drive his tractor up the mountain.

Emma led. Barry could hear the sound of her breathing as they proceeded up the hill. They passed through a small dark wood and then came out the other side. The path suddenly became steep as it wound its way higher and higher.

'Mind your shoes,' she said. 'It can get quite mucky.'

'It's so quiet.'

'Aye. But sure anything would be quiet after that party.'

They stopped for a moment and looked back. They had been climbing steadily and the lights of the town were now visible in the distance.

'The air up here,' he said. 'It's so fresh.'

'Aye.'

'And just look at the sky. When the moon flashes through the clouds.'

'Aye.'

'It's eerie. Is it always like this?'

'Well, no,' she said. 'But sometimes.'

'Gosh.'

'Barry?'

'Yeah?'

'You're not used to the country, now, are you?'

'No, I'm not, I suppose. We lived in Boston. And now we live in Dublin.'

'So. Do you, well, miss the States?'

'Yeah.'

'I would hate to have to leave home. The way you did.'

'Why?' he asked, looking over at her.

'We moved house,' she said. 'Just a few weeks ago. We used to live very near here, in a lovely wee cottage. But we moved into a new estate in town. And even though it was only a few miles, I hated moving. I still hate it, I'm not settled in at all. It must be difficult to move to an entirely new country. Especially for someone quiet, like you.'

He looked down at the ground.

'I'm sorry,' Emma said. 'I hope I didn't say the wrong thing.'

'You didn't,' he said, looking up at her.

'I'm always doing that,' she said as she walked ahead. 'Saying the first thing that pops into my mind. Shooting my mouth off like some kind of eejit.'

'It's okay. I mean, don't stop saying whatever you want to say. Please. Just always say what you want to say.'

She stopped. He could see her eyes looking back at him in the half light, the moon shining on her face. And then she turned back to the path and said, 'Come on. We've a ways to go yet before we reach the lake.'

They walked for another few minutes in silence. Barry felt as though he had never been in a place so dark, so far from anything human. As they walked, he drifted into himself, feeling strange and disoriented, as if he had been cut off from the world and time and everything that he knew.

'Here it is,' she said, 'just through here.'

She pulled a loop of barbed wire off a post and pushed the wooden gate ahead of her. Barry followed, helping her close it behind them.

And then they stood on the shore of the small lake, more like a large pond. The water was black, surrounded by low black hills. There was no wind. The surface was glassy and silent, as if it absorbed sound and light into its heavy darkness. They looked across the water and felt like explorers who had found a new land.

'It's called Loughnagalla,' she whispered. 'It means the Lake of the Strangers. It's said to be filled with minerals, full of life. The older people come up here with jugs and pitchers to collect the water. They say it cures illness.'

'The water is so dark,' Barry said.

'Yes, it's always this way. Even during the daytime there's a blackness in the water.'

They stood for a moment looking out across the glassy surface of the lake.

'Emma,' he said.

'Yes?'

'Why did you bring me here?'

'I don't know,' she said. 'I just wanted to.'

'But why?'

'Well, you seemed so sad,' she said. 'Back there, at the party. I thought you might prefer it here.'

'Oh, I do,' he said. 'I feel like, I don't know. I just want to stay here.'

'Do you?'

'I feel as if I'm somewhere totally new.'

'You are somewhere new,' she teased. 'You've never been here before.'

'That's not what I meant.'

'What did you mean, then?' she said softly.

He looked at her. Her ironic smile was gone. She gazed at him steadily, openly, waiting for his answer. She looked suddenly as if everything he said meant a great deal to her.

'I don't know,' he said, scraping the ground with his shoe. 'Sometimes I feel like no one listens any more.'

'Sometimes no one does,' she said, still looking at him.

He returned her look then. He wanted to say something to her, something directly to her, something that he had never said before and that she had never heard before. Something that would make this a deep, shared moment between them. But no words came to him. And he felt suddenly anxious, as if he was expected to say something, say the right thing at this moment, in this sacred place. But nothing. The words wouldn't come. He looked at Emma looking at him beside the black water, but no words came into his head.

But then she smiled, as if she understood his anxiety. And then she took his hand. They stood quietly together then, looking out across the water. He could feel her fingers, the soft surface of her skin in his hand. The clouds were reflected on the water and there was deep silence around them as they stood.

'Barry,' she whispered.

'Yes?'

'Let's remember this.'

'Okay.'

'Just being here, at this lake,' she said.

'Okay.'

'Promise me you'll remember this always.'

'I will.'

They looked at one another, then, without smiling, for a long, slow moment.

That was two years ago. Barry's mind was sunk into his memories of that time, he noticed nothing around him as he cycled home through Rathgar. He approached the house, slowed, got off his bike and walked it through the gate.

It was two years ago. We were only fourteen, he thought. And yet we felt so much older. So grown up, just for those few hours. The two of us, walking back down that hill. Holding hands in the dark night, as if we had known one another for months.

She had kissed him then. Outside, just before they went back into the house. Just a brief peck, but on the lips. And then they had sneaked back into the kitchen. The place was filled with empty bottles, ashtrays, plates of crisps. There was still music on low but the party was over, everyone had gone home. They looked into the sitting room and saw Emma's mother asleep on the sofa.

Barry remembered Emma's voice in the kitchen before she went inside to wake her mother. She must have been getting a cold, he thought, her voice was so low, sounding like a woman, someone in an old movie.

'Barry,' she said.

'Yes.'

'You'll be leaving in the morning,' she said. 'To go back to Dublin.'

'But we'll come up again soon,' he whispered.

'No, you won't,' she said. 'Your dad, Uncle Denis. He doesn't get on with Uncle Michael. Your dad is embarrassed by Uncle Michael.'

'How do you know that?'

'Because I live here. I'm family. Auntie Anne tells me everything.'

'But we'll come back,' he insisted. 'Or I'll come on my own.'

'No, you won't. They won't let you.'

'Well, then, you'll just have to come to Dublin.'

'Stop, be serious. We're not going to see each other again. For a long time.'

'But I have to see you.'

'No. Don't say it. It won't happen.'

'Why not?'

'Just listen,' she said. 'You have to write to me.'

'I will.'

'I mean it.'

'Okay. I'll try.'

'No, you can't just try. You have to write to me. Every week. Every day if you can.'

'I will. I promise.'

'That's all I want. For you to write to me. Until I see you again.'

Emma had looked at him steadily as they stood in that dark

kitchen, as if she had extracted a solemn promise. And then, she turned and walked into the sitting room. He stood alone and watched as she gently woke her mother. Then he watched them talk for a moment in low tones. And then they left the house. And that was all.

Since that time, two years ago, Barry had not seen Emma or heard her voice, except deep in his imagination.

He did write. All through the spring and summer months he wrote to her every week. Short letters, mostly, on blue-tinted sheets. He wrote to her about his summer holidays and the lads at school and what he was reading and what he'd seen on telly. And she wrote back, too, but less frequently than he wrote to her. She wrote about working at the hotel and a party she had gone to and her mad friend Lorna.

His dad teased him about receiving letters from a girl, but his mom told him that it was a very nice way to have a girlfriend, and that this girl, whoever she was, would cherish the letters and that Barry, too, should keep them all, for ever.

He had few friends during that first summer in Dublin. He looked forward to writing to Emma, telling her everything that had happened during his week. He wrote about his impressions of his new home, and his attempts to find a way to fit in, and his loneliness. And Emma wrote back, encouraging him to keep going, assuring him he would feel more at home soon. Her letters grounded him, made him feel less misunderstood. They made him feel that, very far away, he had at least one friend.

Then school started again, and the rugby season came with it, and during practice in September he broke his wrist. He sent her one scrawled note with his damaged hand, but then he stopped sending letters because writing was very slow and his homework was taking twice the time it usually took. As the weeks passed, he felt badly about his long silence but he couldn't dredge up the courage to write to her again. At Christmas he sent her a card with a very brief note that took him twenty minutes to compose, but she didn't write back. And so it ended.

He was tired now from running and from cycling home in the heat. The house was empty and hollow-sounding. He went inside and drank a large glass of juice. Then he went into the back garden, ablaze in the afternoon sun. He eased a garden chair into a reclining position. He took off his shirt and lay back. He looked at his taut abdomen in the sunshine, flexed his stomach muscles. Smooth and hard.

He relaxed again and thought about Emma, and how he would see her in three days. He tried to imagine how they would meet at Uncle Michael's house or at the party in the hotel. And he thought about how it would be now, when he saw her again, two years later, both of them two years older.

The sun shone on him as he thought of her. He thought that now, two years later, things would be different. It would be more this time, more would happen. He would be with her alone, and maybe they would kiss, and he would touch her face and her hair, and feel her thin body beneath her clothes.

Sitting in the sun he could feel his body respond to his thoughts, thinking of her, there at the lake, where they might be in just a few days. But then, as his sensations began to focus and the vividness of his thoughts began to flow into his body, he stopped himself, stopped his mind from thinking about Emma. Because he never allowed himself to think of Emma that way, the way he thought about girls when he was alone. Other girls, yes, but not Emma. Although he longed for her still, he never, never allowed himself to think about her in that way.

Even now. Not Emma. Not that way.

CHAPTER 9

Denis O'Donnell was trying to conclude a lengthy telephone conversation at the office. As the voice on the other end droned, he gazed through the glass door into the open-plan area. Suddenly Peter Fagan appeared. He wore an Italian suit and his silver hair was perfectly groomed, as always, even at the end of a long day. He paused outside Denis's office to eavesdrop.

'Yes,' Denis said. 'Okay, that's grand, first thing Monday morning I'll get Johnny to . . . Yes, we'll come back to you with the August campaign . . .'

Peter began pulling faces at Denis through the window. He crossed his eyes and strained his tongue upwards towards his nose.

'No, it's not too late to change the focus,' Denis continued. 'Yes, of course, but at the last meeting . . . But as I was saying, at the last meeting we agreed . . .'

Outside the window Peter began to hang himself with his tie, his face twisted in mock pain.

'Look,' Denis said, 'I'll be passing this over to Johnny on Monday . . . Right, that's grand . . . Yeah . . . Yeah . . . Okay, look, I'll put this in an email, just so we're all straight . . .'

By the time Denis replaced the receiver Peter was halfway

through an elaborate striptease dance. Denis sighed and waved Peter in.

'Why hello there!' Peter said. 'So sorry to interrupt! Were you on the phone?'

'You're an awful bastard.'

'Bastard? Moi? But I was only trying to brighten your day!'

'That was our friends at the bank,' Denis said, gesturing towards a chair.

'Oh? And are they happy?'

'Oh God, don't start.'

'But I must start, my leetle friend,' Peter said, breaking into a French accent. 'I am so sorry for you, but ze bank it eez our biggest prospect. We need to close ze new campaign tout de suite . . .'

'I know, I know, I know.'

'So. Any progress?'

'Oh, yes and no,' Denis sighed. 'I met with them again yesterday afternoon. Had a session with John Quilty.'

'And how did you get on?'

'Bored the fucking trousers off me. How he ever got a job in marketing is beyond me.'

'Yes,' Peter said. 'But did he say what he wants?'

'Eventually. We discussed financial vehicles. Product positioning. Demographic profiles.'

'Okay. So?'

'It's more or less as we thought. They're aiming at the nouveau riche. They want an ad campaign that appears to be highbrow and sophisticated, but it has to appeal to the instincts of a well-heeled Neanderthal.'

'Sort of a fancy chocolates campaign?' Peter said.

'Yes, that's the idea.'

'So,' Peter said. 'Are you making any progress?'

'Yes, I think so. I'm getting somewhere with the slogan. By Monday morning I'll have it nailed down and, assuming Johnny is back, his team can work it up and we'll be away in a hack.'

'Okay . . .' Peter said, 'so do you want to bounce it around?'

'No thanks, mate. It's all right, I'll get there. Oh, by the way, on top of everything else I'll be out of the office on Friday.'

'What's up?' Peter asked.

'Family do. In Donegal.'

'Family?' Peter asked. 'But I thought your mother . . .'

'Yes, but my brother. He's still living in the house.'

'You've never spoken of having a brother,' Peter said.

'I know.'

'You don't get on?'

'We did once upon a time,' Denis sighed. 'Apparently Stephen Deane is throwing a party . . .'

'Whoa, cowboy!' Peter said. 'A movie star? An estranged brother? A party in the wilds of Donegal? What a story!'

'Yes.'

'But you're not looking forward to it?'

'Basically, no. Not at all.'

'Because?'

'I don't know,' Denis sighed, leaning back in his chair. 'It's a bit messy. Maybe it's a guilt thing.'

'Guilt!' Peter said. 'Haven't heard that one for a while. I thought we threw out guilt with the Catholic Church and boiled potatoes.'

'I thought so too.'

'But Denis, my son, we always feel guilty about our families.'

'Do we?'

'Of course,' Peter said. 'You grow up. You move away. You get your own life. You make a few bob. And there they sit, mammy and daddy and the black sheep and the white sheep, right back where you started from.'

'Yes?'

'You think you should do more,' Peter said. 'You think you should be there for them, making them comfortable, sorting out their problems. But unfortunately, my friend, it's not that easy. You have to live your life.'

'Yes,' Denis said. 'I suppose that's it, really.'

'Well, look,' Peter said. 'You go off on Friday and enjoy your little party. And if you need a bit more time for this campaign, we can always beg for mercy.'

'Thanks. But I'll get it sorted.'

'Okay, my son. But the offer stands.'

'Thanks, mate.'

'Don't work too late,' Peter said, standing.

'I won't.'

'And enjoy yourself.'

'Always do.'

In the early days of his career, Denis earned a good reputation for generating ideas and getting campaigns off to a strong start. In the States he had originated nationwide projects for all sorts of products. Yoghurt. Panty Liners. Computer hard disks. He became known for his ability to get it right, understand the audience, tease their interest, capture mind share, make them hungry.

But since he returned to Ireland to run the Dublin office, his management responsibilities cut him off from the creative side of the business. He spent his days sucked into contract negotiations and crisis management. He tried to take time to guide the junior staff, share their ideas, help them clarify their thoughts, act the counsellor if they needed some encouragement. But generally the creative teams did their work, and he did his. And as a result of this division of labour, he hadn't generated a pitch on his own for years.

But now the onus was back on him. The team was worn out, the bank had wrung them dry. And just lately business had slowed. Advertising spend was falling across the country. And so they needed this contract.

Denis looked up at the clock: ten past seven. It was warm in his office, the summer's heat hadn't eased at all as the day lengthened into evening. He loosened his tie, rolled up his sleeves. He began to rummage in his desk for a clean pad of paper, found one, threw it on his desk. He dug out some coloured pens from the top drawer, he wrote 'Invest!' in fancy script across the top of the page, filling in the letters as he went. Then in the centre of the sheet he drew a picture of the sun with fanciful rays and an enigmatic smile. He wrote a few phrases in the margins.

Sunshine days.

Golden rays of warmth.

Summer's warmth.

The Sunshine Bond. You and summer's warmth.

Shit, he thought. This is a fucking disaster.

He crumpled the sheet and fired it into the bin at the far end of the room. Then he looked at the phone on his desk. He thought about picking it up and dialling the number, his old home number, the number that would put him through to Michael. He wondered what would happen if he simply phoned Michael and told him about the campaign. The products. The audience. The angle. Knock it around for a few minutes. Wouldn't it be lovely? Denis thought. To be able to pick up the phone and ring your brother and chat about business, about the weather. Anything. Like they used to do. But he couldn't do it. Not any more. Too much time had passed. At first he had just stepped back, waiting for Michael to snap out of it, come to himself, become normal again. But it didn't happen. The old Michael never really came back. And the division between them stuck, hardened into a rift. And now he didn't know how to begin to bridge the divide.

He stood up and began to pack his things into his briefcase. A minute later he was on his way out of the office.

'Ah, Fiona,' he said as he drifted by the reception desk. 'Still working?'

'Yeah.'

'Don't overdo it,' he said.

'I won't,' she answered. 'Just catching up on a few things. Good night.'

'Good night, Fiona.'

He walked out the glass doors and into the car park. The evening sun was still warm. He got into his Mercedes.

He sighed as he drove out onto the road. He felt tired. The traffic crawled along Appian Way.

Security, he thought. That's what these investment products are for. You think if you buy into the right fund, you'll never want for money. And your kids will grow up perfect. And your wife will remain irresistible. And you'll stay close to your family, and your friends will always be there, and no one dies, and no one gets hurt.

That's it, he thought. That's what the bank is selling. And it's all rubbish. You're never more than a breath away from losing it. All of it, the whole lot. Your staff can quit, form their own company, steal your clients and leave you penniless. A bad driver can cut off your legs. A young woman, a receptionist working late at the office, can step between you and your wife, your kids, your life savings . . .

His mind wandered back to Fiona at the front desk, to her face, to those exaggerated eyelashes, to that soft suggestion of facial hair above her lip.

He could have asked her to dinner tonight. Could have taken her down to the Japanese restaurant on Baggot Street. Nothing formal, just a chat. Could have ordered a bottle of wine. They could have lingered over their meal. He thought of kissing her for the first time as they entered her apartment.

God. Kissing Fiona. What would it be like?

For seventeen years he had been a thoroughly faithful husband. He hadn't so much as kissed another woman since he met Julia. He'd nearly forgotten what it was like, a first kiss with a new girl. The hesitancy. The exploration in the eyes. The invitation and the challenge. The feel of lips, cool, slightly wet and, that first time, so loose.

He remembered Dotty Geraghty, back when they were sixteen. Drunk on stolen beer, on the bridge over the Finn, late, with the cars passing by, hooting their horns. He leaned into her and their lips met, they kissed, and then they kissed deeper, so deep as he pushed into her, they nearly fell over the wall and into the river. She started to laugh. They straightened up and he tried to kiss her again.

He smiled, thinking of that kiss, the wide eyes of her, the way she laughed, the way she said no, that's grand, thank you very much!

And then, of course, there was Catherine. All those years of Catherine. It was so unexpected, seeing her again at the weekend with Julia and the boys standing by. He never thought about her now. It was hard to believe that, at one time in his life, it had been Catherine, nothing but Catherine. For two long, formative years. Hours and hours of kissing, undressing, having sex like animals. It was like eating. Over and over, every weekend. Sometimes twice in one night. Like a hunger.

All that time, he thought. All those hours spent with her young body, eager and alive. Relentless, that's what she was. All through second year, all the way through third year. Never stopped.

He sighed. That life, back then. So free. Such fun it was, back then, in comparison to now, when everything is timetabled, and the money is never enough, and the worries never seem to go away.

But perhaps it wasn't really like that. It couldn't have been. Not as third year wore on. We were all nervous about the exams, would have done anything to escape. Drink. Fuck. Just drop out, like Stephen did. Anything to get away from that feeling of pressure. Sure we were all a bit beside ourselves at that time. Towards the end we were hardly speaking. None of us.

Mad. Mad situation altogether, the whole scene was mad. It's little wonder Michael finally slipped over the edge.

*

During their boyhood years in Donegal, Denis and Michael were just one year and one inch apart. They went to the same school, wore the same grey uniform, ate the same lunch packed in identical plastic containers. When they were growing up everyone assumed they were twins.

'Such lovely boys,' they would say, those women in town, or benign Father MacNeice after Sunday Mass.

'And how old might you be?'

'I'm six,' Michael said.

'And I'm seven,' Denis added.

'But surely you must be mistaken? Aren't you . . .?'

'No actually,' their mother would break in. 'They're not twins at all. Denis is a year older.'

'Sure you'd never know it,' they'd say, a confused smile creasing their faces. 'Very alike, so they are. Very alike indeed.'

The house in the hills offered space, comfort, and endless territory to explore. His father was often away, spending his time between Dublin and his constituency office in Letterkenny. His mother remained at home: loving, indulgent and quite incompetent. She never mastered the business of feeding, bathing and tidying up after her boys. She relied instead on an ageing housekeeper who arrived early enough to make breakfast and left just after tea had been cleared away. And so the boys had plenty of everything and enjoyed utter freedom to follow their interests.

They were inseparable. On summer days they ranged the wilds behind the house, captain and first mate, seeking pheasants in the fields, playing lookout in the big beeches on Trooper's Hill, or fashioning rafts to sail across Loughnagalla. From the early days

Denis was the leader. He took charge of Michael and then he took charge of their schoolmates, heading up every team the school could muster. Michael was the quieter one and infinitely more academic, so far ahead of his peers that he leap-frogged Second Class and moved directly into Denis's year. Denis grew increasingly protective of his younger brother, especially as puberty approached and the boys in the class came to mistrust Michael's successes at school.

'Oy, Denis!'

'What?'

'Your brother.'

'Yeah?'

'He knows everything.'

'Yeah?'

'Why's he such a swot?'

'He's not. You're just thick.'

'Sorry?'

'I said piss off and leave him alone, right?'

As they neared the end of school, the boys grew into men, with blue eyes and wavy hair the colour of sand. Despite their diverse interests – Denis won the Young Entrepreneur award, while Michael came first in Art – they still enjoyed one another's company. Even now Denis had vivid memories of the two of them invading the kitchen on wintry Saturday mornings as the rain poured and the wind howled outside. They positioned themselves side-by-side at the cooker frying up breakfast while Joni Mitchell sang or Rory Gallagher jammed on the stereo. Then came the announcement, the shouting from the base of the stairs to rouse their parents out of bed, urging them to come down and eat while it was hot: rashers, sausages, fried eggs, black and white pudding, grilled tomatoes and the old china coffee pot filled with strong, freshly brewed coffee. The mess was slapped onto plates and set on the table as their parents stumbled into the kitchen, still blind with sleep, mumbling their thanks and begging the boys to please turn down the music.

Captain and first mate. They were brilliant times.

At that time Denis mapped out his life like an architectural drawing. He was going to take up a career in marketing, get a job in the States, make his money fast and enjoy what life had to offer. Michael was less sure, dithering over his decisions, fretting over what course to take. Denis came into Michael's room one morning as Michael lay gazing at the ceiling. He surveyed the room's contents. The prints by Blake and Leonardo. The statues lining the shelves: a man smoking a pipe, a woman pointing her finger at the sky. A black-and-white photograph of their mother standing beside a tree, the Donegal countryside spread out behind her like a quilt.

'Mick,' he said. 'Look at this room. It's the nearest thing to a gallery in the entire county.'

'Yes?'

'You know you love this stuff.'

'Aye.'

'So why don't you do it?'

'Do it?'

'Yes. Do what you like doing. At college. Art, for fuck's sake!'

And so it was decided: Denis would study commerce at UCD, and Michael would go to the College of Art and Design. They would find a house to share. It would be great craic.

Denis remembered that final summer before they moved to Dublin, the two of them holding court at the hotel, standing at the bar in their jeans and sweaters, gathering girls around them like birds to a feeder. They had an unconscious routine that played itself out like a well-rehearsed two-hander – Denis charming and witty, Michael softly ironic – and they knew they were a dishy pair, the stuff of schoolgirl dreams: those gorgeous O'Donnell boys.

Word of their plans to study in Dublin spread through town. One Saturday afternoon Stephen Deane arrived at the house, skinny and nervous, with his large, square-jawed mother stationed behind him on the doorstep. Denis answered the door.

'Ah, hiya,' Stephen said into the door saddle. 'Are you going up to Dublin?'

'Sorry?' Denis said.

Stephen's mother pushed him aside, backing Denis into the front hall.

'Denis O'Donnell,' she said in a heavy Donegal accent. 'Are youz goin' up to Dublin to study?'

'Yes,' Denis said. 'In September . . .'

'That's grand so,' Mrs Deane said. 'My Stephen will be going up as well, and we've a house organised, and we'd like youz to share that house with him.'

'Oh . . .'

'It's a grand big house, there's four fine big bedrooms, and you won't find cheaper rent in Dublin.'

'I see,' Denis considered. 'I'm sure that would be grand, Mrs Deane, but I'd need to check with Dad . . .'

'Don't you go worrying about your Daddy. He'll be thrilled to have you so well looked after.'

'I, I'm sure . . .'

But before Denis could object she had turned and pushed Stephen towards the car.

'Now that's settled so,' she said as they walked away. 'We just need one more for that fourth bedroom and we'll be doing rightly.'

They drove off leaving Denis open-mouthed in the doorway.

Within a week the fourth member materialised in the form of Mary Moran. The boys knew her vaguely from inter-school functions. Michael had always liked her but Denis had reservations.

'Her parents are Nazis,' he protested. 'They'll make her hang a sacred heart in the hall.'

'That's why she's going to college,' Michael said. 'To escape them.'

'But surely she could find a nice tidy house filled with virgins . . .'

'She doesn't want to live with women,' Michael said. 'She says women are impossible. Too bitchy. She's convinced her mother she'll be safer living with us.'

'Safer?' Denis exclaimed. 'Have you seen the size of her? She's as safe as a fucking vault.'

'Denis . . .'

'Seriously, if we have to share with a girl, why couldn't we find one with a bit more . . .'

'Oh, give it a rest,' Michael said. 'She's going to be your housemate, not your concubine.'

And so they settled into the big house in Donnybrook. Within a short time, the house earned a reputation as the ideal student haven: a place to go at weekends, to get pissed, to get off and to sleep through a hangover. A gang began to form around them, growing outward that first year to encompass a multi-provincial, multinational assortment: Mary Moran and Stephen Deane from Donegal, Gerry and Evelyn from Cork, Bob and the lads from Blackrock College, the two sisters from the States, a big Danish guy who tried to pounce on every girl he met. And, at the centre of it all, the O'Donnell boys.

God, it was good fun.

Denis fast installed himself as the captain of the squad, just as he had at school. He oversaw provisions, administered a rota of jobs and duties, kept the noise levels down during the week and the volume up during the Friday night parties. Michael took on a supporting role, offering guidance to his peers with wisdom well beyond his years. And so when Mary Moran had yet another row with her mother, Michael was there with tea and cigarettes and a steady, positive regard. He even accompanied Mary when she bought her first packet of birth control pills.

'You did what?' Denis asked Michael.

'We went to the Well Woman Centre,' Michael said. 'It's where you go to get the Pill.'

'I know what it is,' Denis said impatiently. 'But why?'

'What do you mean?'

'Mary Moran will be the last girl on this planet to get shagged.'

'I know. She told me she's not quite ready to go all the way.'

'So why in the name of God . . .?'

'It's about taking charge,' Michael said. 'She wants to take control of her destiny.'

'Oh, right,' Denis considered. 'Look, you're not planning to, you know . . .'

'Jesus, Denis! She just needed a bit of support. It doesn't really concern you, so don't go troubling yourself about it.'

'Okay,' Denis sighed. 'Very thoughtful of you. Very touching indeed.'

Stephen Deane, too, quietly consulted Michael about his problems. He felt he needed to come out of himself, he wanted to try something challenging and out of character. And so he determined to audition for the UCD Drama Society. Michael set to work to find something that would suit Stephen's personality as well as his accent. They settled on a scene from a Brian Friel play, a monologue offering endless opportunity for dramatic interpretation. Stephen lost himself completely in the role, his wiry arms and legs forming shapes to reflect the contorted thoughts of his character. And then Michael coached Stephen with his lines, over and over. And over again. But despite the exhaustive rehearsals, Stephen never got the actual script into his head. To Michael's horror Stephen improvised his way through most of the audition, slaughtering the sensitive script and filling the gaps with ex tempore asides. But the effect was nothing short of brilliant. Stephen landed a role in the first play of the season, the first of the twelve roles he would play over the next three years.

And so a sense of order prevailed in the house, with the boys at the helm, and visitors aplenty, and a series of Friday-night parties that had become the best that UCD had to offer.

Despite the new-found freedom, Denis never lost his focus. He took his studies seriously, he encouraged everyone else to do the same, told them to get their exams and get on with their lives. He said the world was growing smaller and Europe was getting closer and business was going to pick up and very soon Ireland would no longer be the sleepy marginalised backwater that everyone knew and loved. And he really believed it. Positive energy seemed to flow around him, people noticed it all the time. As first-year exams were drawing to a close he won a competition for marketing, something a third-year student was expected to win. There was money involved, two hundred and fifty pounds. Back at the house the music blared and soon the gang was wildly drunk beneath a haze of cannabis smoke.

And during that wild, pumped-up, end-of-year party, Catherine presented herself to Denis like an unexpected gift. She was from Ballyshannon and he had seen her around the college canteen but they had never spoken before. He still remembered how she materialised, late into the party, wearing a short skirt and a pink three-buttoned top out of which her generous bosom threatened to burst every time she inhaled. He didn't remember how the conversation started but suddenly he was staring into a pair of dark eyes and seeing hair like he'd never seen before, hair like a forest, something you could get lost in, soft and dark and welcoming. They talked about nothing, he could hardly hear her voice above the music, it didn't matter what they were saying, he just loved looking into those eyes, feeling the presence of those breasts as she spoke, as she breathed, exposing the white skin where one, two buttons were undone, those breasts lurking there below, pulling him, drawing him towards her. And then she started backing out of the room and she turned away and his face was focused on her thighs as he followed her up the stairs, trying not to stare up her skirt as she lifted one leg and then the other up the narrow, steep stairway to his room, and then there they were, he was with her, they were half-undressed and he was on her, feeling a joy he had never known, moving gently, oh so gently over that full, gorgeous, generous white body.

The college years passed quickly and suddenly it was spring term of their final year. Ireland was disintegrating all around them. The economy was dying, the jobless rate soared. The pressure was on to perform well, everyone was studying hard, cramming late into the night and then falling into bed, only to be back at the books the next morning, scratching the sleep from their eyes.

Everyone felt tense and vulnerable in the knowledge that, if they survived the exams, they'd immediately be off to London or New York or somewhere where they spoke English to find some kind of a job. They were burdened with the awareness that major changes would soon be upon them, the life they had come to love was soon to end. The friends, the people they depended on, the parties and the generally mad routine were about to be pulled from under them. And there was no parachute, no safety cord and no way back. And it was frightening, really frightening, though everyone was afraid to admit just how frightening it really was.

Mary Moran, heavy and satiric, sank into a public depression, sobbing that she couldn't do it, that Psychology was beating her, she'd never pass, she'd never get a job, her mother would never accept her back into the house and the whole thing was an enormous waste. They took it in turns to comfort her – Michael, Stephen, and even Denis – to listen and provide whatever support they could, before rushing back to another intense round of exam preparations.

And then one evening Stephen Deane announced to his housemates that he was opting out.

'Sorry?' Denis said.

'I'm not doing the exams,' Stephen said. 'It's a film. I've been called for a second audition.'

'A second audition?' Michael said.

'Yes. In London. They say it's going to take two days, it's the same time as my exams. I'll miss three of the papers. So I'm not doing them.'

'Don't be daft,' Denis said. 'You have to sit the exams.'

'He's not daft,' Mary said, with her eyes lighting up. 'Stephen, well done! This is brilliant!'

'I know,' Stephen said. 'It's exactly what I've wanted.'

'You're making a huge mistake,' Denis said dryly.

'But Denis,' Stephen protested, 'this is it! It's a *film*. They need an Irish character. They even want my accent. I can't turn this down.'

'But what if you don't get it?' Denis asked. 'Then where will you be?'

'I don't know,' Stephen replied, looking away.

'Well I do,' Denis said. 'You'll be serving coffee into your forties with all the other useless star-struck failures . . .'

'I can't miss this, Denis.'

'I've never heard such moronic shite!' Denis exploded. 'You're passing up the chance to finish your degree, you're actually going to mess up your life on the odd chance that some sad bastard would give you a part in a film? For fuck's sake, you can't memorise ten lines!'

Stephen stood up and met Denis's gaze. 'You've got this wrong. This is all I've wanted for the past three years. I'm going to go to this audition.'

'Michael,' Denis said impatiently, 'would you ever say something here?'

'I think Stephen knows what he wants to do,' Michael said softly.

'And I'm telling you all,' Denis said, 'Stephen Deane is making the biggest mistake of his life.'

Stephen looked at Denis then. He was shaking. Tears of frustration were forming in his eyes. Then with a dramatic sweep of his arm he grabbed his jacket and walked out of the house.

Later that night, after everyone had gone to bed, Stephen quietly returned to the house to pack his things. He was composing a note to say goodbye when Mary Moran came downstairs and pleaded with him in anxious whispers to reconsider. But Stephen said he'd had enough of college, enough of exams, and enough of Denis O'Donnell, and he was going off to live his own life.

And two weeks later Stephen Deane landed the role.

Meanwhile, Michael was preparing for his final exhibition. He spent his days in the studio on his own, returning to the house ashen-faced, collapsing on the sofa like a released prisoner. He brought home a series of sculptures, explaining that they were a study of humankind based on mediaeval humours. Weird stuff altogether: a man's head spitting brown ooze with his teeth sticking out at impossible angles; a woman in white ceramic with creamy skin but bleeding vibrant scarlet. Each piece was suffused with singular, riveting agony.

Denis noticed that Michael was losing weight but he wasn't particularly worried about him. They were all skinny as rakes and even Mary Moran was shedding pounds as the tension increased. But then at the Friday-night party, one week before the exams were due to start, Denis was stepping across the bodies on the floor when he saw Michael and he sensed for the first time that something was going wrong.

Michael had positioned the sofa directly in front of the stereo. Music was blaring out of the speakers at high volume: Queen, Freddie Mercury screaming over a wild chorus of voices. Michael was sweating profusely. Across him lay a blonde girl wearing a chain of earrings and an Indian skirt. Michael had pulled her on top of him and was explaining something as he held onto her, shouting passionately to her about some nonsense, dialogue and dialogic and materialism and the hidden order of art. Denis had never seen the poor girl before and Michael was practically screaming into her face and she looked stunned, as if she didn't know how to escape. Denis felt he had to intervene, so he reached over and turned the stereo down and told Michael to lighten up and let her go. Michael just stared back as though he didn't know what he was saying. And the whole room seemed to stop for that moment as the two brothers stared at one another, and everyone thought there was going to be a row. But then Denis simply told Michael to go easy on the jar, and someone put Madness on the stereo, and the dancing started again, and that appeared to be the end of it.

Unfortunately, as Denis later realised, that encounter signalled the beginning of a deterioration in Michael's grip on his surroundings, but at the time Denis didn't recognise the signs. Two days later he came into the kitchen to find Michael, wide awake, still dressed from the day before and looking pale and uncertain.

'Hey Mick,' Denis yawned. 'What's wrong with you? Didn't you sleep?'

'What?' Michael replied.

'Sleep. Didn't you get any sleep?'

'No. Sure, how could I?'

'What do you mean?' Denis frowned.

'I'm working on the argument. For the exams.'

'What argument?'

'The argument,' Michael said earnestly. 'In the Bacon.'

'Sorry?'

'Francis Bacon. The Pope. You know, the Velasquez. There's two sides to that story. Definitely. I just have to sort it out.'

Denis stared at him for a moment. 'Are you sure you're not dreaming?'

'No, Denis, don't be daft. I'll be grand. It's for the exams. I just have to get this sorted out.'

'Okay,' Denis said hesitantly. 'I'm going to boil the kettle. Can I get you anything?'

'No, thanks.'

'Right. But maybe you should try to get some sleep?'

'Yes. Right. Later.'

Michael sat there on the sofa, then, as Denis made breakfast and ate it and did the washing-up. And Michael hardly moved except that his lips twitched occasionally, as though he was about to say something, if only to himself. Denis went into the college library for the day and forgot about the incident, thinking Michael was just following his artistic impulses.

Then that evening the phone rang in the house, and it was his mother back in Donegal.

'Denis, have you seen Michael?'

'Yes, but not since this morning. Why?'

'Where is he?'

'I don't know. He's probably still at college.'

'Well he's just after phoning me,' she said. 'He must be at a phone box somewhere. I could hear traffic in the background.'

'Right. What's the problem?'

'He's asked me to look for a book. In his bedroom. He kept talking about some writer. Back-teen, something like that. I can't find the book in his room.'

'Sure you know Michael. The book is probably here in the house somewhere.'

'But Denis,' she said, 'it seemed terribly important to him. Could you tell him I've tried? I've looked everywhere.'

'Right. I'll let him know.'

'Maybe he should try to buy himself another copy,' she said. 'He seemed very concerned.'

'Don't worry. I'll make sure he gets sorted out.'

'Thanks, lovey.'

'Plonker,' Denis said to himself as he put down the phone. 'Making her dig through all that shite in his room. Selfish fucking bastard.'

Denis didn't see Michael that night or the next day and he was too wrapped up in his own work to worry about Michael and his bloody book. By then Denis was facing problems from another corner as well. The exams were about to begin and Catherine responded to the pressure by becoming increasingly demanding. She was getting clingy, he thought, calling to the house every evening, sitting in the kitchen and staring at him over the counter as he studied. She had her English literature all sewn up, was totally prepared for every paper, so her studying consisted of a cursory glance at her notes between cigarettes. Meanwhile, Denis was giving it every ounce of energy he could muster.

And so, when she arrived at the house, she had nothing to do. She developed a new facial expression, a sort of vulnerable half-smile, as if she were seeking Denis's approval but was at the same time ready to lash into him for ignoring her. He was getting annoyed about it, too, especially because his libido was non-existent due to lack of sleep. And when they did climb into bed she went all silent, expecting him to direct the show, to take it slowly and make it meaningful, and all he wanted to do was get on with it, release whatever sexual energy he could locate within himself, and then get back to the books.

They were, he noted to himself, at cross-purposes.

The night after his first exam, he was especially shattered and he couldn't take it any longer.

'What is it?' he said angrily.

'What?' she asked from across the table.

'What do you want?'

'Nothing. What do you mean?'

'Look,' he explained. 'I'm sorry, but I'm wrecked. I've got my strategy paper tomorrow. I really need to swot this stuff one more time.'

'God. More studying. It's all you do. All the time.'

'It's the exams! What do you *expect* me to do?'

'There's a life out there, Denis. Life! Outside the exams!'

'Yes, and it starts the day the exams are over. Not before.'

'Not for Stephen it didn't.'

'Leave Stephen out of it.'

'Okay, okay. No need to snap. I'll just go for a walk or something.'

'Right,' he said testily.

Then he watched her leave the house. For some reason the image stuck with him: a navy jumper, the collar of a pink polo shirt half sticking out the top. Her voluminous black hair subdued in a massive pony tail. Her shoulders looking small and fragile as she walked out the door without looking back.

Denis was angry, so angry he couldn't study. He threw his books across the room, grabbed his jacket, walked down to McCloskey's, had two pints at the bar, watched the match, smoked. He returned around ten and studied for another hour, still annoyed about Catherine, before collapsing into bed.

They didn't speak for two days. Then, on Friday night, she showed up at the party. Denis got drunk and felt very relaxed and they spent the night together. It was tender, more tender than it had been for some time. They smiled at one another. They felt free from everything: the recent rows, the exams, the future. It seemed simple, as simple as it had in the beginning. But then, the next morning, as he slipped out of bed and looked at her, still asleep, he knew it was coming, the end of the two of them.

By the following Monday night Denis had finished all but two of his exams. The house was quiet, everyone was exhausted. Mary Moran had Joan Armatrading on the stereo and Denis sat down with her on the sofa. They shared a box of chocolates. They talked about Catherine, a subject that had always been taboo between them. Denis listened to Mary attack Catherine's wardrobe and her fake accent, the one that sprang from somewhere between

Donegal and Dublin 4. He found himself laughing and feeling that maybe the timing was right for a break. And then the phone rang, and it was his mother again.

Michael was totally off the rails.

It was 9:30 and Denis didn't know where to begin looking.

His mother was nearly hysterical. She said that Michael had phoned, he was talking total rubbish, blathering on about dialectics, saying he was getting married. She had tried to calm him down but he wouldn't listen, he couldn't tell her where he was. She begged Denis to take this seriously, she was very worried, would he please go out and find Michael, for God's sake?

He took a taxi into Michael's college. He was sweating when he reached the front desk.

'Yeah,' the porter said, pulling on a cigarette. 'He was here today. This afternoon.'

'Right. You see, I need to find him. I'm not quite sure where he is. I think he might not be well.'

'Well sure, you'd never know where Michael would be off to.'

'Sorry?'

'Your brother, Michael, now. He marches to his own tune, if you know what I mean. Marches to his own tune . . .'

Denis phoned his mother to see if Michael had phoned again, but he hadn't, so he started to run towards town. He finally made it to Neary's, asked around, no one had seen Michael, so he ran around the corner to Peter's. He pushed his way to the bar, panting, perspiring freely, begging Aidan for any news of Michael's whereabouts.

'Yeah, he was in all right,' Aidan yawned. 'Had some new bird with him. Never saw her before. A blondey one with loads of earrings. Somebody said she was at Trinity. She tried to light up a jag, right here at the bar. Gas. I had to send her outside. Michael seemed well pleased with himself and this bird. Talking nineteen to the dozen at her. He followed her out the door and that's the last I saw of them. If I were you, now, I'd check out her rooms at Trinity. I'd say you'd find him there. Sure you know Michael . . .'

Denis left the pub, ran back to Grafton Street. He tried to tell himself this was a load of bother over nothing but something in the back of his mind told him it was serious. He hadn't seen Michael in three days. He knew Michael had been a bit unsteady lately, but sure he'd always been that way.

Always had his own ideas, Michael. But he wasn't *mad*.

Shit.

He stopped at a phone box, rang his mother again, calmed her down, told her Michael had been in the pub, had probably had a few jars too many, said he'd find him soon, told her not to worry. Then he tore off down Grafton Street towards Trinity.

He didn't know what her name was or where the rooms were but he decided to go in the front gate and start asking around. As he rounded the bend, he could see scaffolding, green netting covering the front of the college. Sandblasting. They'd been at it all summer.

And then, as he neared the front gates: the crowds. Looking up. He searched the pink evening sky, looked over College Green, over the portico of the Bank of Ireland. Nothing.

He pushed his way through the crowd, approached the railings, looked up again, asked someone what was going on. He followed the gaze of the crowd up into the scaffolding, up to the blue clock, up above, to the pinnacle. Then he saw a man, his chest bare, standing on the apex of the roof, shouting. Waving his arms, gesticulating. Denis couldn't hear the voice over the sound of the traffic. Then he saw a girl below him, standing on the scaffolding, looking up at him, listening, as if frozen against the sky.

And then the face, Denis finally saw the man's face. And it was Michael.

Denis shouted up but Michael couldn't hear him. He didn't know where to turn, where to go to get up there, to get Michael down. He watched as Michael swayed above the clock, waving his arms against the sky, the crowds below reeling with fear and fascination. But then three gardaí climbed from the tiny window at the top of the building, edged their way across the scaffolding. They grabbed the girl, shouting up to Michael to calm himself, ordering him to sit, to stay there, to sit down, while they climbed up, around, behind him. Then a big garda appeared on the roof, grabbed Michael from behind and wrestled with him, the breathing of the crowd suspended as they watched the garda struggle with Michael, swaying momentarily against the vibrant sky, until Michael finally collapsed in his arms and they sat, the garda holding him: a pietà, high above the city, heaving, breathing, on that rooftop, safe, finally safe.

'Fucking bollix,' Denis said to himself as he watched from below in the midst of the crowds, amidst a murmur of voices asking who it was, who is the mad fella nearly killed himself, the eejit.

Fucking stupid fucking bollix.

The next two weeks were an unfocused mess of sleeplessness and unease as Denis's separate worlds crashed into one another.

Denis travelled with Michael in the garda car to St John of God's hospital. Michael was talking non-stop, peering into Denis's eyes but not seeing him, not connecting with anything around him. They admitted Michael sometime around midnight, dressed him in white and injected him with tranquillisers. For a few minutes he remained awake, asking over and over where Una was. But Denis knew that Michael was not really there, that his mind was now wrapped in a haze of blurred ideas and sensations. The nurses said very little to Denis except that Michael was safe now and he should go home, there was nothing more Denis could do.

His parents drove down from Donegal in a panic the next day. When they arrived at the house and entered the front door, they found Mary Moran in tears on the sofa, wearing her black pyjamas. Denis drove with them to the hospital. The three of them met Michael in the patients' lounge. For two hours they sat with him as he stared into space, smoked, sipped a grey cup of tea. His mother cried and his father paced the room and then tried to command the staff to let Michael come home. Finally, they were shown into the office of a consultant with an English accent who explained that Michael was experiencing a severe episode of schizophrenic delusions, that it was too early to provide a complete prognosis but that, with appropriate care and treatment under his direction, Michael's condition could be controlled.

'Controlled?' Denis's father exploded. 'But when is he going to be himself again?'

'I'm sorry, Mr O'Donnell,' the consultant said looking at his watch. 'But control is the best we can hope for at this stage.'

Denis and his parents had a silent steak dinner at a stuffy

restaurant. He returned to the house to be confronted by Catherine, who wanted him to take her out to escape from all the tension.

They sat across from one another at a low table in Madigan's. They were surrounded by RTÉ types in formal wear, obviously after a function. Denis felt small and weak.

'So what are you going to do?' Catherine said.

'Do? What *can* I do?'

'He's your brother. You can't just leave him there.'

'I can. It's a hospital. A psychiatric hospital. They look after lunatics.'

'He's not a lunatic. It was just a bit of fun. He had a bit too much to drink. That blonde cow put him up to it.'

Denis didn't respond.

'So,' she persisted. 'What are you going to do?'

'I told you I'm not doing anything.'

'That's so like you,' she said. 'It's his problem, it's nothing to do with you . . .'

'For fuck's sake . . .'

'No, I'm serious. You're going to go back and finish your little exams, then you're going to fly off to Boston to carry out your little plan of world domination. And to hell with Michael, to hell with Stephen, to hell with the lot of us.'

'I don't need this right now.'

'It's true, though, isn't it? The world can be falling down but as long as you're on track nothing matters.'

'Yeah. Okay. Maybe you're right. And so what if it's true?'

'Nothing at all,' she said, sipping her brandy. 'It's just that you're an awful selfish bastard, Denis O'Donnell.'

He looked down at the table, shook his head, felt angry, was going to lash out, but then retreated into himself and said nothing.

Denis drove towards home now, on this June evening, twenty years later, in a sour but reflective mood.

In two days he would see them again: Catherine. Stephen Deane. Mary Moran. And of course, Michael. There would be stories, of then and now. Nervous laughter. Attempts to hide the signs of age. Hints at love affairs, suggestions of wealth and success. It would be interesting, certainly. Maybe even a bit of fun.

But right now Denis felt as though his life was on trial.

Stephen Deane wasn't really the problem. Denis regretted their argument long ago and he admitted feeling raw envy at Stephen's success. Undoubtedly their reunion on Saturday would be awkward and Denis expected to receive a long-overdue 'I told you so'. But he actually looked forward to having the chance to speak with Stephen, maybe to patch things up. It would be worth the effort. When you're in advertising, you can never have too many friends in Hollywood.

As for Catherine, well, seeing her again would be difficult. The break-up had been managed badly. There had never been a final scene, no explosive row, no formal tear-stained goodbye. They had simply gone in different directions, Catherine to London, Denis to Boston. Within a few years Denis had met Julia and they began seventeen years of more-or-less blissful marriage. Denis knew he could never have been happy with Catherine in the long run, not after his experience of her temperament during their time together at college.

But the way they parted, after two years of being together, meant that a great deal remained unsaid. It was like a play ending without a final curtain. And now there was the chance that Catherine would choose the party on Saturday night to drag it all up again. It could be awkward for Denis, and painful for Julia, and embarrassing for the whole lot of them.

And then, in the middle of it all, there was Michael. For Denis, Michael remained a focus for feelings of deep-seated remorse. Because Denis could never, ever forgive himself for letting that relationship lapse.

He had gone over it in his mind a thousand times, how the hiatus between them had developed, why they lost contact the way they did. There was the initial break when Denis travelled to Boston. Then the litany of lame excuses: Michael was schizophrenic, he wasn't the same person he had been before, he tired easily, there was nothing for them to talk about. Then the continuing self-justification, like a recital of legal evidence. Denis phoned Michael occasionally. He took Michael to dinner whenever he was in Ireland. He offered Michael money, regularly, but Michael always declined. He saw Michael at his mother's funeral, and signed over the house to him, kissed his share goodbye, let it all go Michael's way.

But nothing, Denis knew, could really justify the way he had turned his back on his brother. And now he didn't know where to begin.

And so, now, driving home on a warm Wednesday evening, Denis suffered a gnawing sense of self-doubt. His mind was awash with painful memories, and he simply could not predict what would happen when he and Michael were together again, in a few short days, at the party, with so much unresolved conflict between them.

And, to make matters worse, he also knew that by Monday morning, when the party was over and all the reunions complete, he had to present his slogan for National Bank's new exclusive line of investment products.

Julia sat up in bed, staring at the mirror across the room. Denis was curled up beside her, facing the wall. Blue light hung in the late-evening sky.

'Denis?' she said softly.

'Yeah,' he mumbled.

'Are you still awake?'

'Not really,' he said.

'Are you okay?'

'Mm. Bit tired.'

'Is work going okay?'

'Yes.' He turned towards her. 'Work is grand. Why?'

'Oh, nothing,' she said. 'Just, we haven't really talked. About Donegal or anything.'

'What's there to talk about?' he yawned. 'Do you not want to go?'

'Yes, I do,' she said. 'But I wish I knew what to expect.'

'Expect?'

'Yes,' she said. 'I feel like I don't know anything. About the scene in Donegal. You and Michael. Your gang.'

'There's nothing to tell. They're all boring, middle-aged farts by now. Just like us.'

'Yeah, but . . .'

'Look, it's just a party. We'll go and see what happens. There's no need to prepare. Just be yourself. You'll be grand.'

He rolled back towards the wall.

'Maybe we'll talk about it later in the week?' she said. 'When you're more awake?'

'Yeah,' he yawned again. 'Later in the week. That would be lovely.'

In a few minutes she could hear him breathing beside her. The slow breathing of early sleep. She tried not to recall what Catherine looked like on Sunday, in the hot sunshine, looking up at Denis in that way, with that look of challenge in her eyes. She felt alone. She wished she was tired.

CHAPTER 10

Emma Gallagher sat on a plastic chair at the black table in the staff room of the Northern Hotel. The rest of the daytime staff were gone for the afternoon and she too was ready to leave, but she was waiting for Lorna to balance the till so they could walk out together.

She leaned forward on her elbows examining a new blue packet of cigarettes. She read the government warnings on the side of the packet: 'Pregnant Women Should Not Smoke'.

She took off the plastic wrapper, crushed it and tossed it at the ashtray in the middle of the table. She watched it unfold like a waking animal. She pulled the gold foil off the packet and took out a cigarette. She held it in both hands, suspended between her fingers, considering it as if it were a bank note. She ran it under her nose and inhaled the sickly sweet smell. Such an elegant little creation, she thought. So smooth against your fingers. So perfectly white. A lovely, white, tubular, virginal thing.

Funny, she thought. So poisonous.

Then she yawned, feeling drained. Again. Like so many afternoons lately.

She dug a lighter from her pocket, flicked it on, lit the cigarette, inhaled deeply and felt an immediate tingling rush through her body, a sudden joy.

The only good part, she thought. That first drag.

A moment later Lorna Nolan walked into the staff room, tall and willowy, with large grey eyes that made her look slightly dazed.

'Hiya,' she said, pulling off her hostess apron. 'Sorry it took so long. I'm terrible at balancing the cash, it always takes me ages.'

'Let's go,' said Emma.

The two girls walked out of the kitchen. They passed through the car park and onto the footpath out of town.

'Such a lovely day,' Lorna said dreamily. 'Fancy a drive to the beach?'

'I wish I could. I have to go shopping with Mam. She wants to buy something for the party.'

'Oh, of course, the grand affair! When is the crowd from Dublin arriving?'

'Tomorrow,' Emma said. 'They're staying with Uncle Michael.'

'And what about your wee friend?'

'Sorry?'

'Don't *sorry* me,' Lorna said. 'You know who I mean. That Yankee cousin of yours.'

'He's not my cousin,' Emma said. 'He's my second cousin.'

'All the better,' Lorna said. 'So he *is* coming.'

'Aye.'

'So tell us, how long has it been?'

'Nearly two years.'

'And do you still have all those letters?'

'Aye.'

'They were lovely,' Lorna said, swinging her arms.

'Yes. They were lovely.'

'Sure he was mad for you back then.'

'I don't know,' Emma said, looking down at the path. 'We got on, like. We didn't really know each other.'

'Why did he stop writing?' Lorna asked.

'He broke his arm. Playing rugby.'

'No! Is that the reason?'

'Aye. He wrote one last note. Said he couldn't write for a while, it hurt too much. Then he never really wrote again. Except for a card at Christmas.'

'Bastard.'

'Ach, well, I don't think so,' Emma said. 'We were only young. And we only met the once. He had his life and I had mine.'

'Emma Gallagher!' Lorna laughed. 'You sound like an old maid. He was a bastard to you and you know it.'

'Sure that's just the way fellas are. Short memories. No point in fighting it.'

'But he's coming up for the party anyway?' Lorna urged.

'Aye.'

'And so? Are you going to see him?'

'I don't know,' Emma said. 'I'd say I'll see him all right. I don't know if we'll have much chance to talk.'

'Of course you will,' Lorna urged. 'Corner him. Make him squirm a bit for being such a shite. What are you going to wear?'

'My uniform, you loony. I'll be working.'

'Oh, of course. Well, wear your sexy top anyways – the low one. Let him know what he's missing.'

'Ah now, Lorna. He's hardly pining over the likes of me. I'm sure he's a rake of Dublin girls to keep him occupied.'

'Sometimes you forget how gorgeous you are. Apart from those bags under your eyes.'

Emma smiled at her friend.

'Look,' Lorna continued. 'Tell Mam you can do the shopping tomorrow. Go home and get your togs. We'll head up to Rathmullen. My sister's driving, we'll collect you in twenty minutes. This might be the last good day we have this summer.'

Emma shook her head.

'Sorry,' she said as they reached the house. 'We'll have to hope for another day.'

'Oh, hi, lovey,' her mother said as Emma entered the house. 'How'd you get on today?'

'Grand.'

'Would you like a bit of lunch? I could make you up a nice roll and a cup of tea . . .'

'No, thanks, I had something at the hotel.'

'Are you sure now? You look a bit peaky.'

'I'm just a bit tired. I couldn't sleep in the heat last night.'

'Ah, you poor thing. There's nothing worse than a bad night.'

'I might have a wee lie-down,' Emma said.

'Of course. Do you think you'll feel up to shopping later?'

'Aye. Later.'

'There's no hurry now. It's Thursday so there's late shopping tonight. I just need your opinion, you know. Something for the party. For Saturday night.'

'Yes, Mammy. We'll go shopping later.'

'That's great. No hurry now. You have a nice wee rest and we'll head into town whenever you like.'

Emma trundled up the stairs. With each passing year, she thought, Mammy becomes more like a child, and I become more like her mother.

A few minutes later she was lying in bed. The afternoon sun streamed through the lace that covered her window. Despite her mother's promises, she still had no proper curtains. Emma knew the O'Hare boys across the way could see her. Every night she hid behind the door to undress and turned off the light before crossing the room.

Now the space was lit up brightly by the sun. So warm. She could feel the perspiration on her neck as she lay back in bed and closed her eyes.

Barry, she thought. Here, in Ballyfinn. Tomorrow.

It had been so long, over two years now. She wondered what he looked like. Taller, perhaps. More like a man. There was a photograph downstairs, a family portrait that had come with in a red Christmas card. Uncle Denis in his suit with his advertising-agency smile. Aunt Julia looking like something on the telly, with her perfect blonde hair and her gleaming teeth. Little Jimmy in his jacket and tie, scrubbed clean, his smile so happy and natural.

And then Barry, standing behind Julia, in a navy jacket with his shirt open at the neck. His golden hair curling above his lovely clear eyes. A half-smile. Not forced, but not happy either. A bit distant.

Emma tried to imagine him there in the studio as it was happening. A quick-witted photographer with a Dublin accent telling them where to stand, making a fuss of Jimmy's tie, flirting with Julia, treating Denis with mock deference. Barry being pushed and prodded and positioned, feeling foreign and wishing it was over. But saying nothing.

The same shy boy who stood with her at the lake, with the moonlight in flashes all around them. It was all so innocent, she thought. We thought it could last for ever.

But sure we were only fourteen then, she thought. It's only natural that, after so long apart, you forget one another. And the pressure, then. You can't save yourself for someone far away when there's the pressure all around you.

It shouldn't matter, she thought, but it does. When you seem to be the only virgin in town.

Marie Hegarty does it with Conor Jackson. Jenny Murphy does it with Jim Conroy. She'd even seen Peter Quinlan buying condoms in the chemist's the other day. Then there's Gillian Courtney with her baby, he's nearly two now. Even Lorna, Emma thought. Lorna who can't even handle a bank note. Even *she* did it. At her parents' New Year's Eve party, for god's sake, with that eejit Jacko Bonner from Letterkenny. The only reason she let him near her was because he was so tall. They lasted a few days into the new year, and then it was all over.

Gas, Lorna. Describing the details. The look of horror on her face, then splitting her sides laughing, almost crying at the same time.

Emma closed her eyes, feeling her mind loosen and her thoughts drift. Those girls, the girls at school. So predatory. There's no waiting around, it's like a power thing. The fellas think they're calling the tune but it's all mapped out for them. Pulled in like fish from the sea.

That was my problem, Emma thought, suddenly wide awake. That really was my problem.

I wanted to be like them. Like all those other girls.

The one in charge.

*

It had happened six weeks ago, the night of the concert.

The town was awash with posters hanging from every lamp-post and in every shop window. Some band from Scandinavia: the latest in European jazz. They were touring Ireland, and someone on the town council had a connection with some cultural committee in Dublin and managed to book them to play Ballyfinn.

Emma quizzed Uncle Michael about them one night after tea.

'You've actually heard of them?' she asked.

'Oh yes,' Michael affirmed quietly. 'They're a quintet. Norwegian. They're quite good. Very intense, but still accessible. Here, bear with me a moment. I might just have something inside . . .'

He went into the sitting room as if on a mission. A few moments later music began to play from the speakers on the walls and Michael returned, his face animated by his discovery.

'Listen to this,' he said, leaning across the table. 'It's called "Coffee". Listen to the Bach, the polyphony, just there, beneath the melody . . .'

Emma listened. She didn't understand what Michael meant and she wasn't sure if she liked the music. But she could feel the energy of the playing. She heard them move together, the five of them, building slowly at first, and then louder and with more fire. It was a haunting, foreign sound.

'Listen to the bass here,' Michael said. 'The way he pulls away from the group . . .'

'Lovely,' she replied hesitantly.

She studied the stark black-and-white photograph on the CD

insert. Five of them positioned before a bleak landscape, their faces as impassive as the grey Nordic countryside.

'But Uncle Michael,' Emma said. 'They look so miserable . . .'

As Emma walked through Ballyfinn on the day of the concert, she could sense the anticipation on the street. It was as if everyone in town had suddenly turned into a jazz fan. The usual 'Hello' and 'How yaz doin'' was replaced by a new greeting: 'Are you going to the gig?' As she passed the shoe shop, she could hear Jason and one of his customers in animated conversation about the CD. Then she encountered a group of office girls standing before one of the posters, blocking the pavement, pointing at the saxophone, laughing in hysterical chorus.

Walking on, she saw Jenny Murphy ahead of her in her school uniform. Jim Conroy strode beside her in his black jacket and jeans. Emma watched them walk together, watched Jenny look up to him with her phoney smile, the smile she reserved only for boys. She watched Jim's thighs as he walked, muscular and slightly bow-legged. He worked the night shift in the factory during the week. He was a footballer, played in the matches at the weekend, had a reputation for his speed on the pitch. Jenny didn't make a secret of the details of their relationship. She smoked outside the school-yard and made not-so-subtle comments about her weekends and what they had got up to.

Emma didn't like Jenny. She didn't like her fake confidence, her smug, know-it-all attitude. But there they were, she sighed. Jenny and Jim. One of the town's darling couples. It was as if a sign had been embossed on their foreheads – 'Sold. Strictly hands off'.

She turned up the drive for her house. When she entered the kitchen she found a note on the table.

Hi, lovey

Hope you had a good day. I'm doing my bit at the hospital, will be home by 7. We'll have dins then.

Daddy says he's short of staff, he needs you to work tonight at the concert. It's in the big function room at 9. Hope this is okay. Your uniform is clean.

See you soon,
Mammy

Emma felt a sudden rush of energy come upon her. She hadn't expected to be going to the concert. The tickets were very dear and she was still too young to be served in the bar, especially with Daddy about. And so she was pleased to have an excuse to go to the big event.

It would almost be like playing with the big girls.

The Northern Hotel was transformed for the occasion. Theatrical red lights had been installed in the function room and black curtains covered the walls. A semi-circular platform had been set up at one end of the room with a Norwegian flag framed tautly behind the stage.

By the time Emma arrived, the atmosphere was already heavy with anticipation. Every male in town was there wearing dark glasses and black shirts. The girls were there, too, posing in leather trousers or short skirts, trying to look relaxed and sophisticated, positioning themselves to be seen.

Lorna caught Emma's eye when she entered the kitchen and waved her back towards the staff room.

'I've got some vodka,' she whispered.

'You haven't!'

'Sure we might as well enjoy ourselves. Everyone else will be having the time of their lives.'

They huddled together as Lorna poured vodka and Coke into plastic cups and downed her first drink.

'Ah, that's lovely,' Lorna said in a husky voice. 'You'll never believe who pinched me outside.'

'Who?'

'Bill Doherty.'

'The fella in the butcher's?'

'Aye. And I babysat his kids only last week.'

'Oh, God,' Emma said, swallowing. 'That's disgusting!'

'Aye! And the music hasn't even started!'

Emma and Lorna were busy taking orders when the players finally arrived on stage. As the lights went down and the saxophone tuned up, the audience began to applaud, but tentatively, as if unsure what would happen next. Someone in the crowd said something and nervous laughter filled the room.

But then they began to play. And from the first note the music rushed out like an attack, big and loud and fast, with a heavy primitive beat that filled the room with sound like a train racing from a tunnel.

Emma stopped to take in the spectacle: the band in their sombre clothes behind their blazing, brassy instruments, the lights glaring off them as they played. They made a powerful sound and yet they remained removed from it all, introverted and tuned into themselves alone, ignoring the room, the crowd, and even each other. The only contact between the players was the occasional nod of the head, each in their own world as the music blazed through the room.

Her eyes were drawn to the bass player. He was slender and very tall, and his large, full double bass shone with the richness of a red-brown chestnut. He had a tightly trimmed beard and long black hair drawn back into a ponytail, his black shirt open at the neck, and a silver earring glinted in the stage lights. He was the only one to display any pleasure in the music, the only one to smile. From the beginning Emma noticed his quiet smile, such a lovely, benign smile as he played and as he listened to the others play, as if he was happy with the sound, happy with the way he was playing. Happy just being there.

And all the while she watched his hands, his long fingers stroking the strings, up and down, so fast, so strong and so light, calling forth low sound from the instrument almost like an echo from deep within, making the rich wood moan in his hands.

Emma turned then to take in the audience. The men were transfixed, motionless and staring as if paralysed by the music, while the women swayed side to side with the beat. Emma saw Lorna threading her way through the room and bending to serve each table, her hips moving subtly in time with the pervasive, captivating mood of the music.

Two hours later it ended. The band disappeared from the stage, the applause, the whistles and hoots eventually died down, and the lights came up on an exhausted crowd.

She was disappointed that it was over. She had enjoyed the music and the atmosphere, enjoyed the banter with the customers. She and Lorna had been drinking steadily throughout the concert and she felt she had been part of something adult and animal and alive. She was still wide awake and she wished the night could continue. And so when Gerry at the bar asked her if she'd serve for another hour up in the residents' lounge, she didn't object at all.

The lounge was full when Emma entered, and she had to walk carefully between the crowded tables. On her way across the room, she passed Jacinta Quigley who worked at the bank. Jacinta sat beside the piano player, the buttons of her blouse open low and her hand brushing his knee whenever she gestured. And Emma saw other women there too, women Emma didn't know, probably from Letterkenny, drawn to the musicians, surrounding them, engulfed in the feeling that the music had set off, something deep and primal and urgent.

Emma saw the bass player standing with Dr Jackson. She approached and offered him a pint of stout, which he accepted with a curt nod.

'Ah, Emma,' Dr Jackson said. 'On duty tonight, are you?'

'Yes, Dr Jackson.'

'And did you enjoy the music?'

'I did surely,' she said. And then she looked up at the tall musician and said, 'Your music was really lovely.'

'Oh, thank you,' he smiled shyly. 'Do you like jazz music?'

But before Emma could answer, Dr Jackson cut in.

'We wouldn't get much jazz up here, Eric. I'm sure Emma has never heard anything quite like your music before tonight.'

'Ah, now,' Emma protested. 'We're not as bad as all that. I hear a bit of jazz now and again. My uncle Michael, now, he has a great collection of jazz CDs.'

'Oh, really?' Eric asked politely.

'Aye,' Emma said directly into his eyes. 'He was telling me once about a bass player. Scott something. He died in a car crash. He was very young, it was ages ago, like. Uncle Michael said he was a lovely player.'

Emma took a breath then and she watched as Eric's benign expression darkened, his fingers stroking his beard as if drawing the benign smile from his face.

'Ah, Scott Le Faro,' he said in a soft voice. 'You are so right. He was the most beautiful, sensitive musician ever to play the bass. And he died so young.'

'Yes,' Emma said. 'It was tragic, like. That's what Uncle Michael says anyway.'

'He has always been my inspiration,' Eric said with a sad smile.

Emma could feel the blood rush into her cheeks. She tightened her grip on the tray in her hands. And she looked at Eric again, studying that tender sadness in his face. Emma could sense Dr Jackson beside her as if he was trying to protect her from her own thoughts, but she kept looking at Eric, his lined face, his sad, clear eyes.

But then Emma heard her name being called. She looked over to see Jacinta Quigley signalling to her, shouting to come and take their order.

'You'll have to excuse me,' Emma said. 'I'm needed across the way. But I'll be over again shortly.'

'Take your time,' Eric smiled knowingly. 'We're in no hurry here.'

Emma was dizzy. Although she continued to function – she still took orders, filled her tray at the bar, returned to the room, served drinks, made change – for the next hour her brain, her body was pulsating. With those few quiet, sensitive words, she had been seduced. She had never experienced desire like that before. Her mind slipped into fantasy, she lost touch with her surroundings. She felt he knew everything, everything she wanted. She felt he was the one to take her across that line and become the woman she longed to become.

It all happened so quickly. By one o'clock the lounge was beginning to empty and Eric sat alone, surveying the scene, looking lonely, sitting forward as if he was about to leave. Emma walked to his table, then, and bent down to collect the glasses. She felt nervous and found it difficult to look at him.

'So,' he said, sitting forward in his low seat. 'You enjoyed the concert tonight?'

'Aye,' she said shyly.

'Maybe you would like to hear us play again?'

'Aye,' she repeated. 'That would be lovely.'

'But you hesitate,' he said. 'Perhaps it is difficult for some people to understand the language of jazz.'

She felt embarrassed then, as if her ignorance of his music had suddenly been exposed.

'I'm sure everyone can appreciate music,' she said petulantly, 'if it's good enough.'

'I'm sorry,' he smiled at her retort. 'Perhaps you think I am too elitist.'

'I'm sure I don't know anything about you.'

'I am easy to understand,' he said, sitting back. 'I just travel, and I play the bass. People seem to like it. But I don't know why. I don't know what it means to them.'

'Does it have to mean something?'

'I think everything has a meaning, Emma.'

'Even music? With no words?'

'Yes,' he said softly. 'I think the times without words can be the most meaningful times.'

She studied him again. She was fascinated by the way he spoke, his accent, the way he said her name. His eyes were narrowed in the low light, as if he was studying her reactions. She looked at his long body in his dark clothes, and she looked again at his face, so focused on her, as if she was all that existed for him in the room.

'It's very late,' she said. 'I should be finishing up.'

'And then what?'

'Then I should be going home.'

'Should?' he said softly. 'You keep saying should. But is that what you want to do?'

She inhaled then, and set the tray down on the table beside her, and straightened herself. She smoothed her skirt nervously with her hands. And then she looked at him directly. She tried to speak, tried to think of a smart reply to his invitation, but nothing came. Suddenly she didn't want to speak at all. She felt his eyes on her and suddenly her sensations became blurred and out of focus, as if she were existing out of time.

Then she caught herself. She looked cautiously around the room. People were talking in small groups, leaning forward over the low tables, their backs visible in the low light. She looked back at Eric but tried to avoid his eyes.

'I don't know,' she said. 'Maybe we might . . .'

'Yes,' he replied without changing his expression. 'I think maybe we should.'

She walked ahead of him and left the room. She heard him walking behind her as she walked down a deserted corridor and up a flight of stairs. She stopped to let him pass as they entered the corridor and he led the way towards his room. As she followed him, she could feel perspiration forming on her palms. They passed room 28 and she could hear Jacinta Quigley's voice from behind the door, and Emma knew Jacinta was inside with the piano player with whom she had sat all evening. She paused for a moment then, not to listen, but just to check herself, to take stock one final time.

Was this what she wanted? To go into a hotel room with a touring musician? Some man who travelled the world, who didn't care what happened to any of the women he seduced?

She looked at Eric ahead of her. She watched him reach into his pocket for his keys. She looked behind her for a moment, she thought about turning and walking away and saving herself from this lunacy.

But then she heard voices from inside that room, a woman's voice talking low and a man's deep voice crooning softly in response. She couldn't make out what they were saying, only the sound, the rise and fall. And then the blur came on her again, and she could hear an echo of the music in her mind, and she could see Eric now as if in a haze, standing in the corridor, pleading silently with his deep, clear, sad eyes.

And so she walked forward, she stopped thinking and walked forward with the blood rushing within her, urging her forward to him.

She knew those rooms so well. Since she was a girl she had helped dust those desks, Hoover those carpets, strip those sheets from the beds. But now that familiar place was blocked out, the space crowded out by the man before her, immediately but gently pressing her against the wall with his body as the door eased shut behind them. He bent his head and began kissing her, his large hands holding her face as he moved his body against her. For a moment her mind resisted and she stopped him, holding his arms, looking into his face, seeking an invitation in his sad, lonely eyes. Then she listened to his breathing and she felt his hands on her skin, and she let it become hazy and loose once again, and she pulled him towards her and they kissed, harder now, and he reached beneath her and lifted her, carrying her quietly to the bed like an instrument, a beautiful, delicate instrument.

The sun was risen by the time she returned home. It was a bright morning but it had been raining in the west and there was a rainbow against the black clouds rolling in. She crept in the back door, relieved that every hinge in the new house was well-oiled and silent, every step on the staircase secure and free from creaks.

Her parents were asleep.

She lay in bed then, so tired, recalling the feeling of his skin against her body. He had been good to her. And she had found it comforting, for a while, to lie with him, when it was over. He wanted to talk then, but then they really didn't have much to say. And so she tried to act like the women in the films, women who stood and began to dress, confidently, as if this sort of thing happened to them every day. And then she forced a smile and said goodbye, trying to get her voice just right. And then she left the room and, like the music, it was all over.

*

Now, six weeks later, Emma lay in her bed on a hot June afternoon. Her thoughts went down into her body, trying to feel something different, trying to understand what was happening to her. She didn't know how she could be pregnant. She had been safe, the timing was perfect, she should have been in the clear. And yet she was late. And she felt exhausted all the time. Such dire, rotten bad luck.

She thought about Barry again. She thought about how she would see him on Saturday night and how distant they would have to be, because there was nothing for them to say now. She had waited to see him for such a long time, and now that it would finally happen, there was nothing more that she could say to him.

She felt angry, then, so angry with herself. For giving in to the pressure of Jenny Murphy and those stupid girls in town. For letting that man be with her, and take advantage of her feelings. For giving in to the pressures outside herself, and the pressures inside too. All too much pressure.

She became afraid, then, feeling so tired but so afraid of herself and what had become of her body. As she lay there on her back the tears began to run down her cheeks and down her neck and into her pillow. She could feel them there, cold, drying against her skin.

And she was afraid to wipe them away, afraid even to move.

'Oh Barry,' she sobbed softly. 'What in the name of God have I done?'

CHAPTER 11

Jimmy O'Donnell sat at the kitchen table wearing a blue baseball cap and a Den TV T-shirt. A deck of playing cards was spread out before him. He was leaning two cards against one another, trying to stand them up into a house. Denis came into the kitchen in his dressing gown.

'Hi, Jimmy,' he said. 'Are you ready to go?'

'No. Mom's still in town.'

'I know, but she'll be back soon. We'll head off then.'

'Dad, will you play cards with me?'

'Not now. I have to finish packing. What are you building?'

'I'm trying to make a house,' Jimmy said. 'But it keeps falling down.'

'Why don't you have yourself a game of patience?' Denis asked.

'I don't know how.'

'Don't you?'

'No. Besides, I don't see the point.'

'Of what?' Denis asked.

'Playing cards. With yourself.'

Denis carried a mug of coffee to the table. 'Sometimes you're on your own,' he said. 'Or you're cheesed off with your friends. So you play patience.'

Denis sat down beside Jimmy and gathered the cards into a tidy pile.

'You watch how I set these out,' he said.

He placed the cards in a row across the table.

'Dad?'

'Yes?'

'What happens if parents get cheesed off?' Jimmy asked. 'With each other, like.'

'Nothing. It happens all the time. Why?'

'But what about if they get *really* cheesed off?'

'I suppose they have a row. Then they sort it out.'

'But what happened to Sally and Declan?' Jimmy asked.

'That was a bit different. Declan, well . . . Declan decided he wasn't attracted to Sally any more.'

'So they got a divorce, right?'

'No. They're just separated. Now look what happens here . . .'

Denis put a red card on top of a black one.

'So how does it happen?' Jimmy persisted. 'How do you go from being cheesed off to being, like, separated?'

'Oh, I think that takes a while.'

'How long?'

'At least twenty minutes.'

'No, seriously.'

'Seriously, it probably takes a while,' Denis said. 'A few years maybe. Now, why are you asking all these questions?'

'No reason. It's just that . . .'

'Yes?'

'Well, you and Mom. You seem a bit cheesed off yourselves.'

'She's just a bit preoccupied,' Denis said, returning to the cards. 'She just needs a bit of a rest. She'll be grand.'

'I hope so.'

'Don't worry,' Denis said, setting another card on the table. 'We can't get separated.'

'Why not?'

'Because,' he explained, turning towards Jimmy, 'we've only got one deck of cards.'

Julia walked through the door to the kitchen. She was burdened with two bags from a boutique in town and two more bags filled with groceries.

'Hi,' she called without enthusiasm.

'Hi, Mom,' Jimmy said from the table.

'Where's Daddy?'

'I think he's in the shower.'

'And what about Barry? Is he up?'

'I don't think so.'

She set the bags on the floor and surveyed the kitchen. 'And what about all these dishes?'

'I dunno.'

'Have you finished packing?'

'I couldn't find my swimming togs,' Jimmy replied.

'What do you need swimming togs for? We're only going for two days.'

'Daddy said we might go swimming.'

'Okay,' Julia said. 'So. Did you pack everything else?'

'Yes. Well, no. Not really . . .'

'Look, honey,' Julia said with frustration in her voice, 'I can't do everything around here.'

She walked out of the room and up the stairs. Jimmy could hear her shouting into the bathroom, something about getting the boys ready. He couldn't hear his father's muffled reply. A few minutes later Julia returned to the kitchen.

'Now, I want you to put those cards away and go up to your room and finish packing. I've laid everything out on your bed. All you have to do is put the stuff into your case. And then pack any books that you want to bring.'

'Okay,' Jimmy said, pushing the cards to the side. 'Oh, Mom?'

'Yes, Jimmy.'

'Did you get your hair cut?'

'Yes, I did.'

'It looks lovely.'

'Thank you. Now, up you go.'

Jimmy left the room as Julia began removing groceries from her shopping bags and packing the food into a large plastic cooler. Denis came into the kitchen. He was still wearing his dressing gown and he was rubbing a towel across his hair.

'Hiya,' he said. 'What's all this?'

'It's what we're bringing to your relatives.'

'Surely we don't need all these things.'

'Yes we do.'

'What? Shampoo?' he said, lifting the bottle from the table. 'They'll have shampoo.'

'We shouldn't use theirs,' Julia replied. 'There are four of us and only two of them.'

'And what's all this? Apples? Eggs? Bread? Danish pastries?'

'We're not going to go up there and eat them out of house and home. They don't have much money. You know that.'

'They're grand,' Denis protested. 'Michael got the house, didn't he? He's never had to pay for a roof over his head.'

'Yes, that's correct, as you've said many times. But he's not making any money now and you can't eat a house.'

'Righty-o,' Denis retreated. 'I'll get dressed, so.'

A moment later when the food was all packed into the cooler, Julia lifted the other bags onto the table. She reached into the largest bag and pulled out a cocktail dress. Sleeveless, black satin. She held it up against her body. It reached just above her knee. She glanced at the price tag hanging off the shoulder. Then she folded the dress and replaced it gently into the bag.

'Don't know why I bothered,' she sighed. 'He didn't even notice my hair.'

Jimmy was sitting in front of the television. It felt strange to be home on a school day. Everyone was rushing around and everyone was in bad form. They were supposed to have left for Donegal hours ago and now it was almost time for lunch.

His mom and dad were running up and down the stairs carrying cases and bags and shoes. Barry was in the kitchen doing the washing-up from breakfast, Mom's orders. Jimmy heard Barry drop a glass and he jumped as the shatter rang through the house. A moment later it happened again, this time with a plate. It was even louder than the first crash. His mom started shouting.

'*Barry!*'

'Sorry.'

'What are you *doing* in there?'

'It just slipped.'

'Well, *please* be more careful.'

'Okay, I will.'

Jimmy flicked through the channels. Australians on the beach. A show about buffalo that he had already seen. People sitting on a sofa talking. Jimmy was about to switch off when a man appeared who had the same accent as Daddy.

He was a movie star. He was being interviewed by a woman with long hair who kept leaning forward and laughing. The man was talking about growing up in Donegal, about the craic they used to have, the music in the pubs, the laughs. He looked so perfect, he had such a perfect smile and a lovely deep voice. Then they showed bits of some of his movies, action movies, and Jimmy recognised them, he had seen the videos. First he was chasing the guys in Africa who shot the rhinos. And then the one where he had to rescue the nuns from the avalanche.

He looked so cool in them, Jimmy thought, with his shirt ripped and the blood on his shoulder. Then they were back in the studio and he looked cool there, too, tough and tanned and handsome.

Then the ads came on and Jimmy switched the telly off. He could hear his parents outside packing the car. They said his name, something about whether he needed to bring something. Jimmy got up and went out to them.

The boot was open and it looked almost full but there were still cases and bags sitting on the ground. His mother was rubbing her forehead, his dad was trying to shove something else in.

'Jimmy,' Julia said. 'Do you need to bring this adventure set? The box is awfully big and we're running out of room.'

'Well, I just thought . . .'

'What?'

'Well, I just thought outside, in the garden. At the house. I could set it up there.'

'But, Jimmy,' Denis said, pulling his head from the boot. 'We can't take every bloody thing you own.'

'It's all right,' Julia said. 'It'll fit on the back seat. Put it between the boys. It will keep them from fighting.'

She looked down at her watch. 'It's nearly time for lunch,' she said. 'Should we eat before we go?'

'We can stop on the way,' Denis said. 'We'd better get on the road if we intend getting there before . . .'

Just then Denis's mobile phone began to chirp.

'Oh hello, John. No, I'm not in the office today. We're heading up to . . . Yes, okay. I'll have Fiona send that over to you . . . Right, I'll have her send it straightaway. Righty-o. Look, I'll be away from my desk but I'll keep the mobile switched on . . . Okay, good luck . . .'

Denis rang off and began dialling another number.

'Can't someone in the office take your calls today?' Julia asked.

'Sorry? No, not today.'

'But you won't be able to relax on the drive if you're trying to organise things at the office.'

'I can't drop everything just because of this party. I'll only be a sec.'

Jimmy and Julia looked down at the pavement while Denis spoke on the phone.

'Mom,' Jimmy whispered.

'Yes, honey.'

'Are you okay?'

'I'm fine. I just wish we could . . .'

'What?' Jimmy asked.

'Nothing. Could you go see if Barry is finished with the dishes? Tell him to hurry, we'll be leaving soon.'

'But the car's not even packed and Dad's still on the phone.'

'I know that, honey, but could you please tell Barry to hurry?'

Jimmy walked back into the house. He pushed the door so it nearly closed behind him. Suddenly the house seemed very empty. He thought for a moment that he was in a new place, somewhere he had never been before. He felt like he was in a film. He pretended he had to get through to the kitchen, to rescue the man, the man chained to the wall, just like the actor on the telly. He pretended to hold a gun out before him in both hands. He dashed through the hall, paused, burst into the sitting room swinging his gun before him, then pivoted around to face the kitchen. Then he got down, shimmied across the floor and got up slowly and gazed through the glass in the doors. And then he saw Barry. He was leaning forward and staring out the back window, absolutely motionless. His hands were still in the dishwater as he stared blankly into the empty back garden.

CHAPTER 12

Anne sat in her car before the Northern Hotel, drumming on the steering wheel with her fingers. School had finished early. The sun continued to blaze, the heat strong and unnatural for so early in the summer. She rolled down the window, wishing there was a breeze.

A few minutes later, Michael emerged from the hotel. He looked especially well, she thought, in his cream-coloured shirt, open at the neck. Summer suited Michael.

'Hi,' he said as he sat into the passenger seat.

'Hiya,' she responded, leaning over to kiss his cheek. 'Did you enjoy your swim?'

'Yes. It was lovely.'

'Good. Have you eaten? Do you want to get something?'

'No. I'm not hungry.'

'Right,' Anne said. 'Well, off we go then.'

They crawled through the busy town, stuck in the lunchtime queue of traffic.

'It's so close,' Anne said. 'I almost passed out in the classroom.'

'Yes. Dreadful.'

A tall man was walking on the footpath ahead of the car.

'Michael!' Anne called out.

'Yes?'

'That's him. There, in front of the Chinese.'

'Who?'

'Stephen. Stephen Deane.'

'Oh, yes,' Michael said. 'Gosh. I haven't seen him since college.'

'Except in the films,' Anne said.

'I've never seen his films.'

'You haven't? My God. You must be the only one in the Western world.'

'They didn't look like my kind of thing.'

'No, they aren't your kind of thing. But are you not curious?'

'Not really,' Michael said. 'I lived with him for three years. Saw plenty of him back then.'

'You're a gas man,' she sighed.

They parked in front of the SuperValu. A moment later they were pushing a shopping trolley through the aisles of groceries.

'So,' Anne said. 'Where do we start? We'd better prepare for the boys.'

'We don't know what they like.'

'Then we'll have to make an educated guess,' she said. 'They're Americans. They probably eat rubbish. Here. American-style crisps. American-style peanut butter. Toaster Tarts. God, look at the price of these things . . .'

'Yes.'

'And sure they're only sugar-coated rubbish.'

Michael picked up a box of cereal. 'What about these?' he asked.

'Honey Pops?'

'Yes,' Michael replied. 'They're lovely.'

'They're not for you, they're for the wonder boys. Now, I think we've got enough here to keep them happy for a couple days.'

'I'm sure we have.'

'But what about the Queen of Sheba?' Anne said.

'What *are* you on about?'

'Julia. I'd say she takes quail eggs for her breakfast. And she prefers asses' milk for her bath.'

Michael walked on, shaking his head.

'Look,' she laughed as she followed behind. 'We're having the perfect family to stay. You can't expect them to lower their standards.'

'You're not approaching this in the right frame of mind,' he said.

'You're probably right,' she sighed. 'We'd better stock up on drink, though. You remember the last time Denis was up. For the funeral. He was scuttered the whole time.'

'Yes, but that was different.'

'It wasn't. He's coming up here for a hoolie. He'll probably be worse than ever.'

She loaded three bottles of wine into the cart and reached up for a bottle of Irish whiskey.

'Anyway,' she continued. 'That gang of yours. They might end up back at our house.'

'They won't. The party is at the hotel.'

'But what about the wee hours of the morning?'

'You're taking this far too seriously.'

'I am not. I want to make a good impression.'

'They're just ordinary people.'

'Ordinary people? I don't think so, my love. There's your high-flying brother and his mail-order wife, straight from the US of A. There's Stephen Deane, the Hollywood legend. Then there's Catherine what's-her-name – apparently she's made a fortune in London.'

'Catherine?' Michael stopped. 'How do you know about her?'

'Ah, now, I have my sources.'

'Who?'

'At school. All the teachers know about this party and this notorious gang of yours. And I'm glad, too, because you haven't told me a thing.'

'What did you hear about Catherine?'

'Oh, nothing,' Anne said nonchalantly. 'Just that she was part of your crowd, that she made her fortune in London, and that she is, well, rather well endowed.'

'Hmm. I suppose that's Catherine, all right.'

'Can't wait to meet her,' she said.

'You know, by the way, that she and Denis were . . .'

'Oh, really?'

'Yes. For quite a while, actually.'

'Interesting,' Anne said. 'I wonder does the Queen of Sheba know?'

'I doubt it. I don't think Denis would tell her. It was a fiery sort of relationship.'

'Gosh,' she said. 'This party gets more interesting by the minute.'

As Michael and Anne wheeled their heavy trolley through the car park they were hailed by a silver-haired man walking towards them with a healthy stride.

'Hello, Dr Jackson,' Anne said. 'That's another lovely day.'

'It is indeed,' he replied, stopping to mop his forehead with a handkerchief.

'I don't ever remember such heat in June,' Anne said.

'Unusual weather altogether,' Dr Jackson said. 'Bad days for our fair-skinned race. I'd say you're quite sensitive to the sun, are you, Michael?'

'Yes, a bit,' Michael replied.

'I was thinking about you the other day,' Dr Jackson said. 'It's been some time since you've called in to see me.'

'Yes,' Michael said.

'I wish you would, you know,' Dr Jackson said. 'I think it's time for us to have a wee chat.'

'Right, I will. I'll call in soon.'

The doctor studied Michael. 'You're still on the Chlorpromazine then?' he asked.

'Yes. Every month.'

'And how has he been?' Dr Jackson said, turning to Anne.

'Oh, right as rain,' she replied.

'A bit tired, perhaps?'

'Yes, well,' Anne smiled tightly. 'He does need his sleep.'

'Because you know my views on these medications.'

'Yes, Dr Jackson,' Anne said.

'I don't like to see people subjected to unnecessary, long-term treatments.'

'No,' Anne said. 'No, not at all.'

Dr Jackson gave them both a final, admonishing look.

'You will come in now, won't you? If you don't want to queue in the clinic, call round to the house. Any time. Now that my wife is no longer with us, I don't mind visitors.'

'Yes, okay.'

'Well,' he said, smiling. 'Nice to see you both looking so well.'

'Thank you, doctor,' Michael said. 'All the best now.'

And then Dr Jackson gave a little wave and walked off towards his office.

'Gosh,' Anne said as she began loading the groceries into the car. 'He's very concerned about you.'

'I know. He's always been that way.'

'But is he right?'

'About what?'

'About your treatment. Those drugs. Should you still be taking them?'

'They say they've got the dose as low as it can be,' he said. 'No point in messing about with things.'

Anne looked at Michael for a moment. Then she smiled a brave smile, gave his arm an affectionate rub, and returned to the groceries.

Michael sat behind the house in a wooden garden chair. The ground was still damp from a shower during the night but now strong, oppressive heat burned through the hazy sunshine. A stillness covered the garden. It was like a burden, stifling the afternoon: a weight of hot, sodden air. It felt almost tropical, Michael thought, with the grass steaming around him and no wind, no hint of a breeze in the trees, their fresh, early-summer leaves drooping like wet hair. So unusual, he thought. So unreal.

A perfect start to the weekend. All of us, all of this. Draped in a haze. Like a memory.

He folded his newspaper loosely in his lap, closed his eyes, let the warmth soak into his face. Dr Jackson, now, he wouldn't like this at all. Chlorpromazine and sunshine don't mix, he'd say. Heightened chance of melanoma. Skin cancer. Bad medicine, Chlorpromazine. Should really do something about it.

Strange that we saw him today, of all days, he thought. Like Hamlet's father bursting on stage and stirring everything up. Sure it's bad enough already, with the weekend bringing it all back again. Bringing *them* all back again. The people who were there, when it all happened, when it all started.

This strange life of mine, he thought.

Michael had read all the books when he was younger. Even when it was difficult to concentrate he had forced himself to gather information, a few pages at a time. Schizophrenia. The symptoms, the causes and, of course, the various chemical treatments.

In the early days he had sought out someone or something to blame, but there was nothing there. No single event, no person, no combination or pattern that he could identify as the cause of his problem, the thing in his head. His muddle.

Of course there were incidents, unhappy memories. His father had been a brute. A tough businessman turned politician. But nothing unusual in that. And his mother was, he thought now, a bit absent. Not cold, exactly. But removed. An inspiration rather than a support.

He still recalled them, those terrible meetings, twice a year, when school reports were issued, and every other child was

rushing home with a sense of freedom. He recalled the shouts
around him as he walked towards the car where his mother would
be waiting for them. Denis, with his tie askew and his trousers
dirty from some friendly scuffle, laughing, shouting back to the
lads that he'd see them soon; and Michael, the perfect one, his hair
tidy, his clothes in order, his books neatly arranged in his school
bag, with no one to shout to as he pulled the car door closed
behind him.

Mam would greet them, offer them her cheek, give them a
formal welcome to their holidays. Then they would drive, as they
always did, to Letterkenny. It was meant to be a treat: lunch, then
the cinema. A little end-of-term celebration. But what Michael
remembered most about those days was the first stop at Daddy's
office. The constituency headquarters. They would park outside
and climb the narrow stairs to the small reception room and see
Biddy with her blue hair piled up high on her head.

'There they are,' Biddy would say in her heavy Donegal accent.
'Two fine boys. Two fine big boys!'

Then she would usher them into the office where they would
stand before Daddy's dark, mahogany desk – Mammy behind
them, primly gripping her handbag, and the two boys in front
clasping their school reports.

'Now, Denis, give us a look,' he would say from behind the
desk, using his office voice and looking not at all like their father
but rather like someone on the news. As he did twice every year,
he would reach across the desk to accept Denis's report, position
his glasses on his nose, and then hum tunelessly as he scanned the
results.

'A fine effort, my good fellow. A very acceptable effort indeed.

Might put a bit more work into the handwriting, I see. Very important, you know. Especially if you're the man in charge. You want to make sure they can read your instructions.'

'Yes, Daddy,' Denis would reply as if reading from a script.

'And what's this? A note from Mr O'Grady. Who's he? Oh, yes, the games teacher. Very complimentary. Very good indeed!'

Then he would hand the report back with the usual surprise tucked inside: a five-pound note. The boys never saw it in his hand even though they looked every time. They watched closely but never saw it being slipped into their reports.

'Now, Michael,' he would say. 'How did the young lad fare this term?'

The reach. The tuneless hum. This time the ritual was a bit cursory, sounding a bit bored.

'Yes, very well. Up to your usual standard, I see.'

'Yes, Daddy.'

'A good report, as I would expect. No special comments, but a fine report all the same.'

He sighed from behind his desk and leaned back in his chair. 'You know, Michael,' he said. 'It's not all about books.'

'No, Daddy.'

'I didn't get to where I am by keeping my nose in a book.'

'No, Daddy.'

'It's about getting out there, mixing with the lads. The rough-and-tumble, Michael.'

'Yes, Daddy.'

'Do you not play sport at all in that school?'

'I do a bit, Daddy.'

'Well, good. That's a start. Next term then, Michael. I want

you to get out there on the pitch and give it your all. I tell you, I'd
be so proud. There's nothing like seeing a fellow out there on the
pitch with the other lads, giving it a good go.'

'Yes, Daddy.'

'Giving it your all.'

'Yes, Daddy.'

He would return the report with a sad smile on his face.
Michael remembered the bank note falling to the floor, and
bumping his head on the desk as he reached down to pick it up.
He remembered wincing, holding back the tears as Mam recited
her lines, the same ones every holiday:

'What do you say, now, boys?'

'*Go raibh maith agat*, Daddy!'

And again, that benign, slightly saddened smile from the
ageing man behind the desk as they retreated from the office, past
Biddy, and back down the stairs into the car.

Michael opened his eyes. The garden. The unusual heat. The
perspiration trickling down the side of his head.

He stretched, letting the newspaper slide to the ground.
Shouldn't really sleep, he thought. Denis is probably in the car
now, driving up to see us. So much still to do.

Wonder what it will be like, seeing him again. All so different
now.

He leaned back in the chair, stretched his legs, drifted off once
again into his school days. From an early age he did well in his
studies, well enough to be promoted into Denis's year.
Academically it was the right move but it meant he was a year
younger than his classmates, and he never really bridged the social

gap. At home his father spoke with him little, barked at him to stop messing on the piano, rarely noticed the artwork he displayed on the fridge. His mother was more appreciative of Michael's efforts but she too tended to favour Denis, responding to his easy confidence, his wit and gab. Michael remembered his mother fawning over the lads Denis brought home from school.

Denis was Michael's only companion during those awkward years as they approached their teens. He remembered rambling the hills with Denis, destroying the enemy with imaginary rifles or skipping stones across the smooth surface of the lake. They never spoke about deep subjects, just their favourite meals or who would get the roles in the school play. But Denis was a necessary comfort to Michael at that time, when they were twelve or thirteen, a time when Michael lacked any real engagement with the world beyond home territory.

But then, as an adolescent, Michael's outlook improved. He grew taller. The lads in school started to turn to him for help with their studies. Suddenly there were girls about, and a group formed, a gang of them would meet in town on summer evenings. It was all innocence and good fun, and for the first time in his life Michael felt accepted, comfortable within himself, and with Denis, and with their circle of friends. A bit withdrawn, perhaps, at times. But generally comfortable.

He was painting now, in his room, in the evenings. First watercolours and then oils on canvas. His work was sharp and clear even though he set himself difficult tasks: writing in reverse script to represent the inside of a shop window; detailed anatomical drawings; fragments of ossature, fossil remains of creatures that never existed. He was hungry to learn more, to see more, to expand his range. His parents brought both boys to London for a weekend, and while Denis and his father went to the Tower, Michael scoured the galleries, revelled in the pre-Raphaelites and, most exciting of all, that first genuine Blake. He grew eager to get away from Ballyfinn and so he suffered none of the usual anxieties about leaving home. They joked as the day of departure approached: sure it wasn't like moving at all, what with half the town coming along!

At college, despite the large social circle that congregated in and around the house, Denis remained Michael's only real confidant. Sometimes it seemed so incongruous: Denis the budding executive, Michael the intense artist. People coming into the house would see the two of them together, chatting about a film or throwing something across the room, an orange or a ball of socks, catching it, tossing it back and forth. Messing. Relaxed.

Michael's art flourished. His instructors at the College of Art and Design spotted it straight off, his drive and his talent, his striving to balance opposing forces. He painted a series on 'The Marriage of Heaven and Hell': manic faces caught between joy and anguish. Heads leaning back, mouths open and distended, eyes squinted tightly shut, tears emerging from the cracked lines: happiness, or agony, or both at once?

His media soon evolved into three dimensions. He worked with furniture: chairs taken apart and re-fitted with perfect craftsmanship, but out of place, out of joint, with their arms bending inwards, legs missing, the fabric divided into crazy patterns. Beautifully finished and yet exuding discomfort, like instruments of torture.

A series of large mobiles followed, hung solemnly from the

ceiling in the college canteen, whirling like stately dirigibles above the dirty tables. The most unlikely objects offset against one another: leather-bound books hanging from one end of a steel rod, counterbalanced by a single sheet of poetry, the whole lot gently swaying back and forth. A dirty, rusted sledge hammer held aloft by a tiny antique bird, a blue tit, stuffed, caught in mid flight. His instructors commented that, while the symbolism was a bit heavy, the technique was sublime.

At times Michael became compulsive about his work. It was like a tension within him that could only be lifted and carried away by creative activity. When, after days of uninterrupted effort, he finally finished a painting or a sculpture, a feeling of peace would descend on him. He would return to the house then and drink tea, reconnect with Denis and Stephen and Mary, chat about nothing, feel normal again.

He sometimes sensed that his ideas were a bit out there, not quite in sync with those of the people around him. But it didn't seem to matter. All he needed at that time was to work without distraction, and to know that Denis was there to listen if he got stuck. Chat. Toss an orange around the room. Back and forth, back and forth.

Then, as First Year came to a close, Denis and Catherine became an item. Everyone said they were a natural couple: glib, good-looking and successful, with Denis heading up the Commerce Society and Catherine's legendary First Class Honours in English. Denis didn't talk about her with Michael and Michael sensed the relationship was primarily sexual. At the parties it sometimes appeared as if she and Denis weren't together at all, looking almost like enemies, controlling their patches from opposite ends of the room. And this arrangement suited Michael, because she never really took Denis away from him. Michael needed to know that Denis was there and that, no matter how mad the house got, or how deep into his work Michael went, Denis was still available to him.

But Catherine remained on the scene, hovering like a dark figure in the background, waiting for the party to end and the crowds to disperse. Then Michael would catch them kissing downstairs or hear the not-so-muffled moans from Denis's room. She would be there again in the mornings, showering next door to Michael's bedroom. She would appear downstairs wearing one of Denis's shirts at the breakfast table, her hair wild around her unpainted face, the steam rising from her coffee mug. But then she would leave and the house would settle back into its comfortable pattern once again: Denis cleaning up, getting the place tidy, making sure there was food in the fridge. Stephen Deane trying to memorise his lines, his face tightened in concentration. Mary Moran curled up on the sofa, eating biscuits, sniping at the order of the world.

It was comfortable, and interesting, and engaging, and Michael was content.

College years drew towards a close and final-year exams loomed. The dynamic changed, the routines became unsettled. The gang displayed a new edginess. Denis disappeared into the library for days at a time and Michael often found himself alone. And with Denis preoccupied with his studies, Catherine had to readjust. She didn't want to face up to the changes that were inevitable after college. She appeared self-assured but she hungered for approval, and Denis had up to now always been there to feed her appetite. Without Denis she became like a person with a piece missing, a gap where her nametag should have been. And to fill this gap, to stop the quivering uncertainty, she needed someone there, someone to look at her, to listen to her, to reflect her image back to herself.

Michael became more aware of Catherine as spring approached. He became increasingly uncomfortable when she was around. Her presence in a room, even if she were simply reading a newspaper, spread a sense of unease.

One night she arrived at the house, late. She told Michael that Denis had agreed to meet her but Denis hadn't returned home from the library. Michael made her a cup of tea. They sat together, not speaking much. And then Michael said he was tired and retreated to his room because he sensed that Catherine was embarrassed at being stood up. But then, a few minutes later, he heard her outside his door.

'Mick?'

'Yes?'

'Can I come in?'

'Sure.'

'Hiya,' she said, walking into the room.

'Hi.'

'I'm sorry to disturb you.'

'You're okay.'

'Look. I know this is a bit daft, but do you fancy a pint?'

'What?'

'Just a quick one. Just down to McSorley's.'

'But Catherine . . .'

'I know, look, I'm sorry, but I'm fed up. I'm going mad. Just a quick one.'

'Right,' he sighed. 'Okay.'

'I'll wait outside while you get dressed.'

In the pub her hair was tied back. She leaned towards him, cupping a brandy in her two hands. Her eyes were focused, wide and engaged.

'But what do you two talk about?' she asked.

'Denis and me?' he said. 'God, I don't know. Nothing, really.'

'Does he talk about me?'

'Sometimes.'

'What does he say?' she asked.

'Nothing specific. I can't remember.'

'But you must remember something,' she insisted. 'Anything. Sorry, another pint?'

'No thanks. I've a lot on tomorrow.'

'Oh, come on. Relax. Here, have a fag, for God's sake. You Donegal men never lighten up.'

He took the cigarette, leaned forward towards her lighter. Inhaled. Exhaled. Sipped his pint.

'So go on,' she urged. 'What does he say?'

'He says you're great,' Michael considered.

'Oh?'

'At your studies. He says you're first in your year.'

'Oh, come on. I don't need an academic assessment. What else does he say?'

'He says you're persistent.'

'And what's that supposed to mean?'

'He says you'll get what you want.'

'Sorry?' she asked.

'Out of life.'

'How *interesting*,' she said with sarcasm in her voice. 'I must say, Michael, I'm truly moved. Such intimate views, shared between brothers.'

'Sorry if I've disappointed you. Maybe you should ask Denis what he thinks.'

'I've asked him a thousand times.'

'And?'

'It's always the same.'

'Yes?'

'If I ask your brother what he thinks of me, he says, full of sincerity, "Catherine, you're a grand girl altogether."'

'Right,' he smiled. 'So there you are.'

'Yes, indeed,' she replied. 'There I am.'

The next morning Michael was tired. He wasn't used to drinking during the week. He overslept and was rushing to leave the house when he met Denis in the kitchen.

'Where were you last night?' Michael asked.

'I was at Peter's. We were revising finance.'

'Catherine was looking for you.'

'I told her I'd be out.'

'Right.'

'Why?'

'Oh, no reason. She was just looking for you.'

Two nights later Catherine appeared at the house again, and again Denis failed to show. Catherine cajoled Michael into going to the pub. They found a quiet corner and she leaned back into the curvature of the plush, soft seating. She rested her brandy on her stomach just over her silver belt buckle.

Michael was on his third pint. He was tired and he felt a bit dazed.

'Catherine, it's late. I'm in the middle of my project. I really need to get back.'

'Oh, come *on*. Just one more. Then I'll take you home to your beddy-bye.'

He glanced at her belt buckle. It reflected the light from somewhere in the room. He looked up to try to see where that bright light was coming from.

'You're like him, you know,' she said.

'So I'm told.'

'But you're the dark horse, really.'

'Am I?' he asked.

'Oh, yes, indeed. You give nothing away. You really are the mysterious man from Donegal.'

Michael finished his pint. 'I think we should head.'

'Okay, right you are,' she said, straightening up. 'Wouldn't want you turning into a pumpkin, now, would we?'

When they arrived back at the house, Denis was just inside the door hanging up his coat.

'Cup of tea, anyone?' Catherine sang out.

'Yes, please,' Denis said.

'None for me, thanks,' Michael said. 'I think I'll head up.'

'Right,' Denis said. 'See you in the morning.'

Michael climbed the stairs to his room. He felt drunk, he stumbled as he took off his trousers. He could hear them chatting below, the murmur of voices and the clink of mugs on the table. He climbed into his cold bed and reached for a book, but he could not read. He heard Denis and Catherine coming softly up the stairs, heard the bedroom door close behind them.

Michael remembered the shape of her there in the pub, leaning back in her black jumper. The copper-coloured brandy, that silver belt buckle.

Shit, he mumbled as the heat of his body infused the cold bed. This can't really be happening.

As the exams approached, Denis withdrew into his studies and became increasingly remote. Catherine began to visit Michael regularly.

He didn't especially like her personality. He found her overbearing and insecure and her conversation centred almost exclusively on herself. And yet Michael was attracted. He could feel it when they were together, when he'd had that third pint and she was there with that black hair of hers, sometimes tied back, sometimes free and wild around her face, that hair that he wanted to feel against his skin. And her body, such a fascination of curves, now seeming so firm, now so pliable as she moved, leaning towards him with her cleavage within view and staring into his eyes, as if urging him forward to kiss her, right there, in McSorley's, in plain view of the world, like a challenge.

Michael had kissed very few girls. Since coming to Dublin there had been a few innocent snogs, usually as a party was ending, begun in an affectionate mood but leading to nothing. There was an encounter towards the end of Second Year. He had been in the UCD bar talking to a girl wearing a loose, Indian-cotton dress. Closing time came and they walked out together. She was questioning him about his art as if it were an interrogation, hardly allowing him to pause between questions. She led him to the steps

by the lake and then began kissing him, slowly at first, but then
eagerly and passionately, backing him against the perimeter wall.
Michael could still remember the sweet smell of wine on her
breath as their hands travelled furtively across one another's
bodies. It was brief and exciting as far as it went, but then a
security guard happened along and they stopped, confused and
sobered. They walked to the bus stop together holding hands. He
saw her again a few days later but, strangely, both were trapped by
nerves, and neither could recreate the attraction that had seemed
so real on that first night.

And so, at twenty, and with his college years drawing to a close,
Michael remained a virgin. And Catherine was there, every night,
like a temptation in the desert. He felt guilty and confused. He
wanted Denis to come back into the picture to set things right. He
woke in the middle of the night and lay awake for hours. Then he
would fall asleep heavily as the birds sang outside and the sunshine
streamed through the window. The alarm would go off and he
would sit up, his head heavy and his muscles sore.

He was supposed to be preparing his final exhibition but he
couldn't concentrate at college. He had two works to complete
and he had to submit his layout for the final display, but his
creativity dried up. He spent two days drawing, filling page after
page, trying to design a plan for the room to show his material, but
his designs were bad, there was no spark, he was afraid to show
them to his instructors.

He started taking long walks in the evenings, circling the
playing fields in Belfield. He became obsessed with something he
had read by a Russian art critic about opposing voices.
Unconsciously, he began to apply the theory to the words people

spoke to him, hearing contradictory messages in even the simplest exchange.

'Hiya, Michael.'

'Yeah. Hiya.'

'Enjoy your walk?'

'I will.'

'No, weren't you out? Just now?'

'Oh, yes. I was. Out.'

'And how was it?'

'It? Ah. It was grand.'

'Lovely evening.'

'Ah, yes. Lovely.'

'Are you sure you're okay?'

'Yes, I am sure. I'm okay.'

He took to listening to a Prokofiev piano concerto on the stereo, repeatedly, over and over and over. He began to hear in the music a battle between the piano and the orchestra, between the melody and the harmonies, the rising and falling of the lines. He tried to explain the tensions in the music to Mary Moran, and she nodded and said she heard it too, but he knew she didn't hear it, not the way he did.

He found himself sitting in coffee shops in the afternoon or on the sofa at dawn, wide awake, unable to remember how he had got there, with arguments raging through his brain about antinomies and dialogic and the hidden order of art. He thought that if he just stuck with it and worked it through, then all would be well, and he would finally have the answer.

In the middle of all this there was a row at the house and Stephen Deane walked out, slamming the door behind him.

Michael still remembered Mary Moran's rage as she screamed at Denis and then stomped up to her room, and then the empty, deadly silence.

Then came the last Friday night, the last party of the year. The exams were nearly finished. It would all end the following week, people would leave for home or fly off to their jobs in the States or England or Europe. This was the final hoorah, the last time they would all be together. The house was wild, there was drink everywhere. The Police were blaring on the stereo, people were jumping up and down on the furniture. Clothes were being removed, two guys from Wicklow were in their Y-fronts and one of the girls was bouncing around in a lavender bra.

Michael began talking to a new girl. She said her name was Una but he didn't know who she was or where she had come from. She was blonde and very thin and had a dazed look on her face. Michael tried to explain what his work was about and she appeared very interested. She smelled faintly of hashish and she said very little but her big round eyes seemed to Michael at the time to express a depth of understanding. But then Denis began to shout something at Michael. He said something about letting the bird go and changing the fucking music. Michael didn't understand the problem. He wanted Denis to explain but Denis just walked away. Someone put on some different music and Michael felt confused, he couldn't grasp the problem.

Then Una left the room and Catherine suddenly appeared beside him. She pulled him up off the sofa and urged him to dance with her. She looked into his eyes and held him as they danced, sliding her thumbs down the waist of his trousers so she could feel his skin. Then the music slowed and they were dancing together in the darkened kitchen and Michael didn't know what was happening to him, feeling her breasts against his chest. He had to push her away as she pulled his head down to kiss her. He said no, his head pounding with confusion as he pushed her away, knocking a glass onto the floor.

He walked out of the kitchen and back into the sitting room. Una was there alone, sunk into a comfy chair in the corner. He slid in beside her, knowing that Catherine was behind him standing in the kitchen doorway. He put his arms around Una's tiny waist and held her as the music died down and someone opened a can of beer beside them. He pulled Una towards his face and then the voices became quiet, the voices in his head became calm as he kissed her and felt her tiny body with his shaking hands.

Michael remembered little about the events of the days that followed. He heard parts of the story from Denis and Stephen – later, when he was in the hospital, heavily sedated and fuzzy. They told him that his conversation had gone strange. They said he had latched onto Una as if she were the Madonna and that she never really knew what hit her. They told him something about the portico at Trinity College but he didn't know the entire story.

He remembered the gardaí, though. Big men with country accents who talked amongst themselves as they brought him, handcuffed, into the hospital. He remembered an admissions process, a perfunctory series of questions delivered across a table in a monotone by a young female clinician with an ironic expression on her face. She asked him his name and where he lived and whether he had been in hospital before, and she transcribed the information onto a form as if she didn't believe a word he uttered.

They had to hold him down for the first injection, delivered while he was face down on a table, his trousers forcibly lowered. After that first one, he had no fight left.

The next day his parents' faces were pale. Grey scum formed across their mugs of tea as they sat in the white-walled canteen area, surrounded by dazed patients, smoking, staring. Michael didn't know what to say to them. He felt they wanted him to apologise. He wasn't sure what he had done wrong. He wanted them to take him home.

He had few visitors. Denis came every few days, smoking and drumming his fingers on the table. He said something about himself and Catherine splitting up and that he would soon be off for the States.

'Which states?' Michael asked.

'Don't be daft,' Denis replied, stubbing out his cigarette.

Those early days stretched into weeks. His face broke out in a rash. A staff nurse gave him some ointment. He asked her if Una was all right, but the nurse only said she was sure Una would be grand and that Michael needn't worry himself about her. His stomach was sore and he wasn't sleeping at night but he hadn't the energy to complain. A tall Englishman called on him and said some reassuring words, but then, after a ten-minute interview, he disappeared. Michael didn't see him again for a month.

Michael finally returned to his parents' home in August, long after Denis had left for America. Michael had nothing to do with his time. He tried to redecorate his room. He moved his bed to the other wall, took down the shelves, patched the plaster on the walls, painted everything. His energy was so low that it took two weeks. His father came to see him in his room at the end of each day. He urged Michael to quit smoking and consider his future. It seemed to be good advice but Michael's motivation was gone, he could not think straight, he couldn't begin to formulate a plan.

His father died, then, in November, of a long-overdue heart attack. They could not locate Denis. He had travelled somewhere for the Thanksgiving holiday and they only found him two days after the funeral. He didn't bother to come home. For six months Michael lived in the house with his grieving mother. They read Denis's letters with wonderment. He was, it appeared, doing very well. He wrote home about securing a large contract with an IT company (whatever that meant) and working on a nationwide media campaign (which sounded very important) and getting a major promotion (again, not quite sure what this meant, but it sounded very promising indeed). And all the while Michael and his mother sat in the house, listening to the sound of the wind howling through the trees, as winter slid damp and dark towards spring.

That was twenty years ago, Michael thought.

He sat up and stretched, trying to shake off the lethargy brought on by the afternoon heat. It saddened him to remember those days when everything had started, or rather, when everything had ended. Those final days when he first experienced the confusion that had dogged him ever since. Since that time he had never been free of the doctors, and the injections, and the drug-induced calm that cast a haze over his mental activity. He had lost Denis then. Michael did not begrudge Denis his success. Rather, he simply missed him, as a brother. The companionship. The shared set of memories. The simple enjoyment of each other's company.

He never told Denis what had happened with Catherine. Even though Catherine no longer figured in either of their lives, and even though the two brothers were no longer together, Michael could not yet face the spectre of angering Denis or losing his trust.

Michael looked at his watch. Half three. They would be here in a few hours. The party was tomorrow night, with Stephen Deane. And Mary Moran. And Catherine. And the others. Their memories weighing down upon him like the relentless summer heat.

He looked up into the trees, the sunshine reflecting off the leaves bringing tears into his eyes. Then he stood, and inhaled deeply, and walked towards the house.

PART II:

THE WEEKEND

CHAPTER 13

The sun shone, the countryside was green and alive, the sheep and cattle clean and picture-perfect as the O'Donnells drove north towards Donegal, between the hedgerows, past the irregular fields and through a series of busy villages: Collon, Clontibret, Ardee.

But the mood in the car was sour. Men, Julia thought as they sped through the hilly countryside. So moody. With women you can say something, but not with men. You can't shift them when they get like this. They shut you out completely.

We used to have such fun in the car, she thought. Singing, making up verses. Denis used to come up with the best rhymes, double entendres that the boys didn't really understand. Hilarious. Got the boys laughing, got all of us laughing so hard.

But this is like a funeral procession, she thought. Denis isn't with us at all. I wish he could relax. I wish he would just *say* something. And then Barry doing his morose adolescent thing. He should be happy, glad to be finished with school. There's been no time to talk to him, find out what's wrong.

The border post at Aughnacloy had been torn down and now fresh grass grew along the clean verge. Julia turned towards the back of the car and forced a smile at Jimmy in his baseball cap.

'Hi, there,' she said.

'Hi.'

'How are you?'

'Grand. Mom?'

'Yes?'

'Guess how many sheep I've seen so far?'

'Ah, I don't know. Sixty.'

'Two hundred and eighteen.'

'Really?'

'Yeah. I'm counting them. I'm going to try to see a thousand.'

'Wow. That's pretty good.'

She smiled, turned to the front again.

Well, she thought. At least one of us is happy.

At about half-past seven, the burgundy Mercedes finally crawled up the gravel drive to Michael and Anne's house.

Barry felt as if he were travelling in a dream. He'd spent the past week trying to resurrect Donegal in his mind. Now he rolled down the window and his memories rushed upon him. The sheltered drive. The tall pines and beeches. The fresh-smelling air. The old stone house: the grey porch with the blue front door, the bay window, the bedroom windows upstairs, the steep roof reaching up through the overhanging trees. Everything as he had remembered and yet somehow so different now, in real life.

'Here we are, boys!' Julia chirped as the engine powered off.

The car was suddenly silent. No one moved. Barry watched as his parents turned to one another.

'How are you doing?' Julia asked softly.

'I'm okay,' Denis said as he removed his seatbelt.

'Are you ready for this?'

He looked over at her as if seeing her for the first time that day. 'Yes,' he smiled sadly. 'I think so.'

She smiled back at him. Then he nodded and opened his door. 'Right, lads,' he said, stretching. 'All out.'

Barry stood out of the car. His muscles felt tight. He breathed in deeply. The air was fresher than in Dublin. Uncle Michael and Auntie Anne emerged from the house.

'Well, well, well,' Michael said. 'Who have we here?'

Uncle Michael looked out of place, Barry thought. Living in this decrepit old house, and yet dressed so clean and modern. Like a tennis star or something. He watched him walk towards his dad. They looked alike, with the same nervous smile as they shook hands.

'Anne!' his mom called out in her high voice. 'It's so nice to see you again!'

'Yes, Julia. You're very welcome.'

The women kissed one another on the cheek, smiling tightly. They were like opposites, Barry thought. His mom, tall and blonde and rounded, dressed in cream. Auntie Anne, small and wiry, dark haired, in a blue jumper, like a little blue bird.

Auntie Anne turned towards him. 'Hello, Barry,' she said.

Barry had to bend down to receive her kiss. She smiled up at him, her blue eyes shining.

'Well, now,' she said. 'What a fine young man you've become.'

'Thanks,' Barry said.

'And here's young Jimmy, looking so grown up!' Anne said, holding his shoulders in her hands. 'Would you all like to come inside?'

'Right, boys,' Denis directed. 'Let's get the gear out of the boot.'

A moment later Barry was carrying two large cases into the house. Again he was assailed by long-dormant memories. The sitting room, quiet now, emptied of the activity of that night, the night of the funeral. Without thinking he walked straight through to the kitchen. He was drawn towards the conservatory, wanted to look into the back garden, to be again in that place where he and Emma had last seen one another.

'Barry!' Denis called out. 'Might as well bring those cases upstairs straightaway. Michael, are we in our usual rooms? Jimmy, you go up with Barry and get your room sorted.'

'Yes, Dad.'

Jimmy bounced up the stairs with his red backpack and Barry lugged the cases up behind him. Auntie Anne was already upstairs.

'Now, boys, this is where you slept last time, isn't it? You can decide which beds you want to use. I've put one pillow on each bed – will that be all right?'

'I always use two,' Jimmy said.

'Jimmy . . .' Barry cautioned.

'That's grand,' Anne said. 'I'll get you another one in a moment.' She opened the wooden doors of the ancient wardrobes. 'There's space here to hang your clothes, boys. Jimmy, do you need a hand to unpack?'

'No, thanks. I'll be okay.'

'Okay. We'll see you downstairs in a few minutes. I'm sure you're hungry.'

'No,' Jimmy said. 'We stopped and ate on the way. We had our dinner in Carrickmacross.'

'Oh, did you? I see. Right. Well then. We'll see you downstairs anyway.'

She pulled the door closed behind her as she left the room.

'This house smells funny,' Jimmy said. 'It smells sort of damp or something.'

'It's an old house. That's what old houses smell like.'

Barry raised the old sash window. The breeze rustled the beeches outside. Jimmy sang to himself as he took his books from his backpack.

'Auntie Anne is nice,' he said.

'Yeah,' Barry replied.

'Aren't you going to unpack?'

'Maybe later,' Barry said.

'Barry?'

'Yeah?'

'What's wrong with you? You're like a zombie.'

Then Barry fixed his gaze on Jimmy with his eyes enlarged, grotesque and threatening, as if he was about to attack.

A few minutes later, the boys came downstairs where the adults had gathered in the kitchen. The large, age-worn table was set for six. Small starter plates rested on top of dinner plates at each setting. Bone-handled knives and antique silver forks flanked the plates. Red linen napkins sprouted from wine glasses.

'What?' Michael was saying. 'You've eaten already?'

'I was sure I said it on the phone,' Julia pleaded. 'When we talked on Sunday. We didn't want to impose.'

Auntie Anne stood at the end of the table. 'Right,' she sighed. 'Sure, there will be plenty of food for lunch tomorrow. Would you like a cup of tea anyway?'

'Yes, that would be lovely,' Julia said with superfluous enthusiasm.

'Julia, didn't you buy a cake?' Denis asked.

'Yes, that's right, we've got a nice coffee cake – Denis, did you bring it in from the car?'

'It's just out here,' he said, exiting the kitchen.

'But Anne baked tarts as well,' Michael said. 'Apple and rhubarb.'

'Oh, I see, how nice!' Julia said. 'Well then, why don't we save the cake for tomorrow?'

'Here it is,' Denis said, returning to the room. 'Might as well eat it while it's fresh!'

'Anne has baked fresh tarts for us,' Julia cautioned.

'Oh, right . . .'

Denis stood with the cake in his hand, not sure where to set it down. For a few minutes no one spoke as the dinner plates were removed from the table. Michael filled the kettle. The boys sat down expectantly.

'Now, Jimmy,' Anne said, smiling broadly. 'What would you like?'

'Umm, apple tart, please.'

'There's a good boy,' Anne said as she sliced.

Michael began pouring the tea. 'Oh, I should have asked,' he said. 'Would anyone prefer coffee?'

Denis was about to speak when Julia jumped in. 'No, Michael,' she said. 'Tea would be lovely. It really was a long drive.'

'It's shorter than it used to be,' Anne said. 'What with all the new roads. And of course that hold-up at the border is gone now.'

'What a beautiful pie,' Julia said. 'I'd love to get your recipe.'

'Sure it's only an apple tart,' Anne replied. 'Nothing special about it, I'm afraid.'

'Mmm, really lovely,' Denis said. 'Can't beat a good old-fashioned apple tart.'

For a moment the only sound was the gentle scrape of forks on plates.

'So, Denis,' Anne said, 'what do you think of our tidy town?'

'Sure you wouldn't recognise the place,' Denis said. 'The main street widened, all the shop fronts looking so well. The town seems to be booming.'

'Don't you think it's a little sad?' Julia said.

'Sad?' Anne asked.

'All the changes. Everything bigger and brighter. I remember the first time I came to Ballyfinn, it must be fifteen years ago. It seemed such a nice little Irish town back then.'

'It needed a face-lift,' Anne said. 'It's great to see a bit of prosperity for a change.'

'Yes, I suppose,' Julia said. 'You can't stop progress.'

Another pause. Then Anne said, 'So what do you boys think?'

'The tart is lovely,' Jimmy said.

'Thank you, Jimmy,' Anne said. 'But I meant the town. The new shopfronts. What about you, Barry? Maybe you didn't notice?'

Barry lowered his fork. 'Yes,' he said. 'It's really different.'

'And?' Anne encouraged him. 'What's the verdict? Better, or worse?'

'Oh, better, I think,' Barry considered. 'Sometimes you want to hang on to things. But it's hard to stop things from changing. Even your memories. They change when you see things again for real.'

He looked up. The four adults were staring at him like a panel of interviewers.

'So,' Julia broke the silence. 'I want to hear more about this party.'

'It's tomorrow night,' Michael said, setting his cup on the table. 'We're due at the hotel at half-past eight.'

'Stephen Deane is footing the bill,' Anne said. 'We saw him today walking in the town.'

'Really?' Julia said. 'Is he as handsome as he is in the movies?'

'Well,' Anne withheld judgement. 'He wouldn't be my type.'

'Who else is on the guest list?' Julia asked. 'Any other movie stars?'

'No, just Stephen, I believe,' Michael said. 'But Mary Moran is coming up from Cork. She's a therapist now.'

'And Catherine Sweeney, of course,' Anne added.

'Oh, yes,' Julia said. 'We met her in Dublin last Sunday. Do you know her, Anne?'

'No. But I've certainly heard the stories.'

'The stories?' Julia said.

'I assume Helen will be there,' Denis interrupted. 'Herself and Stephen were sweet on one another when they were about seven.'

'Helen's husband manages the hotel,' Anne explained to Julia. 'And their daughter Emma will be there as well. She'll be working though.'

Barry coughed suddenly.

'Are you all right there, Barry?' Denis said.

'Yes, sorry,' Barry said as he reached for his napkin.

'How old is Emma now?' Denis asked.

'She's just gone seventeen,' Anne said. 'She's a lovely girl. She used to call to the house quite often before they moved into the town.'

'She doesn't visit us very often any more,' Michael said. 'Perhaps she's become interested in other things.'

'It happens,' Julia said. 'When girls get a little older.'

'Are you all right, Barry?' Denis asked. 'Do you need a glass of water?'

'I'm fine, Dad.'

'Would you like another slice of tart?' Anne asked.

'No, thank you. I'm fine, thank you.'

'You're sure now?' Anne persisted. 'More tea? Anything at all?'

'No, Auntie Anne. Thanks very much.'

He flushed, looking up to see it again: four adult faces, smiling politely, assessing him as if he were a painting.

Later that evening Anne and Julia stood side by side in the kitchen. Julia held a tea towel while Anne washed dishes in the large porcelain sink.

'How are things at school?' Julia began.

'Oh, they're grand. Always the same. The year is nearly finished now.'

'And your headmistress?' Julia said. 'I've forgotten her name.'

'Mrs Fowles? Sure she's the same as ever. But of course, you were at the school, you met her. So you know what she's like.'

'I was so sorry, you know, that I couldn't come out to see you. After visiting your class.'

'Oh, yes,' Anne said. 'We were sorry too, of course. But sure that's the way these things happen. I'm sure it's all highly confidential, your work.'

'Well, yes, but . . .'

'You're hardly meant to discuss it with individual teachers.'

'No, that's not it,' Julia said. 'I wanted to come out, but I had to go back. To Dublin. Something came up. It was short notice.'

'Of course, you never know where they'll send you,' Anne continued. 'It must be an interesting job. Visiting a different school each day. Writing up your reports, highlighting all the problems. Then off to the next one.'

'It's not quite like that. We do a follow-up on all our visits.'

'I've known other teachers who have gone on to become supervisors,' Anne said. 'It's great that the department can reward teachers who show a bit of ambition.'

'I'm not a supervisor as such. It's a special commission. To help. Some of the teachers really can't cope.'

'I see,' Anne said as she scrubbed a mixing bowl. 'All the same it's a great position to be in. Sure you were only in the country a few months when you got the job.'

'Yes, it all happened very quickly.'

'I assume you were picked specially for the post?'

'Well, no,' Julia said. 'I mean, I had to apply. But my Master's degree, that's what they wanted. My thesis was on immigrant children.'

'I'd have loved to do a Master's,' Anne said, handing Julia the bowl. 'But I had to get out to work. To support myself.'

'Oh, of course . . .'

'And then, well, I'm the breadwinner now. So there's little chance of me getting time to go back to study.'

Anne pulled the stopper to drain the sink.

'Yes, I see,' Julia said nervously. 'So how is Michael doing?'

'He's grand. He's coping very well, despite his disability. He works every morning at the bookshop. And he's a great man to have around the house.'

'Good. I'm glad to hear it.'

'Sure we're very fortunate over all,' Anne said, drying her hands. 'Now. Will we join the men inside?'

Julia looked at Anne. 'You know,' she said, 'I'm really glad we're here this weekend. I only hope we can, well, get to know one another a little better.'

At that moment Barry entered the kitchen. 'Mom?' he said.

'Yes, honey, what is it?'

'This shirt. I was going to wear it, for the party. But it's all creased. It got wrinkled in the case. Could I maybe iron it?'

'You leave that to me, my dear,' Anne said as she took the shirt from his hand. 'I'll have this for you in two shakes. Now, why don't the two of you go inside and relax? I'll just run the iron over this and then I'll join you. I won't be a minute.'

'Thanks, Auntie Anne,' Barry said.

'Yes,' Julia mustered a smile. 'Thanks, Anne. And thanks so much for the tart.'

'No problem at all,' she said as she reached for the ironing board. 'I'm glad you liked it.'

Denis sat on the sofa as Michael fiddled with the stereo.

He looked around the room. It had changed little since they were boys. The heavy red curtains. The plastered ceiling with the water stain in the corner, shaped like a map of France. The same black fireplace with the same brass fire irons. Even the smell hanging in the air was the same: an aura of damp fibres mingled with smoke from a turf fire.

He wasn't prepared for this. Being in the house again. Sitting at the dinner table, the old dinner table where he had eaten a thousand meals as a child. Seeing Michael again, who sounded the same but looked so much older. Like a familiar voice in a new shell.

He felt tired now. He knew he hadn't been at his best on the drive up. He was annoyed to find himself weighed down and irritable, thinking about work when he should have been focusing on this time, this reunion.

The slogan. He still didn't have a slogan for the bank. Every few minutes it burst upon him. He couldn't keep it out of his mind.

Now low piano music emerged from the stereo. Michael sat across from Denis in an old armchair.

'So,' Denis said, looking around the room. 'The house is so neat and tidy.'

'Yes.'

'Our two have the house in perpetual chaos.'

'They're fine-looking lads,' Michael smiled.

'Deceptive packaging,' Denis continued. 'They're like a pair of lizards, the two of them. Sunning themselves, shedding their skins. Within half and hour of coming into a room they cover it with discarded clothes and tea cups and empty cereal bowls.'

Michael laughed.

'It would never dawn on them to tidy up,' Denis went on. 'Getting boys to look after themselves is like training cats to sing. Sure we were never like that, were we?'

'I don't know about that now,' Michael said. 'We had old Peg about the place to look after us.'

'I suppose we did,' Denis said.

Denis studied Michael for a moment. He was dressed well, he'd had a haircut recently. But there was a tiredness around the eyes.

'Sorry, Denis,' Michael said finally. 'Would you like something in your hand?'

'No, thanks, I'm grand.'

'Anything at all? Glass of wine? Drop of whiskey?'

'I didn't know you kept drink in the house.'

'Anne has a glass of wine in the evenings.'

'And what about you?'

'No. I can't, really. Doesn't mix well with my medication.'

'Oh, of course,' Denis paused. 'So. How's the old house holding up?'

'Grand. I had to do a job on the conservatory. Leaking a bit. October last, it was.'

'Much of a job?'

'Just a bit of sealant. It only took an hour or two.'

'Wouldn't get a professional in?' Denis asked. 'To make sure it's all right?'

'No point really. For small jobs.'

'No, of course. Better off doing it yourself.'

They paused then. Michael looked into the carpet and Denis surveyed the room.

'So how is your work these days?' Michael asked finally.

'Oh, it's grand. Same old thing, really.'

'And business is good?'

'Not too bad. But there's been a bit of a change. Just lately.'

'Oh?'

'Bit of a slow down, really.'

'Right.'

'And how about your work?' Denis said. 'You're still at the bookshop, then?'

'Yes. Just mornings.'

'Right,' Denis nodded. 'And it's busy?'

'Always the same. I enjoy it, though. It gets me out of the house.'

'Yes, of course.'

Another pause.

'And Anne is well?'

'Oh yes. She's great, actually. She enjoys the teaching.'

'Really? She never struck me as that type.'

'She loves the kids. And they're mad about her. Whenever we're in town – the parents. Coming up to her all the time. Saying how great she is.'

'Oh. Good,' Denis said. 'And what about yourselves? Any plans to start a family?'

'I don't know, really. We haven't talked about it in a while.'

'I see.'

'Anne thinks, well, she thinks it might be a bit difficult. She can't leave her job. So it would be me here, on my own. And she's not sure I could, well, cope. With the medication and all.'

'Yes, of course,' Denis said, shifting in his seat.

'It could get to be, well, a bit of a handful,' Michael said, staring into the carpet. 'But I don't know, really. I don't know what it would be like. With children.'

'Yes,' Denis nodded.

'I mean, it might make a nice change, you know. Bit of life around the place.'

'It would make a change all right.'

'You must be proud of your two fine boys.'

'Yes. They're grand, the pair of them. A bit of a handful. But I wouldn't send them back.'

'No,' Michael agreed.

'When they're your own,' Denis repeated, 'you wouldn't send them back.'

Anne stood in the kitchen ironing Barry's shirt. It had an American designer label. She paid extra attention to the cuffs and collar, ensuring the shirt looked as fresh as new.

Such a gorgeous-looking boy, she thought as she laid the shirt on the back of a chair. A real Adonis. Deserves to dress well, I suppose.

She folded up the ironing board and replaced it on the hook in the press.

Certainly doesn't say much though, she thought. A quiet man.

She picked up the shirt from the chair.

Surprising, really, she thought. Two successful types like Denis and Julia. You'd think their boys would be full of themselves. But they're lovely kids.

She stood in the kitchen for a moment, listened to the muffled voices in the sitting room outside. Then she ventured out the door.

Julia was sitting beside Denis on the sofa, leaning forward, obviously stuck into conversation. Anne walked over and stood beside her.

'So,' Julia was saying, 'you guys must really be looking forward to this party!'

Michael smiled politely.

'Oh, come on,' she urged. 'Won't it be fun to see all the old gang again? Memories of that famous house of yours?'

'It's been a long time,' Denis commented.

'Yes,' Michael said, rubbing his chin.

'And what about Stephen Deane?' Julia persisted. 'Aren't you curious to hear about life in Hollywood?'

'Maybe,' Michael said. 'I'd say he's the same as ever.'

'I think,' Anne cut in protectively, 'these things are sometimes hard to judge beforehand.'

'Yes, I suppose so,' Julia retreated. 'But I'm sure it's going to be a lot of fun.'

'Now, young man,' Anne said brightly as Barry came into the room. 'Here's your shirt, fresh as new.'

'Oh, thanks. That's great. Well. I might as well go up to bed then.'

'Good night, Barry.'

They all echoed their good nights as Barry left the room.

'Right,' Anne said. 'We all have a lot of catching up to do. But we've got all weekend to chat, and I, for one, am exhausted. And Michael, how about you? You've got a long day tomorrow . . .'

'Yes, Mother,' Michael said, smiling. 'I suppose it's time to turn in.'

'We should probably hit the hay as well,' Julia said.

'Yep,' Denis said. 'A long day tomorrow indeed.'

'Right,' Anne said. 'We'll go up then. Good night, you two.'

'Good night, guys.'

'Good night, Julia.'

Julia and Denis watched as Michael and Anne left the room. Then Julia looked over at Denis. He looked tired. There were dark rings under his eyes, his chin showed a shadow of stubble.

'Here we are,' she said quietly. 'Back in your old house.'

'Yes,' he smiled weakly.

'Feel strange?'

'A bit.'

'So. Did you bring many girls into this room?'

'Girls?'

'Yeah. The maidens of Donegal.'

'Here? No. Well, maybe a few. Just the Murphy girls.'

'Oh? More than one?'

'Aye. There were fourteen of them.'

'Denis!'

'Grand big Catholic family of Murphy girls.'

'You're terrible.'

'Aye. That's me. Dreadful Denis, they used to call me.'

'You seem tired, love.'

'I am a bit.'

'Is there anything I can do? To make this easier?'

'No, love.'

'I just wish you could relax and enjoy this time. Up here, with your brother.'

'Yes. I know.'

'Are you sure you don't want to talk about it?'

'There's nothing to talk about. I'm just a bit tired.'

'Okay. So. Should we head upstairs?'

'Aye. Probably best.'

'Okay,' she said softly as she patted his knee, before they both stood.

'Denis?'

'Yes?'

She looked at him then.

'I just wish . . .'

'What is it?'

'Oh, nothing. Come on. Up we go. Big day tomorrow.'

'Okay. Big day tomorrow indeed.'

CHAPTER 14

On Saturday morning Julia woke early. She hadn't slept well. She had woken often during the night, turning, drifting off into short intense dreams, and then waking again. Denis was asleep beside her, breathing heavily. Strange, she thought. He was an early riser, usually the first up on Saturday mornings.

She stepped quietly out of bed and wrapped her dressing gown around her. She looked out the window into the trees with their golden, early-summer leaves. The air was balmy already and promised another fine day. She bent down before the mirror on the ancient dressing table and hastily brushed her hair.

A good day, she thought, to be together. And maybe to sort things out. With Denis. And with Anne. If only I had slept a little better . . .

She left the room, pulling the door softly closed behind her. She stood in the corridor for a moment, listening for life, but everyone was still asleep. She walked downstairs.

When she entered the kitchen, she found Michael already seated at the table. He smiled as she walked through the door. He looked very awake. He had showered already and he was dressed neatly in jeans and a light sweater.

'Good morning,' she said in a low voice.

'Good morning.'

'You're an early riser. Just like Denis.'

'Yes. Did you sleep well?'

'Not bad,' she yawned. 'I woke once or twice. Denis is still out cold. Must be the fresh air up here.'

She sat down at the table across from Michael. She felt he was studying her, trying to anticipate her next move. She smiled nervously.

'So,' she said, rising again. 'We brought some coffee, I'm not sure where Denis put it.'

'Oh, here, I'm sorry, I made coffee just a moment ago. It's still hot. I hope filter coffee is okay?'

'Oh, yes, perfect.'

Michael looked into the press and took out a ceramic mug and saucer. Then he poured Julia a cup and sat down across from her.

'It's funny,' Julia said. 'When I first came to Ireland everyone drank tea. And the coffee was terrible, if you could get any. Now everyone drinks coffee and it's good coffee too.'

'We always had coffee. Dad drank it. Was rather proud of the fact.'

'Oh,' Julia said. 'But things certainly have changed, haven't they?'

'Do you think they have?'

'Oh, surely you've seen the changes. Everything. The roads. The stores in town. People have so much more money.'

'Hmm,' Michael considered. 'Maybe some things.'

'You can get everything in Ireland now. From anywhere. American fast food. English high-street shops. Euro trash music. It's hard to find anything that's Irish any more.'

'We've always had imports here,' Michael said. 'In the nine-teenth century it was Italian opera. The bishops complained because arias were being sung at Mass. There were terrible rows.'

Julia laughed. 'I miss it though,' she said then. 'The old Ireland. Now it all seems to be covered in cheap veneer.'

Michael looked at her. 'Have you ever walked in these hills?' he asked.

'No, never,' Julia said.

'Well, then. Why don't we have a look round?'

'Now?' she asked.

'Yes.'

'Okay,' Julia said hesitantly. 'If you'd like . . .'

'You get dressed,' he said. 'I'll find you some wellingtons. We'll take a little pre-breakfast stroll.'

'Are you sure you want to? It's so early.'

'Yes,' Michael said. 'I would. Very much.'

Julia looked into his eyes, now playful and alive.

'Okay,' she said. 'I won't be a tick.'

A few minutes later they walked outside in the bright morning sunshine. An untidy hedgerow encroached upon the gravel drive. They picked their way gingerly between the fronds and stalks that reached out to them as they passed.

As they emerged onto the road, Julia was overcome with a sense of well being. Lush greenery surrounded them and the blue summer sky was mottled only by a few lazy clouds. Birds sang from every direction. The new growth gave off heavy scents in the balmy air: raspberry bushes interleaved with young honeysuckle vines; tender young nettles and primroses working their way through the spiky hedge. Now they walked between fields scraggy with saw-grass and luminous yellow gorse. In the distance sheep and cattle dotted the landscape. Michael walked beside her silently but comfortably.

'So,' she began. 'You've lived here your whole life.'

'Well, yes, apart from the years at college. My father grew up here too.'

'Didn't you ever want to try living anywhere else?'

'No, not really.'

'Even while Denis was off in America?'

'No. That wouldn't be my sort of thing.'

'No? And what *is* your sort of thing?'

Michael turned to look at her. 'I'm better off staying in one place,' he said.

'Better off?' Julia asked.

'Yes. I think so.'

They turned onto a smaller road and began to walk uphill. There was no traffic, nothing to disturb the natural sounds around them. Julia could feel her breathing quicken as they ascended.

'Denis tells me you studied art in college,' she said.

'Yes.'

'What kind of art?'

'Oh, lots of things really. Painting and sculpture. Bits of everything.'

'And did you enjoy it?'

'I did at the time, yes.'

'But what about now?' she asked, her breathing coming heavier as they climbed. 'Do you still paint?'

'No. I haven't done anything for years.'

'Why not?'

'I don't know, really. Maybe that's all in the past.'

'But why?'

'You get older,' he said with his eyes on the ground. 'You don't feel the same need.'

'But surely if you enjoyed it before, you could enjoy it again?'

'Maybe. Back then, though, it became a bit of an obsession.'

'So what's replaced it?' Julia persisted.

Michael smiled sadly. 'Anti-psychotic drugs.'

'I . . . I see,' she stammered. 'I'm sorry. I didn't mean to pry.'

'It's okay,' he smiled benignly. 'It's refreshing to be pried into once in a while.'

The steep incline began to ease off. The trees thinned out and a vista began to open up around them.

'It's beautiful up here,' Julia said.

'Yes. I thought you might like it. You see those trees, down below us? In there, that's the house. We're behind it now.'

Julia looked out across the landscape. She could see Ballyfinn far below, and then beyond were slumbering hills, hazy green through the morning mist.

'What's that over there?' she pointed.

'Windmills,' Michael said. 'They were built a few years ago. They come from Denmark. They power the whole area.'

Julia watched the white blades rotating smooth and silent in the distance. They looked like huge bicycle wheels.

'But that's it,' Julia said. 'That's what I meant, below, in the kitchen. How can you say nothing has changed when you look out over these ancient hills and see brand-new power generators?'

Michael stopped walking and leaned on the stone wall beside the road.

'I didn't say nothing has changed,' he said. 'But it depends on your perspective. You're concentrating on the windmills. But you have to think about the wind.'

Julia looked at Michael. He was speaking to her directly, his sandy hair tossed by the summer breeze. But then his face relaxed.

'I'm sorry,' he said. 'I didn't mean to lecture.'

'No, not at all.'

'I just wanted you to experience this. Because, when you lose your grip — I mean, when nothing seems to fit into context anymore . . .'

'Yes?'

'The wind. It stays the same. It's always here.'

'Yes.'

'You might find it useful, you know. Some time. When everything seems a bit temporary.'

She looked at him again. He appeared older now, caring and wise. Fatherly.

'Right,' he said with a smile. 'Lesson over. Will we go down and have some breakfast?'

'Okay,' she said, nodding slowly. 'Yeah. That sounds good.'

He began to walk back through the field.

'Michael?'

'Yes?'

'Thank you for this.'

He didn't reply. But she would retain that image of him there, standing alone against the backdrop of the distant mountains. And she would remember his eyes, focused on her, as if he were requesting constant truthfulness.

*

Jimmy woke to bright sunshine. He sat up in bed and looked out the window into the trees. Massive pines, beeches with golden green leaves. His eyes stung from the glistening sunshine.

He lay back down on his side. Barry was in the next bed, still asleep. Jimmy stared at the colourless woollen blankets covering Barry's long body. The folds of the blankets looked like hills and valleys. Jimmy followed a ridge that stretched all the way up from Barry's feet to his neck, like a ribbon of road, up and around and over. Something for a Land Rover, with guns mounted on the back. The enemy lurking on either side.

'*Pow, pow,*' he said softly. And then machine-gun fire, *prt prt prt prt*, echoing off into the distance.

'Jimmy,' Barry grunted angrily.

'Sorry,' Jimmy whispered. He lay back in his bed and gazed up at the ceiling. He studied the lampshade, imagined a paratrooper pouncing down to the top of the wardrobe.

The air felt warm, it was warm in bed under the covers. He was thirsty. He pushed the blankets back and sat up. He looked around for his slippers, but then he remembered that he had forgotten to pack them. He left the room and walked down the stairs.

'Good morning, Tiger!' his dad said as he came into the kitchen.

'Good morning, Jimmy!' Auntie Anne said.

'Morning,' Jimmy replied.

'And how did you sleep in this creepy old house?' Auntie Anne asked, putting her arms around his shoulders.

'Okay.'

'Can I get you some breakfast? We have Toaster Tarts, or Frosties, or you can have toast and peanut butter?'

'No, thanks. I'm fine.'

'Or perhaps, sir, you'd prefer American pancakes? Or two eggs, sunny side up?'

'I'm okay, Auntie Anne. I'm just a bit thirsty.'

'Okay. How about a glass of orange juice then?'

'Yes, please.'

Jimmy sat on the edge of his father's chair and leaned into him as Auntie Anne set a glass of juice before him on the table. There was silence for a moment as both adults watched Jimmy sip his drink.

'Dad?' he asked. 'Can I come to the party tonight?'

'I'm afraid not, Tiger. It's only for adults.'

'But Barry is going.'

'I know, but he's sixteen. There won't be any other kids your age. You'd be very bored . . .'

'But I wanted to meet that actor,' Jimmy protested.

'Unfortunately it's just for old people,' Dad said. 'You really wouldn't enjoy it.'

'Your Dad's right,' Auntie Anne broke in. 'I've been to parties with actors before, and they're terribly boring.'

'Really?' Jimmy said.

'Oh yes,' she replied. 'You see, I do plays here in town. I'm the producer. And so I get to meet all the actors. Not film stars, really. But some of them have been on telly.'

'Cool.'

'And actors are the worst people to meet at parties,' Anne said. 'They only talk about one thing. And you know what that is?'

'No. What?'

'Themselves.' Anne said. 'They go on and on and on about themselves, as if they were the only people in the world.'

Jimmy laughed. But then he considered for a moment.

'If I'm not going to the party,' he asked, 'am I staying here?'

'No, you won't be staying here,' Auntie Anne continued. 'That was the original plan. I had a very nice girl from up the road prepared to stay with you. But now she's come down with some sort of flu. It's making the rounds at school, everyone has it. So rather than having you stay here, we've got you something much better.'

'What?'

'Your very own, fully furnished, super fancy, absolutely deluxe hotel room.'

'Really?' Jimmy said.

'Yes,' Denis confirmed. 'With two beds. And your own telly. Very posh altogether.'

'Wow,' Jimmy considered. 'I'll be at the hotel, so.'

'Yes,' Denis answered. 'We'll all be at the party right below you. We'll come and visit you to make sure you're okay.'

'Right. So I might see Stephen after all?'

'I don't know about that,' Denis said. 'But we'll see.'

'Maybe,' Anne said, narrowing her eyes in thought, 'maybe we can get you his autograph instead.'

'Oh,' Jimmy said.

'It's much quicker,' she continued, 'and far less boring.'

Jimmy smiled.

'Now, cowboy,' Denis said. 'Why don't you go upstairs and get dressed. And see if you can raise that brother of yours.'

'Okay.'

They watched Jimmy leave the room, and then they were both silent for a moment.

'Michael tells me you're much admired as a teacher,' Denis said finally.

'Oh, I suppose I do my bit.'

'It must take a lot out of you,' Denis said. 'Teaching.'

'Well, yes, but at least it's a short day. It's great to have the afternoons off. Michael gets tired, though. With his work at the bookshop.'

'Oh?'

'It can get quite busy,' she continued. 'If the school kids are in or if tourists arrive. And we get people from the North. They get great value for their sterling.'

'Oh, yes.'

'His manager wants him to do more,' she said. 'He could do the accounts. Or he could manage the stock, order in the new titles, he could manage the whole shop really. But he's worried, you know. About taking on more responsibility.'

'Oh?'

'It's his confidence,' Anne said as she brought coffee to the table. 'He's very cautious.'

'About what?'

'About everything,' she said. 'He's worried that things will get too much for him. He's quite afraid of any change that might upset his routine.'

'I see.'

'But I think he just needs a bit of support,' she said.

'Support?'

'Yes. Someone to encourage him. To reassure him that if it begins to go badly . . .'

'Yes?'

'It can't come from me, though,' she said. 'Someone else. Someone who would show an interest in what he's doing. Encourage him a bit.'

She looked at Denis, then, as if challenging him to respond. But just then Michael and Julia entered the kitchen.

'Well, well!' Denis said with sudden animation. 'Welcome home, travellers.'

Julia's cheeks were flushed with exercise. 'Good morning, you two,' she said. 'What a gorgeous day. I've had a wonderful walk in the country.'

'Good,' Anne said. 'You're just in time for coffee. Julia, you like coffee in the mornings, don't you?'

'Oh, yes, please.'

Jimmy returned to the room then, still in his pyjamas.

'Good morning, honey!' Julia said.

'I thought you were getting dressed?' Denis said.

'I couldn't find my socks.'

'But you could put on some trousers,' Denis said.

'It's okay,' Julia broke in. 'I'll help you in just a minute.'

Jimmy watched the adults fuss over breakfast. Michael was at the cooker heating croissants in the oven, a patch of sweat on the back of his shirt. Anne was never still, rooting for serviettes in a drawer, pouring coffee, refilling Jimmy's juice (he didn't want any more), pulling her dark hair back into a ponytail.

His mom sat beside his dad, leaning forward, her hands in her lap, her hair a bit messed from the walk. His dad leaned back with one arm over the back of her chair. His mom looked peaceful and happy, Jimmy thought. She pushed her hair out of her face like a woman in an ad on the telly. And her voice was lovely, for some reason.

'It's so beautiful here,' she said.

'Do you think so?' Denis replied.

'Why don't we come here more often?'

'We're never invited,' Denis said.

Anne turned as if about to speak, but Jimmy broke in.

'Mom,' he said. 'Can you help me get dressed now?'

'Okay, honey,' Julia said, standing. 'I'll find those socks for you. Might be a good time to wake that brother of yours.'

'Bye, Jimmy,' Anne said. 'Maybe you'll eat something when you come back down?'

'Okay,' he said.

Julia guided Jimmy out of the room. He turned back to wave goodbye. He noticed that his Auntie Anne and Uncle Michael were watching him. They didn't say anything but they were both smiling. In a gentle sort of way.

Jimmy liked them, Auntie Anne and Uncle Michael. And he liked the big house. And he liked the way everyone seemed so happy here.

CHAPTER 15

Emma sat on the edge of her bed staring at the wall. Her head was like cotton wool and her body felt sore, as if she had been kicked all over.

She bent forward to pull on her tights. Her hair was wrapped in a towel and when she leaned over it came loose and fell down. It felt cold on her skin. She put her left foot into her tights and pulled them up to her knees. Then she did the same with her right foot. She stood and yawned. She stumbled forward with her tights holding her knees together, but then she caught her balance.

She shouldn't be so tired. She'd done very little during the day. She'd even had a lie-down in the afternoon. But that's the way she'd been lately.

She reached down and pulled up her tights, wriggling them up to her waist. Then she sat down on the bed and started again from the feet, stretching them up her ankles, over her knees and up her thighs, trying to make them smooth.

Such an effort, she thought, just to pull on my tights. And I have a night's work ahead of me.

She stood and looked at herself in the mirror. She patted her tummy. Early days still.

'Emma!' her Daddy shouted from downstairs.

She reached lazily for her dressing gown and opened the door.
'Yes?'

'There's a fresh uniform here for you. I've had it cleaned.'

'But *Daddy*,' she whined. 'I have a uniform here. This is the
only one that fits me properly.'

'What state is it in?'

'It's *grand*.'

'Grand? What's *grand*, then?'

Emma saw him standing at the base of the stairs. He wore the
trousers of his good suit and his black shoes shone. His turquoise
shirt was still open at the neck. His tummy had developed quite a
bulge of late, she thought. Must be something in the water.

'My uniform is *grand*. I've only worn it the once since it was
washed.'

'You'll wear *this* uniform then. No half measures tonight. I
want you looking your best.'

'Ach, Daddy, don't be ridiculous. I'll be related to half the
people there.'

'I don't care who you're related to,' he boomed. 'You can do
anything you like tomorrow, but tonight you'll be the
professional.'

He looked at his watch. 'You'd better be off then,' he said. 'You
need to help the lads get the room organised. There was a kids'
party this afternoon and the place is in a state.'

'I know.'

She sighed, walked down the stairs, grabbed the uniform in its
plastic cover and stomped back up to her room.

'And listen,' her dad said. 'It's a party. People want to enjoy
themselves. Try to get into the spirit of the thing.'

'Yes, Daddy.'

She closed the door of her bedroom behind her. She felt tired. She wanted to lie back on the bed, and fall asleep, and be left alone.

This is so unfair, she thought. Having to work at this party dressed like a fecking maid. Such a desperate way to see him again. What am I going to say?

She had rehearsed the scene many times, gone over it in her head, those dreadful opening lines:

'Ach, hiya! Yeah, great to see you too! Sure I'd love to have a chat, get to know you again, maybe go for a wee snog out back, aye, except that well, you see, I'm just a wee bit out of sorts, you know, what with the baby on the way . . .'

She turned on the hairdryer and leaned sideways, running her fingers through her hair. She wished the day wasn't so sticky. She didn't hear her mother enter the room.

'Hiya,' her mother said, tapping her shoulder. 'Can I talk to you for a wee sec?'

Emma turned off the dryer and they sat down on the bed. Her mother had had her hair done and she still smelled of the hairdresser's.

'I know you don't want to work at this party,' she whispered. 'And I know your daddy's driving you spare.'

'Aye. A bit.'

'You know why, though, don't you?'

'No, I don't. He's so nervous about this party. It's just the family, so it is.'

'No, it's not just the family.'

'Aye, I know,' Emma said. 'Stephen Deane, the big movie star.

But sure he's just another lad from Ballyfinn like the rest of them. He's not fecking royalty.'

Emma paused for a moment then. She was surprised to note sadness in her mother's eyes.

'You know your daddy is a very proud man. He's wild proud of the hotel and how it's grown and how it's written up in the tourist guides. And all of that has been down to his good work over the years.'

'Aye, but . . .'

'And he's also very proud of you,' she added.

'He doesn't show it.'

'I know that. He doesn't like to show these things. But he is proud of you. He's very proud of everything you do, and everything you are. And tonight, well. He wants to show off his hotel. And he wants to show off *you* as well.'

Then she stopped and smiled. And it came on Emma, then. The thoughts that she had kept from her mind. The thoughts about her parents. And herself. And the baby. And how their lives would be changed.

And then Emma's shoulders began to heave, and her mother put her arms around her. Emma knew that her mother didn't know what was going on in her head, and she didn't want her to worry, but she couldn't stop herself from crying. After a moment, though, she managed to get herself under control. She wiped her eyes on her towel and mustered a weak smile.

'You'd better be off soon,' her mother said.

'Aye,' Emma replied.

But Emma could see a question forming on her mother's face. She could see it playing about her lips and in the way she tilted her head. And Emma knew that her mother was concerned, that her mother sensed her worry.

Why was she crying so easily? What was happening to her?

Denis found himself alone in the house.

Julia was upstairs having a nap. Barry was out for a walk. Jimmy was in the bedroom playing. Anne was in town getting her hair done. He wasn't sure where Michael was.

He felt hot and edgy. Frustrated.

He walked up the stairs, pushed open the door to the boys' room. Jimmy had his adventure set out across the floor and covering both beds. Green plastic soldiers and tanks and plastic Quonset huts laid out in an elaborate array of battle. A glass of white lemonade rested on the bedside table.

'Hiya,' Denis said.

'Hiya,' Jimmy replied, not looking up.

'How's it going?'

'Fine.'

He drove a tank across a pillow.

'Fancy another drink?' Denis said. 'Your lemonade is probably gone flat by now.'

'Yeah, it's flat.'

'Would you like me to get you a new glass?'

'No, I'm grand.'

'How about a game of cards?'

'No, thank you. Maybe later.'

Jimmy repositioned a soldier bearing a machine gun.

'Right,' Denis said. 'Everything okay, then?'

'Yeah.'

'Okay. I'll go, so.'

'Okay. Bye.'

'Bye.'

Denis left the room quietly. He marvelled at Jimmy's ability to lose himself in his games, becoming involved utterly in an imaginary world. Jimmy had said nothing about the party since the morning, seemed to have forgotten about Stephen Deane entirely. Worked it all out, planned his attack, and destroyed the enemy.

So contented, Jimmy was. The only one in the house.

Earlier that day Julia had expressed her annoyance about having to bring Jimmy to the hotel. She muttered something under her breath to Denis, wondering why there was only one teenage girl in all of County Donegal who might look after Jimmy during the party. Denis explained that Anne probably didn't know many teenage girls in the area, and she obviously wanted to use someone she knew well and trusted. Julia gave in but she was still on edge, exhaling in frustration and running her fingers back through her hair. Denis could sense that Julia was nervous around Anne, she was unhappy about sticking Jimmy on his own in a hotel room, and she was even hinting that she'd rather not go to the party.

That was the only time they had talked that day. They still weren't in tune with one another but he lacked the energy to go into it. He thought it might deteriorate into a row and he didn't fancy trying to sort everything out while keeping his voice down so Anne and Michael wouldn't overhear the whole thing.

Even Barry seemed out of touch. He was ordinarily even-tempered, but today he was noticeably irritable. He buried his head in a book all morning, hardly ate a thing at lunch, went for a walk on his own in the afternoon. Anne was clearly disappointed with the boys' reaction to her hospitality. She had filled the house with rubbishy food – everything the boys loved – and here neither of them were eating a scrap!

Then, of course, he and Michael couldn't seem to find anything to talk about.

So Denis meandered about the house. He went out the front, checking the place to see if anything might need repair. But it was grand, really, the old house. Still the same. So he wandered inside again, sat on a comfy chair, glanced at the paper.

So pointless, he thought: being here, going to the party tonight, putting on a face, trying to impress. Denis the successful businessman. The expensive house in Dublin. The lovely blonde wife.

Such a charade. The agency was in trouble, his biggest account was dissatisfied, he and his wife were on a diet of monosyllables. And deep down he knew it wasn't Julia. And it wasn't Anne, it wasn't the boys and it wasn't the party.

It was the bank. The bank and their fucking slogan for their fucking investment products. It was squatting on him like a toad and ruining his weekend.

He put the paper aside and stood up. He wandered through the kitchen and into the conservatory. He looked into the back garden. Michael was there, asleep on a sun lounger. Denis quietly opened the glass door and tiptoed into the garden. He sat down on a garden chair.

Michael, he thought. Having his afternoon kip. Funny how a sleeping man can look like a boy again.

It used to be such craic, Denis thought. The two of us, with the stereo playing in the sitting room, singing along, doing the guitar thing. Waking the parents in the morning with that Rory Gallagher album. Mam and Dad stumbling down the stairs, sitting down to breakfast, Michael wearing that ridiculous chef's hat he got somewhere, serving them eggs and rashers like a clown, with me pouring them coffee, both of them looking something between exhausted and terrified!

At college, then. Michael was so intense. So creative. The clay and porcelain figures all over the house – all those souls in torment. And then the mobiles, him dragging everyone into the college to see them hanging from the ceiling like bloody flying dinosaurs: books and axes and birds and everything gyrating around the room. Weird things altogether.

Brilliant, so he was.

And then the way he used to talk. He knew the theories, knew what was good. He knew everything back then, everyone said it. Denis was there studying how to make money but Michael, he went for the real knowledge. The depth.

Denis looked at Michael now, lying in the sun.

Drugs, he thought. Anti-psychotics. They must knacker him. Keep his head fuzzy so the thoughts don't break through. It's tragic. It's such a tragedy that it had to happen to him. It's like he's been kept down, sent to sleep for all these years.

Denis looked across the garden. The trim grass, the peonies blooming along the border. The huge pine, its conical shape reaching upwards as it always had, even when they were boys. And the space below the branches, so dark, and cool, and impenetrable.

Maybe the problem is me, Denis thought. Michael is still

Michael. He's still Michael, even now. Even though he's not what we expected. Maybe *I* need to change. Myself. Somehow. Otherwise, the past, the dream, well: it can blind you. The dream can blind you to the way things really are.

He'll wake up now, and that will be him. The real Michael. Here. In the flesh.

And then Denis paused in his thinking. Something began to happen. He experienced a sensation, a release of energy in his mind. Like bubbles in his head, popping, with refreshing coolness, all in a rush.

Dreams, he thought. Something about dreams. That girl in the coffee shop. What was it she had said? *The stuff of dreams.*

What was it, Shakespeare? No matter. It doesn't fucking matter. *The stuff of dreams.* That's it. That's what the bank was selling. *The stuff of dreams!*

And it came over him as he sat there in his old back garden, the way things used to come to him, ideas flowing like water through his mind.

The stuff of dreams. What we are now, what we want to be. Today and the future. Hard reality with a vision of the limitless beyond.

That's it. That's the one. The slogan.

He felt as though a world of colour was rising slowly before him: the bright green of the garden, the blue sky, the little flowers peeping out of the hedgerow. Everything, the garden, the air, the garden furniture, transformed from greyness into colour. He could nearly hear his pulse in the afternoon silence.

Michael was waking now, smiling weakly. Denis looked at him.

'Hello there,' Denis said.

'Hiya.'

'Have a good sleep?'

'Aye.'

'Good for you,' Denis said.

Michael raised himself on his elbow and yawned. 'What are you grinning about?' he said.

'Grinning?' Denis said. 'I don't know. Shakespeare.'

'Shakespeare? That's not like you.'

'No. But you're not like you either.'

They looked at one another. 'My God,' Denis continued. 'A grand sleep in a grand sunny back garden. Isn't it well for some?'

'Aye,' Michael grinned, leaning back on the lounger. 'But sure it's a poor house that can't afford one gentleman.'

'Are you comfortable, so?' Denis said.

'Yes, actually.'

'Can I get you an egg?' Denis said.

'Yes, please. A quail's egg, if you wouldn't mind.'

'Soft boiled or poached?'

'Soft boiled, thank you.'

'Michael?'

'Yes?'

'We're too old for this carry-on.'

'God,' Michael laughed. 'Aren't we just?'

Julia woke to hear men's laughter coming through the window. She stepped out of bed and looked outside for a moment. She shivered nervously. Then she walked out of the bedroom into the hall and walked downstairs. She entered the sitting room as Anne came in the front door.

'Hi there,' Anne said.

'Oh, hi, Anne. Your hair is lovely.'

'Ah sure, it'll do. Were you asleep? I hope I didn't wake you.'

'No, I was just coming down. I think I overslept. I was really tired. What time is it?'

'It's just gone six.'

'Oh dear. I really slept. Where do you suppose the men are?'

Just then Michael and Denis entered from the kitchen, both with several buttons of their shirts undone.

'Would you look at the lads,' Anne said.

'You two could be twins,' Julia said.

The four smiled at one another from their separate corners of the room. But at that moment the phone rang and Denis picked it up.

'Hello, this is the O'Donnell Hotel . . . Why hello, Catherine, it's me, Denis . . . Yes, indeed, we're wild here with the excitement . . . God, no, really? Ah now, we can't have that . . . Well listen, we'll be arriving around eight, so you won't be on your own . . . For old time's sake indeed. Righty-o, Catherine, see you then. Byeeeeee!'

He put down the phone. The others stared at him, smiling politely.

'That was Catherine Sweeney,' he said.

'Oh, really?' Julia replied dryly.

'I said we'd be there around eight.'

'That's great,' Julia said. 'Can't wait to see her.'

'Yeah,' Denis said, tucking his shirt into his trousers. 'It'll be gas seeing them all again.'

'Yes,' Julia sighed. 'Gas, as they say.'

Denis looked directly at Julia, then, trying to read her expression.

Michael squinted into the mirror in the bedroom. He wore a white shirt with pale-blue stripes. He was trying to negotiate the knot on a red bow-tie. Anne sat at the dressing table across the room.

'Are you all right?' she said. 'You could wear an ordinary tie, you know.'

'Nearly there,' he replied, struggling. 'I used to wear this years ago. To all the parties.'

'Did you now?'

'I did,' he said, straightening. He turned to face her. 'How do I look?'

'Rather nice. Fit for anything.'

She bent towards the mirror to affix her earrings.

'Why did you say that?' he asked.

'Say what?'

'*Fit.* Why fit?'

'I don't know. I just did.'

'Oh?'

'Okay,' she said, still facing the mirror. 'I said it because, well, maybe you haven't been feeling very fit lately.'

'Haven't I?'

'You've been self-conscious. All week.'

'Oh?'

'Yes,' she said. 'I think you're a bit worried. About what the others will think.'

He sat on the bed and suspended his hands between his knees. 'It's been a long time,' he said. 'Since we've all been together.'

'I know that.'

'The last time I saw Stephen Deane I was doped up in hospital. He came to visit me.'

She nodded.

'I don't remember much about it,' he said. 'But I probably wasn't at my best.'

'No,' she said. 'Probably not.'

'I just want to erase it all. To be the person I was, when I was with them. In the house. Before.'

'And what person was that?' she said, joining him on the bed.

'I've nearly forgotten,' he said.

'Michael,' she said softly. 'It's only normal. That's what people feel at reunions.'

'Yes. I wouldn't know, really.'

'But try and turn it into something positive.'

'How?'

'Tonight. Be yourself with them. Whatever self you are now. See how it feels.'

'Okay. And then?'

'And if it feels wrong, well then, maybe you can do something about it.'

'What do you mean?'

'If you want to change, I'm not going to stop you.'

He looked at her. She wore a deep-blue dress, and her hair hung long and free. Her blue eyes glistened.

'Just be yourself tonight,' she said softly. 'Be the self you are now.'

'Okay.'

'Because I love you. The way you are now.'

'Okay.'

He looked at her again. 'You're a treasure,' he said.

'I know,' she smiled.

Denis lay back on the bed. He wore a light summer suit of pale grey and an ash-grey shirt with silver cufflinks. He smiled smugly, pleased with himself. He looked over at Julia standing before the mirror. He leaned over and gave her a pat.

'Don't,' she said curtly.

'You look gorgeous,' he said.

'Thanks.'

She stood with her back to him.

'Can I give you a hand?' he asked.

'No, thanks,' she said. 'You should take your shoes off the bed.'

'They're clean. Brand-new. They've never been worn.'

'I see.'

She reached into the wardrobe and pulled out the new black dress. She stepped into it, pulling it up and inserting her arms into the sleeveless straps.

'Wowee,' he said. 'Gorgeous.'

'Thank you.'

'Ah, Julia,' he said. 'What's wrong?'

'Nothing's wrong. I'm just a little confused, that's all.'

'About what?'

She turned to face him. 'You've been in a shitty mood all week.

You won't talk about anything, you've left me totally in the dark about how you feel about this party. Then twenty minutes before we head off you perk up like a sunflower.'

'I'm only trying to get into the spirit of the thing.'

'You'd better put on your tie. We're supposed to be leaving now.'

'It's still early.'

'Not if we're supposed to meet Dolly Parton at eight.'

'Dolly Parton?'

She grabbed her bag and walked towards the door. 'They're all waiting downstairs. I'll get Jimmy organised.'

'Julia . . .'

'Yes?'

'I spent three years living with these people. We were great friends. And they're a grand crowd. I think you'll like them.'

'Yes. Fine.'

'So please, just try to lighten up a bit. You look lovely. You might even enjoy this.'

They looked at one another. 'Okay,' she nodded slowly. 'I'll try.'

He moved to embrace her.

'Denis, my makeup. You'd better hurry now.'

'Right. I'll be right down. I'll just put on my tie. Look, love, I'm sorry about this week. I've just been under some pressure . . .'

But she had already left the room.

CHAPTER 16

Denis unlocked the door and then stood aside as Julia led Jimmy into the hotel bedroom.

'Now,' she said. 'This is where you can sleep tonight. Pretty fancy, huh?'

'Yeah,' Jimmy replied.

'You've got two beds to bounce on,' Denis said. 'And your own telly.'

Julia pulled back the covers. 'Now get into your pyjamas and I'll snuggle you in.'

Denis and Julia watched as Jimmy undressed and climbed into bed. Then Denis looked at Julia. 'I can't remember the last time we were in a hotel room together,' he said.

'It was Athlone. Last year.'

'Was it? Oh, right. After that wedding.'

'Here's the flicker,' Julia said to Jimmy. 'You can watch for a while but then I'd like you to get some sleep.'

'Okay.'

'Will you be all right?' she asked.

'Yes, Mom.'

'We'll be back in a little while to see how you're doing.'

'Okay,' Jimmy replied with his eyes fixed on the television.

'If you need anything,' Denis said, 'just phone me. On the mobile.'

'Okay.'

'You know the number?'

'Yeah.'

'You have to dial nine to get an outside line . . .'

'Jimmy, honey,' Julia said, 'if you need anything, just dial zero for the front desk and ask for us. They'll come and find us.'

'Okay.'

'Goodbye then,' Julia said.

'Yeah. Bye.'

Julia and Denis looked at Jimmy sitting in bed, staring into the television. Then they looked at one another. They smiled together for the first time that day.

Julia shivered as they walked down the corridor.

'Are you okay?' Denis asked.

'Yes. Just a little nervous.'

'Don't be,' Denis said. 'You'll be grand. You're always good at parties.'

'This one's different.'

'I know,' he said. 'But you'll be grand.'

They paused outside the room.

'Ready?' he asked.

She nodded.

'Okay,' he said, swinging open the door. '*It's show time.*'

The room surprised Julia. She had expected a dark and masculine space, something sparse and functional, maybe a bit dirty. But it was light and airy, with an expanse of glass looking out over the River Finn. Outside the evening sun shone on a terrace laid with wrought-iron furniture. Inside, large round tables were set with white linen cloths, white china and art deco-style cutlery. A string quartet played in one corner, two men and two women dressed in black.

The room was only half filled but couples and small groups filed in steadily. Men wore jackets or suits with ties the colours of summer, and women wore dresses or skirts with short jackets and sandals. Many of the guests had deeply tanned skin. Couples stood alone looking stylish and aloof; some joined old friends with elaborate greetings. As Denis and Julia surveyed the scene a waitress offered them flutes of champagne.

'Do you know these people?' Julia whispered.

'Most of them. From years ago.'

'Oh my God,' she said. 'Look at Barry.'

'Where?'

'There,' she nodded. 'With that woman.'

Across the room Barry stood straight and tall in his navy blazer. A woman in her thirties faced him, explaining something, gesticulating as she spoke. He was backed up against a table.

'Our handsome son,' Julia said.

'He looks terrified. Does he need to be rescued?'

'Don't be silly,' she replied.

A couple approached them. He was heavy with a red face, and she was short and prim.

'Ah, Helen,' Denis said, bending forward to kiss her cheek. 'And Danny, how's the form? Great to see you both. You remember my wife, Julia?'

'Yes, how are you, Julia?' Helen said.

'The place is looking great,' Denis said to Danny.

'Ah, well, sure,' Danny replied. 'We do our best when company's expected.'

Julia remembered now: Helen was Denis's cousin, and her husband managed the hotel.

Helen smiled at Julia. 'He's been on pins all day,' she said. 'He's convinced there'll be some disaster.'

'It really is a lovely room,' Julia said.

'I only hope they'll behave themselves,' Danny said.

'Who?' Julia asked. 'The guests?'

'Ach, no,' Danny said dourly. 'The staff! Without me there in the kitchen, the carry-on . . .'

Another waitress appeared to fill their glasses.

'More champagne!' Julia said, raising her eyebrows. 'I'll be tipsy before the party even starts.'

'That's what it's here for,' Helen said. 'Brought in special. From the North.'

'Now, missus,' Danny said. 'Don't be telling our secrets.'

'And how are your lovely boys?' Helen asked.

'Sure they're great,' Denis said. 'Not a bother on them. You can see Barry just over there.'

'My God, what a fine thing he's become,' Helen said.

'You'd want to save him from Jacinta there,' Danny said. 'She'll have him across the table shortly.'

'And is your daughter coming tonight?' Julia asked. 'It's Emma, isn't it? Such a pretty name.'

'Aye,' Helen answered, 'but she's working of course. She'll help to serve the meal shortly, but then she'll be inside in the kitchen.'

'Oh, the poor thing,' Julia said. 'Slaving away while we're out here having fun!'

'Don't you worry about her,' Danny said. 'She's better off where she is.'

'Oh?' Denis said.

'You've no daughters yourselves,' Danny continued. 'But if you did, you'd know surely. Never let them out of your sight.'

'Danny!' Helen interjected.

'I'm telling you all,' Danny pronounced. 'And this is strictly for the record. Let your sons do what they will, but don't let your daughters out of your sight!'

Julia smiled. She liked Danny, and she liked Helen, and she was beginning to relax. She looked up at Denis as he launched into one of his stories about some Dublin hotel. He was so changed now, compared to the man she had married. Still handsome of course, with those blue O'Donnell eyes and that easy confidence. And he was still moody, still had his silent spells. But he never got angry any more. He didn't fuss about money, didn't seem to struggle within himself about who he was or what he was going to become. He had grown up, she thought. They had grown up together. She felt as if she was seeing this now for the first time, in this room, with these people.

Denis's people.

Maybe I was wrong, she thought. Maybe I overreacted today. About Denis and Catherine. And this party. This might even be fun.

She smiled at Denis, then, and laughed with the others at the climax of the story. She felt that maybe things would come together for them. Finally. At this party. Tonight.

*

'Hi. I'm Stephen Deane.'

'Oh, hello! I'm Julia O'Donnell – Denis's wife.'

'Glad you could make it.' He smiled blandly.

'Denis is, he's just outside,' Julia stammered. 'He forgot something. His phone I think. He'll be so pleased to see you again! Oh, this is my son, Barry.'

'Hello, Barry.'

'Hi.'

Stephen Deane didn't look the same as he did on screen, Julia thought. He seemed shorter and his face looked less perfect than it did in the movies. And yet there was something about him, some sort of poise, she thought. He had very direct eyes which seemed to assess you as he spoke. And very nice clothes, a black linen jacket and a soft cream shirt.

'My other son is upstairs,' she said. 'I mean, we got him a room, here, in the hotel. He'd so love to meet you.'

Stephen remained expressionless.

'It's so nice of you to have this party,' she continued. 'And such a pretty room!'

'Thanks,' he said. 'So. You married Denis.'

'Yes, I guess I did. Seventeen years ago.'

'That's a long time,' he said, looking at Barry.

'Yes, it is a long time,' she said. 'Especially in Hollywood terms.'

Stephen looked at her.

'I mean, gosh!' she said. 'Hollywood must be so exciting!'

'Yeah. It's a nice place.'

'I've never been there, but I've heard . . .'

'So how is dear old Denis?' Stephen interrupted.

'He's great, doing really well. I'm sure he'll be here in a minute . . .'

'He was the big man, you know,' Stephen said. 'Back at college.'

'Was he?'

'Yeah. Michael and Denis. The O'Donnell boys. They were the big men.'

'I guess you had a good time in that house of yours,' Julia said.

'Yes,' Stephen said. 'But they were the ringleaders. They acted like they owned the place. Real partners, you know? I haven't seen them in years.'

'Well, I'm sure you've been so busy . . .'

'And Denis is your dad, then,' Stephen said to Barry.

'Oh, yeah,' Barry said. 'I, I saw your movie. About the nuns.'

'Oh. Cool.'

'It, it was really great,' Barry said.

'Was that the one with Kim Taylor?' Julia asked. 'I've always admired her characters. She plays such strong women.'

'She's a funny girl,' Stephen said to Barry. 'You know that waterfall scene?'

'Yeah,' Barry nodded.

'Her clothes,' Stephen said. 'That nun's habit. It kept washing off her. In the spray. It was hilarious.'

'Really?' Julia said.

'Yeah,' Stephen said, looking again at Barry. 'Every time we went into the waterfall her clothes fell off. We had to keep sending guys down the river to get them back. It was quite funny.'

'I'm sure Denis will be here in a minute,' Julia smiled nervously.

Just then a tall, thin woman with bare shoulders took hold of Stephen's arm.

'Stephen,' she said languidly into his eyes. 'I'm starving. Tell everyone to sit down.'

'Okay,' he said. 'Well. Nice to meet you.'

'Yes,' Julia said. 'And thanks so much for having us!'

Julia watched, then, as they circled the room, asking people to take their seats. Stephen's girlfriend stared blankly at every guest who passed, but said nothing.

Michael sipped water from a heavy glass and surveyed the people seated around the table.

This is us, he thought. Here, again. At this table. Twenty years later.

He set his glass down, trying to focus on the scene and take in the conversations. Mary Moran sat beside him, her hair pulled straight back from her broad face, her heavy arms covered in Indian cotton the colour of maize.

'But in the end I just had to watch him go,' she was saying. 'I tried so hard to make it work, really gave it my all . . .'

Mary tried to fix him with her eyes. Michael shook his head in sympathy but then broke away from her consuming gaze. He looked at the faces around the table. He was trying to feel the depth of them, to sense in their faces the time that had passed. Those years long ago, the electric leap to the present. The synapse of time.

Stephen Deane sat across the table, relaxed and self-assured, like California. Everything about him was California. An expensive shirt open at the neck. His new California accent that carried across the table. Even his hair was California, so perfectly California.

Beside him sat a blonde girl with a deep tan and thin shoulders. She had a wide red mouth that never fully closed and dangling gold earrings with a pattern that led to nothing. She hardly ever spoke, simply stared, and nodded, and stared again.

My God, Michael thought. Our sensitive Stephen. He's become a photo from a magazine.

Michael thought back to that house, to that sofa where Stephen used to sit holding his mug of tea in his lap. That nervous boy in faded black jeans. A boy who couldn't memorise his lines. He thought he loved Shakespeare but couldn't grasp what it all meant.

Michael took another sip of his water. His eyes moved across to Catherine. Denis's Catherine. She had changed very little. Those large, direct eyes. Her hair, still a wilderness. And that creamy, welcoming bosom, draped in black. She sat beside Barry. Denis's son. God, if that boy only knew who she was, what she had done with his father!

Poor Barry, Michael thought as he watched them in conversation. Look at him there, averting his eyes from that cleavage. Polite young man.

Then, momentarily, Michael felt afraid. Looking at Catherine, remembering the way she used to make him feel. Manipulated. Trapped. Like Barry was now. A sense of anxiety came over Michael about what had happened, the way she had tried to seduce him, the confusion in his mind still so vivid, such a strong image.

He looked over at Denis and a memory flashed upon him: Denis and Catherine kissing on the stairs as he entered the room, seeing Catherine looking up at him as she wrapped her arms around Denis's neck, a cold emptiness in her eyes. What was that vacuity in her face? Boredom? Or deep satisfaction?

He looked down at the table and inhaled deeply. Mary Moran droned on beside him, unaware that he had removed himself from a large swathe of her narrative.

'God, when I think back,' she continued. 'What might have been, Michael. What *might* have *been*! He destroyed everything for me, Michael. Oh Michael, you've no *idea*.'

She was drinking steadily. He could smell the wine on her breath. Her hand brushed against his as she spoke. He nodded again in sympathy.

He looked over at Julia, watching her with Dr Jackson. Interrogating him about his dead wife. Funny, he thought. How she enters so freely into his private life. But he doesn't seem to mind.

Mary Moran continued to narrate about her abusive boss, and then another man she met on a trip to Brazil. Michael nodded, tried to listen. But then he became aware of Anne sitting beside him. He could sense his wife there even though he couldn't see her, even though Mary would not let him turn to see Anne, sitting alone, speaking to no one. And for a moment it cut him in half, he felt divided between two women, two times: the people who once mattered to him, and Anne, who was now all he had. She, now, was the person who could help him stay here, in the present, where he needed to be: now, and one, and together. Not in the past. Not back there.

And just then a picture welled up before him, a powerful image. It came to him the way things used to come to him back in college. A vision: a group of people gathered together before some sort of event, like 'The Last Supper', an array of people at a table, their faces twisted with age. But the bodies, yes, yes, their naked bodies were young and vital, fresh broad flesh on show below their aged, wizened faces. Cold ageing heads on flushed, pink bodies, still, captured at a moment of gesture and surprise and revelation. The image was coming to him, blotting out Mary Moran and the table and the guests and the room. And Michael allowed the image to suffuse his mind as the light ebbed from the evening outside the windows, and the river flowed darker and fuller, and Mary Moran's story continued beside him, the trials of her years colouring these faces, tinting the room.

Barry looked nervously at the cutlery. He was perspiring and he wanted to take off his jacket. He wished he wasn't here at this stupid party. His dad had said that some people his age were going to be here but there were only two little kids as far as he could see and everyone else was at least forty.

He tried to remember what his mom said about the cutlery: Start from the outside. But he had used his soup spoon for the melon and then they took it away and now they were coming around with soup and his spoon was gone.

He was sweating. He tried to think of something to say to the woman beside him. She had a black dress on and lots of hair and makeup and jewellery. He was reaching for his glass for more water and he bumped her arm.

'Sorry,' he said.

'Not at all. You're Barry then, aren't you?'

'Yes.'

'You don't remember me. I'm Catherine. We met last week in town.'

'Oh yeah. Hi.'

'I knew your father,' she said, smiling at him provocatively.

'Really?'

'Back when he was a bit older than you are now.'

'Oh.'

'He was quite a ladies' man back then.'

'Oh.'

'Quite a ladies' man indeed. And what about you? I suppose you've a string of girls, have you?' She tilted her head sideways in challenge.

'No,' Barry swallowed. 'None.'

'I see. Well I'm sure that won't last long. So what do you do with yourself, then, if there are no girls around?'

She turned towards him a bit in her chair. He noticed, for the first time, that she had full round breasts.

'Well,' he said. 'I run a little.'

'How interesting. Tell me more. How far do you run?'

'I, well, not very far. Middle distance.'

Just then a voice came from his right shoulder. 'Sorry, sir, but could I serve your soup, please?'

Something happened then. A shock. Something. That voice. He jerked his head.

'Oh, mind now,' she cautioned. 'Wouldn't want an accident, sir, now would we?'

And Barry turned to see Emma as she leaned over him and set

a bowl of soup on his plate. She straightened and gave him a queer little smile, and proceeded to serve Catherine. Barry could feel the blood rush to his face, his heart working like a man skipping rope. Emma moved around the table, now standing behind his Uncle Michael, teasing him about his tie. She didn't look up, though, didn't respond to Barry's gaze. Then she finished serving and turned to leave the room.

Barry turned in his seat to face Catherine. She smiled at him openly, as if she could read his thoughts, with those red lips, that abundant black hair and that ironic, challenging smile.

The soup was finished. The guests had begun with champagne when they arrived and now the first empty bottles of wine were being removed from the tables and replaced with fresh stock. The string quartet continued to play but the volume of conversation had increased so the music couldn't really be heard. Occasionally the noise levels rose, as a joke told by someone at a particular table reached its peak, and the laughter surged and filled the room, and people seated at the other tables turned their heads momentarily and smiled as if in harmony with their fellow guests, and then turned back to their places.

The doors to the terrace had been opened but there was no breeze and the room was becoming uncomfortable. Some of the men had removed their jackets and placed them over the backs of their chairs. They told stories of golf or sailing or politics to the other men around them: some were old friends and some were just acquaintances. The women too talked to one another, holding one another with their eyes as they discussed some mutual friend or explored some situation, a disease or an indiscretion or some problem of behaviour to be assessed for right or wrong. At one table a twelve-year-old girl sat quietly between her overweight parents. At another a ten-year-old boy made everyone around him nervous as he tried to balance a wine glass on his knife.

In the background, the staff were busy preparing to present the dinner. The buffet tables had been cleared of drinks and laid with stiff, clean white cloths and steel dish holders and heat lamps to keep the food warm. Stacks of dinner plates appeared like round towers at the end of the display and a woman carried out a heavy tray with a pyramid of cutlery wrapped in white napkins.

Now the kitchen girls began to appear carrying in an array of salads and starters: filo pastry squares stuffed with crabmeat; carrot and hazelnut salad seasoned with red-wine vinegar; couscous dotted with red currants and nuts; a smoked trout terrine; a tray of spinach and cheese tartlets; several containers of cream sauces and a fragrant raspberry vinaigrette. A rustic basket woven of dark reeds held breads of whole wheat and tomato and olive and sweet breads stuffed with raisins. Another basket displayed round and oblong rolls, fresh from the oven and dusted with white flour.

Then a team of older women and young men in chefs' outfits processed in with the hot courses: roast potatoes and potatoes boiled with their skins on and steaming leeks and carrots dusted with golden sugar and seasoned rice yellow with saffron. Then there appeared an earthenware dish containing chicken breasts in a fragrant creamy lemon sauce. And then followed the greatest of all: a large dressed salmon on a platter surrounded by lemon slices and colourful stuffed tomatoes and sprigs of fresh herbs, wheeled in by a tall chef exuding confidence and pride in his work.

And suddenly the aroma of food filled the room. Women

turned towards the food and men leaned back from the table or craned their necks over the tops of their neighbours, trying to glimpse the dinner that lay ahead. A row of hotel staff took their places behind the buffet table. Then, as the last dish was set down, the hostess nodded to the first table of guests. People began to stand then, and a queue formed, it was slow and orderly, and the scene was governed by a mood of pleasant expectation.

A waitress bent down to remove Denis's empty dinner plate. He looked up at her and smiled.

'I didn't enjoy that at all,' he said.

'Oh dear, I'm so sorry,' she replied. 'I can see you were suffering.'

'Don't pay any attention to him,' Julia said. 'It was really lovely.'

'Thanks very much now,' the waitress said as she moved on.

Julia rested her hand on Denis's.

'How are you?' she whispered.

'Grand. And how about you?'

'Fine. I'm really enjoying this.'

'Good,' he smiled.

'And look at the desserts!' she said, nodding towards the buffet. 'This is like a food marathon.'

'We're a hearty folk and we enjoy a grand big meal,' Denis said. 'Will we go up?'

'I'm just going to the ladies. Bring me back something.'

'What would you like?'

'Surprise me,' she said.

Denis watched Julia walk away from the table in her black

dress. Then he looked outside to where the remains of the evening still hung in the sky.

'Denis?' Catherine mouthed from across the table. 'Are you going for dessert?'

'Aye,' he nodded as he pushed back his chair.

Catherine stood and Denis followed as she crossed the room. She walked lazily in her high shoes and Denis looked at her shape as she walked before him. He remembered the way she used to saunter when they were out together long ago. Then he felt self-conscious for a moment, as though people were watching them as they crossed the room.

'Isn't it amazing,' Catherine said, 'that so many people could make it tonight?'

'Yes. It's a great turnout.'

'It's almost like fate. Old friends gathering here. Looking over the River Finn, watching the water pass by.'

'Yes.'

'It makes me feel, I don't know, as if something is happening.'

'Yes?'

'Something very powerful,' she said dreamily. 'Very freeing.'

'Right.'

She looked at Denis with her eyes wide. 'Or maybe it's just the wine,' she laughed.

They stood before the buffet table assessing the array of sweets.

'My God,' Catherine said. 'Would you look at this spread! I didn't think Irish hotels had come so far. What have we got here? What a lovely cheese cake, it smells like amaretto! Isn't it divine? And look at this confection of chocolate. Gorgeous!'

'Yes, isn't it just.'

'And I want it *all*!' she laughed in her alto voice.

The waitress served Catherine thin slices of several tarts and a messy dollop of tiramisu. Then Denis took two plates, one for himself and one for Julia, and requested a sample of desserts on each.

'Oh, look, it's such a lovely evening. Let's sit outside, shall we? I want to inhale that fresh Donegal air.'

Denis glanced over at the table but Julia hadn't returned yet. 'Okay,' he said.

They found a small table on the patio and sat down to eat their dessert. Catherine had put two glasses of wine between the plates. She dabbed at her mouth with her serviette. The dark water of the Finn flowed behind them, inaudible above the hum of the party.

'That was scrummy,' she said, setting down her fork. 'Really delicious. Do you still smoke?'

'No,' he replied. 'Just the occasional cigar.'

'Good for you,' she said, rummaging in her bag. 'I've given it up a thousand times. But never for more than a week.'

She lit a cigarette with a gold lighter and then leaned back in her chair, blowing smoke upwards. 'Ireland, Denis,' she sighed. 'You really can't beat the auld sod.'

'You think so?'

'Oh, yes. Sure where would you get this? The people, the food. The *countryside*. Compared with England, Denis. It's so relaxed. I've only been back here a week but I feel like I've left London behind forever.'

'It's tough, that London grind,' Denis said knowingly.

'Oh, dreadful. Mind you, the money's good, and the taxes are so much lower. And I have friends there now, really close friends. I've been on the phone to them all week. Even tonight I've got three text messages so far. They all hope I'm enjoying myself – as if I wouldn't be!'

'That's great.'

'But, all the same. My life. It's grand, it really is. But it doesn't compare.'

'Compare?'

'I can't forget those days at college. There was such an intensity about that time. Those horrible grey walls at UCD. That dreadful antiseptic smell in the loos!'

He laughed.

'And then tonight,' she said. 'Seeing everyone here. It brings it all back. So many memories! It's lovely to see Michael again, and he's looking so well, and his wife is *lovely*. And as for Stephen Deane, *well*! It's unbelievable. It simply beggars belief to see how far he's come.'

'It's like a fairytale,' Denis said.

'Sure that man wouldn't be what he is today if it weren't for us,' she said.

'What do you mean?'

'We helped him, Denis. We helped each other. We were a great team, the lot of us.'

'Yes. We were, I suppose.'

'It's so sad, really,' she continued. 'The way things have to change.'

'Yes. But things have to move on.'

'But why? Why do we have to lose that feeling? That *intensity*?'

'What do you mean?'

'You *must* remember. The way it was, back then. It was fantastic. It was *life*.'

'Well, yes . . .'

'Ah, Denis. The parties! The studying! *Learning*! Can you really tell me you've learned anything since then? Anything that stayed with you? Anything that has *mattered*?'

'Well, I don't know now.'

She leaned forward, speaking quietly but directly.

'And there was love. Do you remember *love*? Do you remember what it felt like, to really love the people around you?'

He paused. 'I'd have to think back,' he said. 'I don't really think about it much any more.'

'But you can't deny what happened. It's with you, it's still there. It's *part* of you.'

He looked at her.

'God,' she continued. 'This life, at whatever age we are today – what *is* it? What does it consist of? Getting up. Getting dressed. Going into a bloody office, sitting at a bloody desk all day. Coming home again knackered, falling into bed. A week goes by, you lose a month here, a month there. The years pass. You meet people, you forget them. Good God, it's not the same as it was.'

'I don't know,' he said. 'It's not so bad, now.'

'Oh, God! You poor man. It's even worse than I thought.'

'Sorry?'

'I shouldn't, but I really have to say this. You've changed. You really have changed! You were so *hungry* back then. You were so *driven*. You wanted to throttle the world, you were going to get out there and hit the States and make it happen *big time*. I remember you, Denis. I remember everything about you.'

'Catherine . . .' Denis said hesitantly.

'I remember what you were like, with that fire in your eyes. You were divine, Denis. I still measure the men I meet now against the man you were then. I really do.'

'Catherine, look, I . . .'

'When I saw you last week,' she said softly, 'I really couldn't believe my eyes. There you were with your wife and your boys and your middle-class job and your tired face – I was shocked. I was really *shocked*. I just wanted to *rekindle* you. I wanted to shake you up and make you that man again. *That man you used to be.*'

He looked at her. Her wild hair brushed against her neck and her eyes were bright with emotion. He turned from her and looked out across the water for a moment, inhaling the evening air. Then he turned to her again.

'Catherine.'

'Yes?'

'I have Julia's dessert here. I think I'd better go inside.'

A look of disbelief crossed her face. 'Denis,' she challenged. 'You can't be serious.'

'I'm afraid I am.'

'Dear God. Did you hear what I was just saying? I've just said a whole string of dreadful things to you. I've accused you of becoming old and boring and lifeless.'

'I know. I heard you.'

'You're not really going to let me away with it?' she pleaded. 'You're not just going to walk away?'

'I'm sorry, Catherine. All that was a long time ago. This isn't really the place for this conversation.'

She stared at him, then, like a teacher looking at a guilty child.

'Maybe I was wrong,' she said finally. 'You haven't changed a bit. Same old Denis. Evasive as ever.'

He looked at her, his face as empty as if he had been slapped. For a moment a deep silence settled between them, and he could hear the river flowing gently behind the terrace. But there was a noise then, a rough scrape as a chair was moved across the flagstones. Denis looked up to see Julia approach their table.

'Oh, so *here* you are!' Julia said. 'I *wondered* where everyone had gone to!'

Her voice sang up and down the register.

'And I was waiting at our table for my *dessert*. Well, it's kind of *chilly* out here, don't you think? Should we go inside, honey?'

Julia cast Catherine an icy smile.

'Oh, dear,' Catherine said, looking up into Julia's eyes. 'I'm so sorry. I didn't mean to deprive you of your dessert. But I simply *had* to speak to this husband of yours and find out what he's been *doing* with himself all these years.'

'Yes,' Julia said. 'It's so nice for old friends to see each other again.'

The two women shared bitterly forced smiles.

'Right,' Catherine said. 'We'd better scurry back to our little nests, then, shall we?'

Julia stood aside to let Catherine pass. She reached behind for Denis's hand. He could feel the nervousness in her cold, stiff fingers.

'I was only aideen years old,' she said in an Australian accent. 'I was a bit young to be awl on my own. But life on the beach was so great! Awl we did was pahdy pahdy pahdy awl the time!'

Michael nodded his support. Stephen Deane had left the table and his girlfriend had turned to Michael and begun telling him all about her life. He didn't know her name.

'There jist seemed to be this gang of us, and we became really, really close, awl of us. We shared everything, everything we had, awl summer long. I've niver experienced anything like it. It was jist so amazing . . .'

Anne was bored. Everyone else had left the table. She'd had a few glasses of wine and now she was bored. She knew that Michael would listen to that stick insect drone on for hours and he would give her the impression that he was fascinated by every word. She was an attractive girl with huge eyes and far too much skin on display.

Maybe Michael did enjoy listening to her, Anne thought. Good for him. But she was bored. She looked around the room and spotted Helen alone at a table in the far corner.

'Michael,' she said. 'I'm going over to see Helen.'

'Okay,' he said.

'Come and join me,' she whispered. 'Unless you get a better offer . . .'

Then she stood and walked across the room.

'Ah, Anne,' Helen greeted her. 'I haven't seen you for *ages*.'

'I know. It's terrible. When I think how it was when you lived nearby . . .'

'Ah, sure I know,' Helen said. 'We knew *all* your news then. And now we don't see you at all. You'd think we'd moved to Siberia.'

Anne smiled. 'How's Danny?'

'Sure he's the same as ever,' Helen said. 'Spends all his time at the hotel. They're wild busy now that all the function rooms are open. They're doing fourteen weddings this month.'

'*Fourteen?*'

'Aye. Sure he's five next weekend alone. They're coming from everywhere. It's like Las Vegas.'

Anne looked out through the windows to the river. She saw Denis and Catherine sitting at the edge of the patio. Helen followed her gaze.

'Is that Denis on the terrace?' Helen said. 'I left my glasses at home.'

'Yes, at the far table.'

'And who's that girl he's with?'

'Her name is Catherine something. Apparently she grew up in Ballyshannon. They were doing a line back in college.'

'Oh, dear,' Helen said. 'She's a grand big girl. Julia won't like that one bit.'

'No, I'd say she won't.'

'Julia's a lovely person,' Helen said.

'Do you think so?'

'Oh aye. So friendly. Very down-to-earth.'

'Mmm, I suppose she is.'

'Oh, Anne, *everyone* says so. They're a lovely couple, so they are.'

'Yes, they are,' Anne agreed. 'They seem to be doing well for themselves.'

'Oh, aye,' Helen said. 'Doing *very* well. But of course she's had her share of troubles, just like the rest of us.'

'Has she?'

'Aye. But sure you know the story.'

'No – what story's that?'

'Sure you were there on the day! When she came to the school!'

'Yes, I was there. She came to my classroom.'

'Well, you know the story so.'

'No, Helen, I don't know a thing. All I know is that we invited her round to the house for tea. She was supposed to spend the night. But then she phoned and said she needed to go back to Dublin.'

'Aye,' Helen said.

'And I know I shouldn't really care about these things. But she never even *apologised*. She just left us a message on the machine and then she didn't arrive.'

'But Anne, surely you know what happened? I told you myself.'

'I'm telling you, I don't know anything. What *is* this famous story of yours?'

'It was on the day after she visited the school. I was at the hospital, you know. Doing my voluntary work.'

'Yes?'

'Well, as you know, I help with the admissions at the front desk. When I checked the records for the day before, I saw her name, right there in the book. *Julia O'Donnell, Kenilworth Square, Rathmines, Dublin 6.*'

'At the *hospital*?'

'Aye. She'd gone in the night before. Then she was let go first thing in the morning.'

'What was wrong with her?'

'She'd lost a wee baby, poor thing.'

'Oh God . . .' Anne inhaled sharply.

'But surely you knew that already?'

'How could I know anything if you didn't tell me?'

'But I *did* tell you. Sure I phoned you as soon as I got home. I shouldn't have, but I did it anyway.'

'Helen, you never did.'

'Oh, maybe it was Michael so. That's it. I must have been speaking to Michael.'

'Michael?'

'Aye, now that I think of it, it *was* Michael. I told him that Julia lost a wee baby. I really shouldn't have told anyone, but I thought since it was Denis's wife and all. It must have been on account of all the travelling she does.'

Anne looked down at the table as the story began to sink in. Why Julia had cancelled the visit. And why she never spoke of it. Tears came into Anne's eyes for a moment as she thought back to how she had been treating Julia, how she had been shutting her out since she arrived. But then she blinked the tears back.

'I suppose Michael,' Helen was saying, 'well, maybe he just forgot to tell you. Sometimes he's a bit . . .'

'Absentminded,' Anne supplied. 'It's the medication.'

'Aye,' said Helen.

Anne suddenly felt a surge of protectiveness towards Julia, as if she realised for the first time that such a confident, successful, attractive woman could herself be vulnerable, and struggle with circumstances, and suffer pain, just as Anne had in her life.

'Oh God,' she said softly. 'I've been so bloody awful.'

It was the in-between time, the indeterminate space when the meal had concluded and the next stage had yet to begin. The serving dishes had been cleared and the tables at the end of the room were being dismantled somewhat noisily to make room for the dance floor. Heavy black sound equipment, hidden during the meal beneath white sheets, was now uncovered and pulled across the floor into prominent display. Members of the band rushed in as if just on time, carrying their instruments and laughing comfortably amongst themselves, disregarding the guests milling around them.

Julia had left the room to check on Jimmy upstairs and Denis was on his own. He stood at the edge of the room surveying the guests. He couldn't see Barry anywhere and assumed he had found someone to talk to. He fumbled in his jacket for a cigar, but then he noticed that no one was smoking around him so he stopped. He looked again around the room.

He felt on edge, unnerved by his conversation with Catherine. Such a leap through time, as if a conversation begun twenty years ago, when Michael had first been admitted to hospital, had somehow continued, without interruption, here tonight: the same attraction, the same danger, the same tone of accusation. And then Julia arriving in the middle of it all, taking the scene in and immediately icing up, as if reacting to a cold wind. She hadn't displayed that intense jealousy in years. He felt stupid and weak and irritated by the whole event.

He decided again to take a cigar from his jacket. He lit it and inhaled deeply. He put his hand in his trousers pocket and tried to appear relaxed. He wondered where Barry had got to.

He looked across the room and saw Mary Moran speaking earnestly to Stephen Deane. Apart from greeting him at the dinner table, Denis hadn't spoken to Stephen all evening. Denis felt he should go, now, and get an autograph for Jimmy. It was time to get the whole thing over with.

He caught Stephen's eye for a moment and mustered a smile of recognition. Stephen returned his attention to Mary Moran, nodding in sympathy with her long story.

Denis hesitated. He knew that asking for Stephen's autograph was in effect asking for forgiveness for what had happened twenty years ago. It was an opportunity to finally lay that unpleasant memory to rest. But he couldn't bring himself to move. He felt overcome with a sense of shame, as if he had been exposed as a weak, small-minded little man.

He pulled again at his cigar, but then he stubbed it out in an ashtray on a table and wiped his mouth with a serviette. He straightened his jacket and prepared to cross the room. But as he moved forward Stephen's girlfriend appeared and took Stephen's arm, leading him away from the bar and leaving Mary Moran open-mouthed, cut off in mid-sentence.

Mary looked up to see Denis. She realised he had seen the entire episode. She smiled and gave him an embarrassed little shrug, and then took a long sip from her drink.

Barry was outside in the hotel car park. He put his hands in his pockets and strolled back and forth. He was bored. He wanted to leave the party and walk back to the house, or find a taxi somewhere, if they even had taxis up here. The windows of the hotel were open and he could hear voices issuing from inside the lounge: men telling jokes, women laughing.

'He *didn't*!'

'I'm telling you he *did*!'

'No *way*! Not when she was standing right *beside him*!'

'I'm telling you I saw the *whole fucking thing*!'

He shivered. He had left his jacket inside. His wallet was in his jacket, so he couldn't get a taxi even if there was a taxi. He cursed. He felt tired, deflated. He hadn't seen Emma since the beginning of the party. He didn't think he would get to see her again. And now he was stuck out here with nowhere to go and no one he particularly wanted to talk to.

He went back into the hotel feeling like a guilty child. He entered the function room and scanned the crowd. A dance band was tuning up in the corner where the quartet had been. He began to walk back to his previous place, but then he saw his Auntie Anne sitting alone at a corner table, waving him over. She had a glass of wine in front of her and there was a half-empty bottle on the table. As he sat down she smiled at him with parental concern in her face.

'Now, Barry,' she said. 'How are you?'

'Fine, thanks.'

She frowned, studying him. 'You're not really, though,' she said.

Barry watched as she sipped her wine and set down her glass. 'I saw you,' she said. 'Earlier tonight. When you saw Emma.'

She paused then to gauge his reaction. 'I know all about it,' she said softly. 'Emma told me. We were great pals, once upon a time.'

She paused again. Barry looked at her nervously.

'What age are you, Barry?'

'Sixteen.'

'Right. And how long do you think you'll stay sixteen?'

'Ah, another few months.'

'No,' she said. 'That's not what I meant.'

'Sorry?'

She leaned towards him, speaking just above a whisper.

'You're a fine young man. You only have this time once. Use your time, Barry. Be yourself. Say what you want. *Do* what you want. Don't wait for things to happen.'

She looked as if she was expressing something of utmost importance.

'Emma is in the kitchen, just through there. She's hovering. She's waiting for you. You weren't here, she couldn't find you. If you don't go now, she'll go home. And that will be the end of it. Go on. Get into that kitchen and find her. I'll deal with your mum and dad. *Just go.*'

Barry sat back. He looked around behind him. Then he looked back at his Auntie Anne for reassurance.

'But listen, Barry. One last thing.'

'Yes?'

'You're still young. But she's young too. You wouldn't . . .' She paused, then, searching his face. 'No,' she said softly to herself. 'You're a good lad. Go on, for God's sake!'

He looked at her, and looked around the room, and then returned his face to her imploring gaze.

A few minutes later the band began to play, a four-piece with a guitar-player who sang country tunes in a nasal tenor voice. As soon as the music started, couples stepped onto the floor and began to dance. The tunes were slow as the band started off, the music just loud enough to inhibit conversation. Couples on the dance floor whispered breathy words directly into one another's ears and the intimacy of their voices felt like skin touching skin.

Julia and Denis had just sat down at their table. Julia still felt nervous and out of place. Seeing Catherine made her feel threatened, almost physically. She looked over at Denis. He was studying the dancers on the floor. He looked distant and sad, as if trying to reconstruct a memory from the movement of the bodies. She reached across to touch his arm. He turned to her with a tired, questioning look. But then he comprehended her meaning, and he stood.

The music was slow and relaxed but they hadn't danced together for years and Julia felt self-conscious in her movements. Denis's hands around her waist felt stiff and she could smell smoke on the lapel of his jacket. Dancing with him now she felt small and insignificant.

'How are you, my love?' he said.

'I don't know.'

'Tired?' he asked.

'Yes. I think so.'

And she realised that she was tired. Her brain was worn out from making polite conversation and attending to everyone around her. She tried to stop thinking for a moment. She leaned into Denis and ignored the singer's nasal voice. She felt the slow beat and moved with the rhythm, in tempo with Denis's body. And after a few steps she began to relax, feeling safe in a womb of warmth and sound.

But she could still sense something between them. They weren't together. Denis was dreaming, he was elsewhere again, just as he had been all week. They had been doing well as the party progressed but now something was there between them. Perhaps it was Catherine. Something, she sensed, had sent them both back into their solitary, separate selves.

She wanted to get Denis back, to be together with him, to enjoy this dance together now. She knew they would be tired tomorrow and the boys would need looking after, and then they would face the long drive home in the afternoon. And so now was the time, now was their chance to connect, to synchronise, if just for a few moments, these few precious moments in this strange and topsy-turvy week.

'So,' she said, forcing a smile. 'You've done well tonight.'

'What do you mean?'

'Two adoring women,' she said. 'At the same party.'

He looked across the room. 'I'm sorry,' he said.

'For what?'

'I don't know. For speaking to Catherine. For leaving you alone at the table.'

'I'm a big girl,' she said. 'I can handle it.'

They danced for a few minutes amongst the couples like themselves, talking, or not talking, moving together with the slow beat.

'Denis,' Julia said.

'Yes?'

'Are you still . . . attracted? To Catherine?'

'That was a long time ago.'

'Yes, I know, but . . .'

'I left her long before I met you. We were finished.'

'Were you?'

'And tonight,' he said. 'Outside. On the terrace. Before you came out.'

'Yes?'

'We were finished then, too.'

She looked up at him. He smiled sadly. 'Are you jealous?' he asked quietly.

'Should I be?'

'No, my love. Not at all.'

'Good,' she said.

They danced for a few moments without speaking.

'But, Denis,' she said.

'Yes.'

'Last week.'

'Yes?'

'I was jealous. Of those women in the newspaper. In their underwear.'

'That's okay,' he said. 'Sure I'm nearly over them now.'

She groaned and squeezed his back with her nails. Then they danced silently for a few moments.

'Are we getting old?' he asked.

'A little.'

'And does it show?'

She looked up at him. She sensed in his eyes something incongruous, out of tune with their surroundings.

'What's wrong?' she asked.

'Ach, nothing I suppose. I just hope I'm not . . .'

'Not what?'

'Finished,' he said. 'Washed out. Too old to change.'

'To change?'

'I just hope I'm not too old to appreciate what we have.'

She looked up at him again. 'You're the most exciting, best-looking man at this party.'

He smiled sadly. 'Then why do I feel this way?'

'What way?'

'As if the best things in life have already happened.'

'There's still time for more,' she said softly. 'There's still time to do whatever you want to do.'

'Is there?'

'Whatever you want,' she whispered, smiling up at him. 'But, Denis?'

'Yes?'

'Just remember,' she said. 'I want to come too.'

He looked down at her, and he sensed her body moving with him, slowly and in time with the music. She leaned into him then and they danced, very close, for what seemed a very long time.

The music changed tempo then and picked up energy. The drummer broke into a heavy driving rhythm and the singer let out a hoot. Julia and Denis made eye contact one last time on the dance floor and then walked back towards their table, moving carefully between the bouncing bodies. They held hands.

Anne and Michael were sitting together at a table across the room, and Anne waved to Julia to join them.

'Bravo,' Anne said. 'That was lovely.'

'And what about you young people?' Denis asked. 'Are you not going to dance at all?'

'It's my fault,' Anne said. 'I can recite my lines to a packed theatre but I won't dance in public.'

'Oh, Anne,' Julia said. 'And I thought you'd be a good dancer.'

Anne caught Julia's eye then, as if about to ask a question. But then she looked at the two brothers. 'Now, gentlemen,' she announced. 'You two fine specimens should go outside. Cool down a bit. Smoke a big dirty cigar or do whatever you men do. I am going to get my friend Julia here a lovely cold drink. And we're going to have a little chat.'

'Oh,' Julia said. 'How nice . . .'

'Now, gents,' Anne said, 'off you go. Your services are no longer required. We'll call you when we need you.'

Denis appealed to Michael, and then tried Julia.

'You heard her,' Julia said. 'Off you go.'

The two brothers shrugged and stood to leave the table. Anne waved with her fingers and watched as the men walked out onto the patio.

'Now my dear,' Anne said. 'What can I get you?'

'Nothing at all,' Julia said. 'I'm just fine.'

'Are you sure? I'm having another glass of wine.'

'You go right ahead,' Julia said. 'There's water here, I'll just pour myself a glass.'

'Okay. So. Cheers.'

'And cheers to you,' Julia said, a bit formally.

'I love wine,' Anne said, setting her glass down.

'Oh, yes. I do too.'

'I usually have a glass of wine in the evenings,' Anne said. 'We don't lead extravagant lives. But it's the one indulgence I allow myself.

'Some doctors say it's good for you.'

'I don't know,' Anne said. 'It helps me unwind. It's just, well, so quiet. In the house. Especially in the evenings.'

'Quiet?'

'Oh God, yes. You should sit there some night in that room. In that house, way up in the hills, surrounded by those massive trees. Sometimes Michael puts on his music, but most nights he's content just to read. For hours. It's so deathly quiet.'

'Yes, I suppose it is.'

'I grew up in a tiny, crowded house,' Anne said. 'There were seven of us all packed into three bedrooms. There were always people about, always something on. But now, with Michael, it's just the two of us. And sometimes I wish there was a bit more life about the place.'

'Yes,' Julia said, as if unsure where the conversation was leading.

'I mean, we do have friends that call now and again. But Michael gets tired in the evenings. And some people are uncomfortable with his disability.'

'Yes, I see.'

'And then,' Anne hesitated as she scanned the room. 'Sometimes, when people do call, I get nervous. I get a bit defensive. I'm protective, maybe, of Michael. And of myself too.'

Anne looked meaningfully at Julia then. 'And so sometimes I mistrust people. People who might, well, have the best of intentions.'

The two women looked at one another.

'There are so many things,' Anne said finally, 'that I've wanted to say to you.'

'Oh?'

'We've been so far apart. I don't think you understand what it's like, living with Michael.'

'No, I'm sure I don't.'

'I mean, don't get me wrong. I'm so happy with Michael. I love him more than I ever imagined I could love anyone. But there are so many things that seem so complicated, and yet for other people it all seems so simple . . .'

'Do you mean, like, children?'

'Yes. God, yes. I think about it all the time. I want children, Julia, so badly. Sometimes it keeps me up at night. But I don't know about Michael. I have to work, I can't be home during the day to look after them. And I don't know what it would be like for Michael. He's so up and down.'

'I know. I'm sorry.'

'But, you know, maybe I'm wrong. Maybe he'd be grand. I just don't know what to do.'

'Anne, maybe there's something you're exaggerating about Michael.'

'Oh?'

'The ups and downs,' Julia said. 'I think, maybe it's an O'Donnell thing.'

'An O'Donnell thing?'

'Oh, God yes. Denis is as moody as a spring day.'

'Really?'

'You've no idea.'

'I'd never have known,' Anne said. 'We really should compare notes more often.'

'We should,' Julia said, nodding in agreement. 'We really should.'

'It's so good to talk. I'm so glad you're here. I've been such an awful cow to you!'

Julia smiled sympathetically.

'I didn't get it,' Anne continued. 'When I met you first, when you couldn't visit us last year. Even when you arrived yesterday. I just didn't understand. I just couldn't see your good side.'

'My good side?' Julia flushed. 'Maybe I should show you my bad side.'

'Maybe,' Anne said thoughtfully. 'But you know, at least I've shown you my bad bits first.'

They smiled at one another, then, as the music droned behind them, and the last of the evening slipped from the sky. And Julia took Anne's hand, squeezing it briefly. And for a moment tears glistened in Anne's eyes as she smiled.

They looked outside then. Beyond the windows the two brothers were leaning against the balustrade and looking out over the river. Smoke was rising from Denis's cigar. They appeared to be deep in conversation.

'That's probably the first time they've talked,' Julia said.

'I know,' Anne said.

'For years.'

'It's so good to see them together,' Anne said. 'God, just look at them. Our O'Donnell boys. Aren't they gorgeous?'

Julia looked at them too, and was about to laugh, about to quip something about their two men. But then a worried expression crossed her face.

'Oh my God,' she said, looking at her watch. 'Where is Barry? I hope he's up with Jimmy . . .'

'No,' Anne said, smiling benevolently. 'I think he's gone out.'

'Gone out? Where?'

'He's with the crowd from the hotel.'

'What crowd?' Julia exclaimed. 'Who are they?'

'Don't worry. I know them. And Barry knows them too. Or rather, he knows one of them.'

'Who?' Julia insisted. 'Where are they? How is he going to get home?'

'Trust me. He's grand. In fact he's probably having the time of his life. He'll get home somehow. He's in safe hands.'

'But . . .'

'Julia,' Anne interrupted. 'This is Donegal, not Dublin. Things work differently up here. He'll be well looked after.'

Julia studied her across the table.

'Look,' Anne pleaded. 'You get to be the mammy all the time. Tonight, just this once, let me be the mammy.'

Julia looked at Anne. And then her face softened. 'Okay,' she said. 'I give in. *Mammy.*'

Anne straightened, smiling. 'That's Barry settled so. Maybe we should go gather our other boys?'

'Yes,' Julia agreed, 'maybe we should.'

The two women turned in their chairs and took one last look out onto the terrace. Michael and Denis remained there still, silhouetted against the backdrop of the darkening sky. And across the room the tenor crooned a slow ballad, holding the microphone close to his lips.

CHAPTER 17

Barry pushed gently on the door into the kitchen. The hum and swish of dishwashers filled the space. A young man in a dirty chef's outfit rubbed down a steel countertop. He looked up without smiling.

'I, I was looking for Emma,' Barry stammered. 'Emma Gallagher.'

'Aye, she's in the staff room. Emma!'

His voice didn't carry over the noise.

'She can't hear me,' he said. 'Go on back there. Straight through.'

Barry's palms were wet as he threaded his way between the racks of utensils. He came to a half-open door. He knocked softly, then leaned his head inside.

Emma stood facing away from him with her head bent down, lighting a cigarette. She still wore her uniform but she had pulled on a black cardigan.

'Emma?'

She turned, waving the match, her eyes widening.

'Barry! My God! Hiya!'

'Hi.'

'Sorry,' she said giddily. 'Here's me smoking. Desperate.'

She stubbed the cigarette out on the table.

'God, would you look at the state of me,' she went on nervously. 'I'm like a wet rat after work. Did you enjoy your wee party?'

'Yeah.'

'I thought it would never end. We're only finished clearing away now.'

She tossed her hair back from her face. 'Jesus,' she said. 'Are you staying, or going, or what?'

'I don't know.'

'Well. What would you like to do?'

'I don't know,' he said. 'We could . . . walk or something.'

'Right. Jesus. Okay, grand. Why don't you wait here a wee minute, and I'll try to find something in the bar.'

'Oh, you don't have to . . .'

'Sure we'll have our own wee party,' she said. 'You sit down there, I won't be a sec.' She gave him a nervous half-smile, grabbed a shoulder bag from a bench and left the room.

He sat down in a plastic chair and surveyed the coldly functional space. On the walls were 'No Smoking' signs and a poster reminding staff to wash their hands.

She was different, he thought. Her face was fuller, her voice was deeper than he remembered. She spoke very quickly. Barry felt a rush of anxiety. He thought he might have made a mistake to try to see her again after such a long time.

But then she returned and stood in the doorway. She seemed to be studying him, at a sudden loss for words. But then she smiled and inclined her head, gesturing him to follow her. They walked back through the kitchen and past the dishwashing machines. She pushed against a heavy steel door and they emerged into the rear car park.

'God, it's great to get away from that place,' she sighed.

She walked quickly away from the hotel. Barry trotted a few steps to catch up. They walked behind a row of houses and came to a footbridge across the river. She continued but then stopped abruptly in the middle of the bridge.

'I'm all out of breath,' she panted. 'I'm not in great shape.'

'You're just tired from work,' he said.

She looked at him briefly. 'I wish that was true,' she said.

Their eyes were still adjusting to the darkness. He could hear her breathing beside him.

'Let's go on,' she said. 'There's a wee place where we can talk . . .'

They crossed the bridge and were soon walking on a dark path beside the river. They passed the hotel on the far side and Barry could see couples dancing through the windows, the lights of the party reflected in the black moiling water.

'How long have you worked at the hotel?' he asked.

'Ach, forever. At weekends. More when we're off school.'

'Do you like it?'

'Sometimes. It's all right, like.'

'What about the customers?' Barry asked.

'Most of them are grand. I suppose the hotel, with Daddy there, it's always been part of us. Sometimes I feel like I'll be stuck there forever.'

'You mean, even after your Leaving?'

'Aye,' she said. 'If I do the Leaving at all.'

'What do you mean, if?'

'Sure you never know what'll happen. Now, there's a wee spot just up here . . .'

They continued to walk. The river beside them widened and the path became uneven. She climbed ahead of him.

'And so,' she said. 'Here we are.'

They stood atop a large rock overhanging the river. The broad, black water was below them, swirling slowly. In the distance were the sounds of the town: cars passing and the occasional shout. She pulled a white tablecloth from her bag and spread it out on the rock.

'Won't it get dirty?' Barry asked.

'It doesn't matter,' she said. 'I'll put it for the wash the next time I'm in.'

She sat down and patted the space beside her. Barry noted that she seemed stiff and nervous in her movements.

'I'm afraid I wasn't able to nick any of our best champagne,' she said, ferreting in her bag. 'But I've got us some whiskey and a bottle of lemonade.'

She poured the drinks into two plastic cups.

'That's okay,' Barry said. 'I don't really drink much.'

'Don't drink much?' she teased. 'What's wrong with you? Doesn't every all-American boy drink whiskey?'

She pushed a cup into his hand. 'You need a lesson in how to survive in Ireland,' she said.

He smiled, embarrassed.

'Ach, I'm sorry,' she said. 'I'm hardly the one to be offering lessons in survival.'

She drained her glass in one long swallow. Then they sat in silence, and she filled her cup again. The water moved beneath them with hushed sibilance.

'So,' she said. 'How've you been?'

'Fine, thanks.'

'We sort of lost touch, so we did.'

'Yes. After our letters.'

'Which *you* stopped writing,' she said.

He cradled his cup in his hands.

'Ah, go on,' she said. 'I'm only slagging you. Sure you can't keep writing letters for ever.'

'I shouldn't have stopped,' he said.

'But you did, and that's the way it goes.'

'No,' he said. 'I broke my wrist. I got behind, in everything. And then I didn't know where to pick up.'

'I know, that's what they all say. And what about the other girls?'

'Girls?'

'Aye, girls. Look, you don't need to be so polite. I won't bite you. I just want to know. About you. About the other girls.'

'There haven't been any.'

She laughed. 'Barry O'Donnell, the god from on high, has had no girls in two years? Jesus, what have you been doing with yourself?'

'Nothing,' he said. 'Running, I suppose. I run a lot.'

She laughed, spluttering her drink. 'Oh Barry! You're gas, so you are!'

Her laughter subsided, then, and she looked out over the water. He turned and looked at her face, watching her smile fade.

'What about you, then?' he asked.

'Me?'

'Yes, you. Any boyfriends?'

'Not really. Not as such. Sure, the mighty men of Donegal aren't what they used to be.'

She drained her glass.

'So you're not going to tell me then?' he said.

'Do you want to know?'

'Not really,' he said.

They could see one another's face in the yellow glow of the distant streetlights.

'That time,' he said softly. 'By the lake.'

'Aye.'

'Emma. That was the first, it was the first time I was ever with a girl.'

'Barry, don't . . .'

'There's been no one since then.'

'But that was all years ago.'

'I still remember. I still think about it. About you.'

'I know, but . . .'

'Please. Couldn't we, maybe, start over again?'

'No. I'm sorry.'

She moved away from him and stood up, looking across the river. He saw her figure against the pale glow from the town. He stood beside her and touched her shoulder.

'Emma . . .'

'No, look, there's something – something has happened.'

'It doesn't matter. I've missed you. I want to be with you. We won't be together long, we can't let this time pass . . .'

'Barry,' she said firmly. 'You don't understand.'

He took his hands away.

'I'm sorry,' he said softly. 'I only thought, I thought you felt . . .'

'But I *do*,' she pleaded. 'Of *course* I do. But for God's sake!'

'What is it then?'

'Oh, God. Do you really want to know?'

'I just want . . .'

'I'm pregnant.'

Her words reverberated across the water like a gunshot.

'*Pregnant*?' he whispered.

She nodded, looking down into the water. The air was suddenly cold and everything seemed to stand out in relief: the rock, the water, the black trees, the lights in the distance. Emma there, her outline, the plastic cup in her hands.

He felt dizzy. He turned away from her and sat down, trying to steady his thoughts.

'How long?' he said finally. 'Before the baby?'

'A good while,' she said.

He nodded in the darkness. He drank from his plastic cup, grimacing at the sickly sweet taste. He looked over at her where she stood, scraping the ground with her foot. Then she turned towards him.

'Are you okay?' she asked.

'Me? Of course I am. I'm just, this just isn't what I expected.'

'No,' she said. 'It's me who's expecting.'

'God,' he laughed bitterly. 'How can you joke about this?'

'I don't know,' she said. 'Nothing else I can do.'

She sat down beside him. They sat in silence for a while, listening to the water flow beneath them.

'So,' he said eventually. 'Who is he?'

'It doesn't matter. He's not important.'

'Of course he's important.'

'He's not. He's not from here. He won't want to have anything to do with it.'

'But he doesn't have a choice.'

'Look, I don't want to go into, like, the gory details. But I was the responsible party. It was a stupid thing, but I chose to do it, and now I have to live with it.'

'You seem fairly sure of yourself.'

'I am.'

'Okay.'

They sat in silence again.

'Who knows?' he asked.

'No one,' she said.

'Not even him?'

'No.'

'So you haven't told anyone?' he said.

'No, no one. Why?'

'Just weird, that's all.'

'This is a small wee town . . .'

'Yes, I know that. I mean it's weird that you've told *me*.'

'Why?'

'Oh, I don't know,' he sighed in a low voice. 'It's just that, we were together once. Back at the lake.'

'Aye.'

'And now,' he said. 'Well, it's happened again.'

'What?'

'We've shared something.'

She turned towards him. 'Barry,' she said softly. 'You're going to make me cry.'

'Sorry.'

'No. Ach, no. It's lovely. I've been so alone. With this whole thing. I don't think you know what this is like.'

'No, probably not.'

'This is the end for me. I can't go on like this. God, my parents!'

'Will you tell them?'

'Sure I'll have to.'

'What will they do?'

'I don't know. They might kill me. That would be the easiest thing. The worst thing is that they'd kill themselves.'

'Emma.'

'You don't understand. You don't know Daddy. He's wild proud of his reputation. And then there's Mammy – she won't understand this, she won't get it at all. It's going to destroy them.'

'Yeah.'

'And the town. How can I face people?'

'They don't matter.'

'Oh, but they *do*! I have to do something soon. I'm tired all the time. I sleep during the day. I'm so thirsty, I can't go an hour without drinking. People are going to suspect, they're going to notice. *Soon*. And I just can't face this.'

Again the silence enfolded them. Barry could hear her breathing heavily beside him. He wanted to comfort her but couldn't bring himself to touch her. He looked at her profile, the downward turn of her mouth, as if this had become her natural expression. So far removed from the girl he remembered. The girl who talked non-stop. The girl who loved foxes.

'Barry?'

'Yes.'

'This is our secret, right?'

'Of course it is. I wouldn't tell anyone.'

'No, I didn't mean that,' she said. 'I meant, it's something. Between the two of us.'

'Yes. Sure.'

'Because I can't go through with this.'

'Do you mean abortion?'

'No. I couldn't face it. I can't face anything now. Except . . .' She turned to him. 'There was a woman in town. Her husband, he used to beat her. And her father – it was dreadful.'

'Yes?'

'She killed herself. She filled her pockets with stones and she walked into the river. And she sank down into the water.'

'Really?'

'It was just there. Just where it gets deep at the bend.'

'Emma . . .'

'We could do it. *Together*. You could help me. We could end all this. Now. *Tonight*. And it would be our secret.'

'Emma, no!'

But before he knew what was happening she was standing. He stood and tried to grasp her hand, and he felt his legs go weak. He could sense panic within himself as she stepped towards the water, pulling him as she went. They stumbled but then he caught himself and he grabbed her arms as she lurched forward. He pulled her back and he held her arms as she kicked and pushed and cried. And then she cried more softly, and he held her there, rocking gently above the black water.

They sat down, then, and held one another, until Emma grew calm, and her breathing slowed, and she lay quietly in his arms.

'Emma,' he said finally.

'Yes.'

'We need to get you sorted out.'

She sat up slowly and faced him. Her hair was tossed and her knee was bleeding from when she had stumbled.

'I think we need to go to a doctor,' he said.

'No.'

'Yes. You need some help.'

'Oh God, please.'

'Look. Things are pretty bad right now, but if we can get you some help it will get better.'

'Aye,' she said sadly.

'I mean tonight. Now.'

'What?'

'We need to go to a doctor *now*.'

'We can't. There are no doctors around at night.'

'But the guy at our table, at the party. He was a doctor. He said he lives in town.'

'Dr Jackson? Sure he'd be asleep.'

'It doesn't matter. We need to see him tonight.'

'Why?'

'Emma, for God's sake. I can't have you throwing yourself in the river.'

'Okay. I won't.'

'I'm not going to let you kill yourself over this baby. And the first thing we need to do is get a doctor and get you seen to.'

'Aye.'

'And then everything will start to get a little better.'

'Will it?'

'Not right away. Slowly. But it will get better.'

She looked at him. He could see her face in the dim light. She was listening to him. Trusting him.

'So, is this a deal?' he asked.

'Aye,' she nodded.

'Can we shake on it?'

'Sorry?'

'I want you to shake my hand on this. Like it's an agreement.'

'Why?'

'Just do it,' he said.

They shook hands.

'Right,' he said, standing. 'Here, brush yourself off.'

'Okay.'

'So,' he said cheerily. 'Which way to Dr Jackson's?'

It was nearly two o'clock when they reached the stone house on Main Street. The streets were deserted and there was a glow of pale orange over the quiet town.

They stood on the porch and faced one another, briefly, without speaking. Then Barry rang the doorbell.

'Shit,' Emma whispered. 'This is so bloody . . .'

'It's okay,' Barry said. 'It's going to be okay.'

He rang the bell again. They could hear shuffling inside and then a light came on. A gruff voice called from within.

'Who's out there?'

'It's me,' she said quietly. 'Emma Gallagher. I'm sorry, Dr Jackson. But I need to see you.'

Dr Jackson opened the door wearing a burgundy dressing gown. He stood with one hand on the door and the other on his hip. For a moment he squinted, assessing the teenagers standing before him. Then he looked beyond them towards the town.

'Well, now,' he said finally. 'That's a mild night for you.'

'Yes, Dr Jackson.'

'Now, Emma. I know you all right. But this young man . . . Didn't I share a table with you at dinner tonight?'

'Yes, sir. I'm Barry O'Donnell. My father is Denis.'

'Yes, yes, of course. Your mother is a very interesting woman.'

'Thank you, sir.'

'Now then. Perhaps you'd like to step inside?'

A moment later they sat alone on a sofa in a comfortable sitting room. They leaned forward, waiting for Dr Jackson to return. Neither spoke.

'Righty-o,' he said, entering the room. 'I'm sorry for the delay, but I always feel a bit more myself when I'm fully clothed. I assume this is some sort of professional consultation?'

'Aye,' Emma said nervously as Barry looked at the floor.

'You've a nasty scrape on that knee.'

'No, Dr Jackson. It's not, well, my knee that's the problem.'

'Oh, I see. Perhaps you'd rather speak to me inside?'

'Aye,' Emma said.

'And this young man . . .'

'Oh, no, doctor,' Emma said. 'It's nothing to do with him.'

'I see. Well then. Very chivalrous, I must say.'

'Sorry?' Emma asked.

'Oh, nothing, dear. Nothing at all. Right, then. I think you had better step inside, and we'll have a little chat.'

A moment later Barry found himself alone in the room. So

strange, he thought. To be in this room, in this place, way up in Donegal. In the middle of the night.

He looked around at the decor. Heavy, old-fashioned furniture and a worn carpet with a red pattern. Above the marble fireplace hung a plaque from a local civic group, thanking Dr Jackson for his years of service. On the wall opposite hung a picture of a woman in her forties, smiling, her hair flying in the breeze beneath wispy clouds.

Barry could hear voices intermittently: Dr Jackson's low hum, Emma's muffled response. Then there was silence. At one stage something fell clanging to the floor. A single car drove by on the street outside and then there was silence again.

When Emma finally came back into the room she had a bandage on her knee and she carried a tissue as if she had been crying.

'Are you okay?' he asked.

'Aye. He says it will take him a wee minute.'

They sat apart on the couch as if they were being watched. They both felt tired. They could hear movement outside and then Dr Jackson came in. He was smiling paternally.

'Well now,' he said, settling into an armchair. 'I'm very pleased you both came here tonight. Perhaps it could have waited until the morning, but you were both wise to get this attended to without delay.'

He sipped a mug of coffee.

'Now, a few comments. First of all, I want you both to promise me that you will control your consumption of alcoholic drink.'

A confused look crossed their faces.

'You smell like you've been bathing in a poitín still,' he said.

'It's a curse for young people, and it leads to nothing but trouble. Now I won't breach my rules of confidentiality tonight, but if I ever encounter either of you with drink on you again, before you are fully twenty-eight years old, I'm going straight to your parents. Understood?'

'Yes, Dr Jackson.'

'Right. Now, young woman, about this more personal matter. I am happy to report that your self-diagnosis is not at all accurate.'

'Sorry?' Emma asked.

'You are not pregnant.'

Emma's eyes widened.

'Are you, like, sure? For definite, like?'

'I am sure, for definite, that you are not pregnant.'

'Then what's wrong with me?'

'I'm afraid I can't say for certain. You are running a slight temperature and I suspect you may simply have the same bug that's wreaking havoc around the schools. For now I want you to go home and get into bed. *Alone*, that is. And in the morning I want you to tell your mother that you are unwell and have her cancel your shifts at the hotel for at least a week. All clear so far?'

'Yes, Dr Jackson.'

'Now then. While you're in bed, I want you to keep filled with clear liquids. Anything at all, but preferably some fruit juice or lemonade. Promise?'

'Yes, Dr Jackson.'

'And then, unless you take a turn for the worse, I want to see you in my office first thing on Monday morning for a full check-up. And at that time, we can discuss, shall we say, the bigger picture. The Emma Gallagher story, if you will. Not a lecture, Emma. But a wee chat.'

He lowered his glasses and looked directly at her, awaiting her response.

'Aye,' she said. 'Yes, aye.'

'Ordinarily, Emma, I don't allow my personal feelings to influence my professional decisions. But I do care a great deal for you and for your family. And I don't want to see any unwanted trouble. Do you understand?'

'Yes, I do. I understand.'

'Now then,' Dr Jackson said as he fumbled in his pockets, 'I have my keys here somewhere. I want to drive you both home. Can't have you gallivanting about, disturbing old widowers along the way.'

'Oh, Dr Jackson,' Emma cried with relief. She leapt up and threw her arms around the old man.

'Now, stop that carry-on. I don't want to catch this thing. Out the door, the both of you. I'm driving you *straight* home. And there will be no snogging on the way, or you will get worse. *Worse*, I'm telling you. Far worse indeed!'

CHAPTER 18

The sky had settled to a deep, rich blue. An infinity of stars hung like a cloud above the black fields. The air outside was warm and still and serene.

Jimmy was tucked into the backseat of the car between Julia and Anne. Denis drove and Michael sat in the passenger seat, scanning the narrow road ahead as they climbed towards the house.

'She was Australian,' Anne was saying in a tired voice. 'She couldn't remember where she met him. God, what a stupid girl. Stephen isn't stupid, is he?'

No answer.

'I didn't think he was that stupid,' she continued. 'She was really stupid, that girl. With that pasted smile. She had nothing to say.'

No reply. Michael shifted in the front seat as if he were about to speak.

'And did you see the dress on her?' Anne continued. 'I'd say it cost her a thousand euro. How can a girl who's so stupid have so much money? Sure you'd have to laugh.'

'Who was stupid?' Jimmy asked.

'No one, honey,' Julia said softly. 'Just a girl at the party. We're nearly home now.'

'I saw Stephen Deane's car,' Jimmy said brightly.

'Well his girlfriend was really stupid.'

'Now,' Julia said. 'Here we are. Home at last.'

Denis got out and held Julia's door open. She stepped out of the car carefully in her high shoes, holding Jimmy's hand for support. He broke free and ran to the house. The adults followed in a funereal procession.

'Now, Jimmy,' Julia said as they entered the house. 'You go straight up to bed. Do you want me to come up and tuck you in?'

'No, Mom. I'll be grand. You stay down and have a nice chat with the grown-ups. See you in the morning!'

Julia gave him a blank look as he dashed up the stairs.

'Well, I don't know about the rest of ye,' Anne said. 'But as they say in these parts, I'm going for a wee lie down.'

'Aye,' Julia said, trying to sound Donegal. 'A wee lie down would – how does it go? – do us rightly?'

'Aye,' Denis said. 'Do us rightly indeed.'

Then the women watched as Denis and Michael stretched, looking like dancers in a choreographed scene.

Anne turned to Julia. 'Is everything okay in your room?'

'Yes,' Julia said. 'Perfect. And is everything okay in yours?'

Anne smiled, and then nodded. 'Yes. Yes, I think so. Yes.'

'Right, lads,' Denis announced. 'I'll give you a shout at dawn, the first crow of the old cock. We'll go for a romp up the mountain, watch the dawn spread over the county. Sure you can't beat the old country living. Ladies, we'll need breakfast on the table – say half past five?'

But the two women had already trudged up the stairs.

*

A few minutes later Anne entered the bedroom. Michael stood at the small hand basin. She looked at his back in his sleeveless vest. She could see the sinewy strength of his shoulders. He wore the bottoms of his pyjamas, metallic blue, the ones she had given him for his birthday. He caught her eye in the mirror and turned to face her.

'Hiya,' he said softly.

'Hi.'

'Did you enjoy the party?'

'Yes,' Anne said. 'I did. Very much. And you?'

'Yes. I'm a bit tired now.'

'I'm sure you are, love.'

She turned towards the wardrobe and began to undress. He sat on the edge of the bed as she removed her earrings and then her dress. She hung it up in the wardrobe, lost in thought. She dug a blue cotton nightgown out of the chest of drawers, but then pulled out a white one. She pulled it over her head.

Then she turned and came to him. He held her gently as she stood before him, rubbing her tummy with his nose, inhaling her.

'Michael,' she said.

'Yes?'

'I really enjoyed the party.'

'Good.'

'But I have to say one thing,' she said.

'Yes?'

'Tonight. At the party. The whole time.'

'Yes?'

'I thought you were magnificent.'

'That's a big word.'

'You're a big man.'

They smiled at one another. Then Michael lay back on the bed and Anne climbed in beside him. For a moment they stared up at the maze of cracks in the plaster ceiling.

'Michael,' she said.

'Hmm?'

'I was thinking.'

'Yes?'

'Watching you, tonight. At the party. You're doing really well lately.'

'Aye. Couldn't be better.'

'And, you know. Maybe I've always been a bit, sort of . . . cautious.'

'Cautious?'

'About us,' she said. 'The future.'

'What do you mean?' he said, turning towards her.

'Children. *Babies.*'

'Oh. Yes.'

'I think we should try.'

'Try?'

'For a baby.'

'Oh. Gosh.'

'I mean it.'

'Really?' he asked quietly.

She nodded.

'But what about . . .?'

'We'll manage.'

'Will we?'

'Yes,' she said. 'We will.'

'But why now? Why all of a sudden?'

'I don't know,' she said. 'Lots of things. Denis and Julia and the boys. The two of us. The party tonight. I just feel like things are going well.'

'Yes.'

'But mostly it's you.'

'Me?'

'You'd be the perfect daddy.'

'Me? But I'm hardly . . .'

'But you are, Michael. You *are*.'

'Gosh.'

'So?' she said.

'You mean *now*?'

'It's as good a time as any.'

'Right. Well then. Right.'

Then he smiled, and she smiled.

'You're a gas, woman,' he said.

'I know,' she smiled.

They kissed then, and then they stopped, reading each other's face, as if searching for an answer. And then she pulled him towards her and they kissed again.

Julia lay propped up on the pillows. She held a novel in her lap. It was a summer read, she'd bought it in a sale and had thrown it into the case just before they left for Donegal. Her eyes danced across the page, skipping every other line but missing little of the plot.

Denis came into the room, still wearing his shirt and trousers. His tie was undone.

'In bed already?' he said. 'Sure the night is only starting.'

She smiled and continued reading. Out of the corner of her eye, she watched him at the sink. He brushed his teeth carefully, as always. Then he gargled with red mouthwash. He crossed the bedroom, taking off his shirt and folding it lazily into the suitcase. He was humming to himself.

'Those songs tonight,' he said. 'Country and Western.'

'Yes.'

'Great lyrics.'

'You think so?' she asked.

'Aye. So evocative. *All my ex-es live in Texas*. Brilliant.'

She smiled and returned to her book. He sat on the edge of the bed and took off his shoes, and then he stood and set them into the wardrobe, leaving the doors open. He sat down again and took off his socks, rolled them into a ball and flung them into the wardrobe.

'Great function room,' he said.

'Sorry?'

'For the party. Great room. You'd never get a function room with such a view in Dublin.'

'No, dear.'

He looked at her.

'What's so funny?' he said.

'Nothing,' she said. 'You're in a good mood.'

'Aye,' he said. 'I am indeed.'

He leaned back on the bed and rested his head on Julia's tummy.

'And why wouldn't I be in good form?' he said. 'Sure I've just been to a great party, and now I've got a gorgeous woman in my bed just dying for me to snuggle in beside her.'

'Have you?'

'Aye. Sure she's holding herself back with the anticipation of it.'

Julia smiled. 'You O'Donnell boys,' she said. 'Full of yourselves, aren't you?'

'Aye,' he said. 'We are surely.'

A moment later he slid into bed beside her. 'So,' he said, putting his arms around her. 'I wonder how our Barry is getting on?'

'I wonder,' she said. 'I think I'd better wait up.'

'I'm sure he'll be grand . . .'

'I know,' she said. 'But I want to wait up.'

'Right,' he said. 'I'll keep you company so.'

She continued reading. He lay beside her with his arms around her middle. She could feel him nuzzling his nose into her shoulder. His foot touched hers at the bottom of the bed. She was nearing the end of a chapter, she turned the page. Just a few more lines.

There.

She closed the book, then, and set it down on the bedside table. Then she turned towards Denis. They lay side by side, facing one another.

'Julia,' he said.

'Yes?'

'I'm mad about you.'

'Are you?'

'But I'm a bit knackered.'

'I know, dear,' she said.

'I'll try to stay awake with you,' he said.

'It's okay. I'll be okay.'

'Are you sure?'

'Yes. Positive.'

'You're lovely.'

'I know.'

She watched, then, as he smiled weakly. And then his eyes began to close. She lay and watched him as he drifted into sleep, his breathing coming heavy and slow.

She reached over then and turned out the light. She sat propped up on the pillows with her arms folded over the duvet. She looked outside into the dark-blue sky, already showing the first hints of morning. A car drove off in the distance.

And she smiled, then, to be here. With Denis as he slept beside her. In this quiet house, the two of them so close to each other, and so far away from everything else in their lives.

Barry watched as Dr Jackson drove away down the narrow country road. He listened for a long time as the car disappeared towards town. The sound of the engine receded and finally died away into the silence of the night.

Barry shivered. He began to walk up the drive towards his Uncle Michael's house. He walked slowly, carefully placing each step as if the soft crunch of his shoes on the gravel might awaken the world around him. Already there was a glow of dawn on the horizon. He brushed against an errant frond from the hedge and the arm of his jacket became dewy wet.

Eventually, step by step, he reached the house, its outline emerging slowly from the darkness. The first bird, a robin, called from the trees on the right. Then, in response, an echoing call

came from the left. The first called again, and again it was echoed.
Barry listened as the calls alternated from side to side, bathing the
house in the sound of the first dawn.

He stood for a moment in the delicate half-light and listened to
the morning. Bird calls now began to issue from all directions.
And as the shadows lifted, the house seemed to move, to rock
gently, to swing back and forth with the rhythm of a nursery
rhyme.

Barry felt tired but he was happy. He had been with Emma
tonight. They had spoken. She had trusted him with the greatest
of her secrets. He had touched her, held her as she cried. He felt
as if he had protected her. And he felt a new strength within
himself, as he stood alone before the house, with the morning
brightening around him.

He approached the hall door and opened it slowly. He thought
everyone was sleeping. He thought no one was awake to hear him
slip quietly up the stairs, and quietly into bed.

CHAPTER 19

Jimmy woke early. He saw the sunshine outside, so bright it hurt his eyes. He looked over at Barry in the next bed curled tightly beneath his blankets. He could only see the top of his head.

Jimmy listened for a moment. The birds outside were going mad. But he couldn't hear anything inside the house. He was starving. He climbed out of bed. He felt confused by something. Oh, yeah, he remembered. He had been asleep in the hotel, and then he came back to this bed.

Right.

He went into the hall and decided to check on his parents. He pushed open what he thought was their door but then he got a shock: wrong room! Uncle Michael was in the bed, his arm hanging down to the floor. His eyes opened. He smiled weakly at Jimmy.

'Good morning,' Michael whispered.

'Hiya.'

'I don't think your mum and dad are awake yet.'

'Right.'

'Give me a minute and I'll come downstairs with you.'

'Okay.'

A few minutes later they were in the kitchen together. 'Now then,' Michael said. 'What would you like for breakfast?'

'I dunno,' Jimmy replied. 'What have you got?'

'Well now, we have a very healthy menu today. Fresh grapefruit, followed by poached eggs on brown toast.'

'Well . . .'

'Or alternatively,' Michael said, reading a box of cereal, 'I can offer you some colourfully packaged, mass-produced sugary rubbish. How about that?'

'Yeah,' Jimmy laughed. 'I usually go for the rubbish.'

'I know,' Michael said. 'I did too.'

Michael made coffee while Jimmy ate. When Jimmy was finished Michael yawned and stretched, and removed the bowl from the table.

'Okay,' he said. 'We won't see your mum and dad for some time I'm afraid. We were all up till blue in the morning.'

'Blue in the morning?' Jimmy asked.

'Yes. That means sort of late-ish. They'll probably have a wee lie-in. So, what should we do now?'

Jimmy thought for a moment. 'Uncle Michael,' he said. 'Do you know how to make card houses?'

'Houses – out of playing cards?'

'Yeah.'

'Sure, Jimmy, I've lived in one of those all my life.'

'Really?'

'Well, sort of. Let me see, now. Where has Auntie Anne hidden the playing cards?'

Michael began rummaging in a drawer.

'You'll find, when you grow up, that women love to play

games. And your Auntie Anne's favourite game is called "Hide the thing".'

He opened a cupboard.

'She picks something that she knows you will need,' he continued, 'and then she hides it so you can never, ever find it . . . Ah, but look here! We've found them! We've won the game!'

He held a pack of cards in the air triumphantly. 'Now,' Michael said. 'Will we go inside?'

A moment later they were sitting on the floor in the sitting room. Jimmy took the first go. He managed to get four cards to stand up in a square. But then down they tumbled.

'Hmm,' Michael said. 'Perhaps we need an architect.'

Michael set two cards upright and then tried to balance a third across the top. Again they fell over as soon as he removed his hands. The two stared at the cards on the floor.

'You're not very good at this, are you, Uncle Michael?'

'No, I'm not. It's the whole issue of gravity. Always pushing you down, trying to keep you underfoot. It's been a particular problem of mine.'

He rubbed his chin.

'But you know, there might be a better way to do this.'

'Really?'

'Yes, I think so. If only we had the right materials . . .'

Anne awoke to find herself alone.

The sun shone brightly. Outside, the birds sang a variegated chorus of chirps and squawks and trills. She looked over to the window and out through the branches. Beyond the trees lay the soft blue hills, like bodies soaking in the morning sun.

She lowered herself back into bed. She felt languid and relaxed, unhurried. She thought back to the party, so filled with events, things she wanted to remember forever. The room with the view of the River Finn flowing by. Stephen and his daft Aussie girlfriend. Her nephew Barry, so fine and handsome, so diffident, looking back at her for reassurance as he walked into the kitchen to find Emma. And her time with Julia: finally speaking with her, feeling close to her. Sisterly.

Finally.

And then Michael, in bed, the first time in so long. And the curling up after, feeling Michael's body as he held her and they lay awake, tired and safe and in love. In love, she thought, after making love, for those precious tired minutes before sleep, where nothing mattered, nothing interfered, nothing could break them apart or disturb that peace, that rare peace.

She felt tired. She tried to sense whether there was a change within herself – silly, she knew. But still. Was there something there? A feeling of languid contentment. The beginnings of that fullness, that sense of completion. Her legs, she felt something in her legs: a tiredness, as if she had been walking a great distance. Her arms, all her muscles: something was there, a pleasant heaviness. A sense that nothing mattered, there was no urgency or reason to move.

The timing was right last night. She wanted him, he needed her, everything seemed to come together for them. But still, it never happens that way, she knew that. Deciding to have a baby and then immediately it comes true.

And yet, deep down, she felt something. She knew it. A girl, she thought. How lovely it would be, how perfect and complete and lovely she would feel if it were a girl – bringing her into the world, feeding her, dressing her, loving her like a part of herself, tender and strong and beautiful!

Maybe, she thought. Maybe it has happened.

She inhaled deeply and sensed her body. She rubbed her hands over her tummy, rubbed them over her breasts, imagined there was a swelling, a filling, a preparing for new life. She smiled to herself. So silly. Even if she were pregnant, there would be no change. Not yet.

And yet, so proud she felt. So proud of herself, and Michael. Their marriage. They worked so hard to make it right. And now, maybe, just maybe . . .

Just then there was a light tap at the door. 'Come in,' she called softly.

The door opened slightly and Julia leaned in.

'Good morning,' Julia whispered.

'Good morning.'

'Is Michael downstairs?'

'Yes. I don't know when he got up. Come in, Julia, come in!'

Julia sat gently on the side of the bed.

'So,' Anne said. 'Did you sleep well?'

'Oh, yes,' Julia yawned. 'I stayed awake until I heard Barry come in. Then I drifted off. And how about you?'

'Oh, yes,' Anne said. 'Like a baby.'

Julia looked at her.

'Oh?'

Anne returned her look and then smiled. 'Sure you never know.'

Julia smiled. 'Denis was exhausted,' she said. 'He was asleep before his head hit the pillow.'

'It was a good party,' Anne said dreamily.

'Yes,' Julia said. 'It was difficult in some ways. But very good.'

'Yes.'

'I'm glad it happened,' Julia said.

'Me too.'

Both women were silent for a moment.

'Do you hear music?' Julia asked.

'Yes. It must be something on the stereo.'

'Maybe we should investigate,' Julia said, standing.

'Yes. I'd love some coffee.'

'Yes,' Julia said. 'Coffee and a good post-mortem.'

'Oh, yes,' Anne agreed dreamily. 'Quite a lot to talk about, isn't there?'

'There sure is,' Julia smiled. 'There sure is.'

A little while earlier Denis had been startled awake. He had heard something from below, the sound of something shifting, a heavy muffled thud.

He opened his eyes and listened. He thought he heard voices, it sounded like Jimmy giggling. What could he be up to, alone downstairs, at this hour?

Better find out.

The morning sun filled the bedroom with light. He looked over at Julia, still heavily asleep. Her face looked angry and sad. So unlike the positive, alert expression she wore during the day.

Sure she must be wrecked, Denis thought. He slipped his leg out from beneath the covers, then rolled quietly out of the bed.

He turned to look at her again. Not a budge.

A moment later Denis walked quietly to the top of the stairs. He could hear voices coming from below but they were punctuated by the sound of something metallic. A clacking and clicking. And then a squeak.

What in the name of God . . .?

He stepped quietly down the stairs and Michael and Jimmy came into view. There were newspapers spread out on the floor. Jimmy held a broom handle and Michael was fixing it into a square wooden base. A moment later Michael took the creation from Jimmy and stood it upright on the floor.

'Now, Jimmy. There's our stand.'

'Okay,' Jimmy said. 'What's next?'

Denis walked down the stairs.

'Dear God,' he said. 'What's going on here?'

'A card house!' Jimmy said. 'We're building a brilliant card house!'

'I see,' Denis said. 'Looks like one of Uncle Michael's card houses all right . . . Right, lads, carry on, don't let me interrupt.'

Denis walked past them into the kitchen. He found the coffee that Michael had made, filled a ceramic mug, and returned to the sitting room.

Jimmy and Michael were busy fixing dowels into holes at different levels on the broom handle.

'Now,' Michael said. 'These will hold our suspension cables.'

'Right,' Jimmy said. 'So where do we hang the whatever-you-called-them?'

'Anywhere you like,' Michael said. 'Just so long as there's a balance.'

'Right,' Jimmy nodded sagely. 'Dad, do you want to help?'

'No, that's all right,' Denis said from the sofa. 'I'll take a supervisory role, if you don't mind. I would strongly recommend, though, that we put on some music to help you work.'

Michael looked over at Denis.

'Yes,' Michael said. 'That would be most helpful.'

Denis busied himself with the stereo for a moment and then the sound came on. A guitar playing a slow, three-chord progression, and then returning to the root. And then Joni Mitchell's young, clear voice, a voice of long ago, singing a gentle love song about the morning.

Denis looked into his coffee. Michael was busy tying strings to pieces of wire, holding them out before him to check for symmetry and balance. But both men, when that song came on, were transported back to those times, in that room, when they had been young together. The music raised long dormant memories of being in that room and joining in off-key and joking and pretending to play along. It brought back feelings of summer days of youth and freedom and being together as brothers, without families or jobs or separation or age between them. Neither spoke as the music played. Denis helped Jimmy punch neat holes through the tops of the playing cards – the kings, the queens and the knaves. Michael hung cords of various lengths onto the geometric framework. Denis finished his coffee and set his mug on the table beside him. Michael strung up the first cards, then sat back, adjusted the string and changed the length of the cross beam. Neither brother spoke, living for that extended moment in the womb of the music, in that room where they had once been, and were now once more, existing in two times at once:

suspended, ageless, weightless.

Then there was a swish on the stairs as Anne and Julia quietly descended. But before they reached the floor they stopped to watch, Anne below, Julia a few stairs above, as Michael tied the last piece in place, stood back, rushed forward again to slide it slightly to the right, just there, yes, that's it.

And then they were all there, admiring the creation that stood on the floor. The pole in the centre. The projections arching out. And suspended, then, circling slowly, the cards, waving back and forth, swaying and rotating with the passing air, showing their royal faces and then turning away again. Now up, now down, now forward, now back, held aloft as if by the air alone in a harmonious dance. Kings and queens and knaves, orderly but not ordered, governed by laws of balance and harmony and yet, apparently, free and random, moving in and out of each other's orbit in a slow, stately, dance: lifted and carried and beautiful.

'So, guys,' Jimmy said brightly. 'What do you think?'